It Wasn't Me!

CJ Gray Novels

Murder comes to Edendale?
It Wasn't Me!

A CJ Gray
Mystery

It Wasn't Me!

CJ Meads

First Published in November 2023
This edition published November 2024

Copyright © 2023 CJ Meads
All rights reserved.
The moral right of the author has been asserted.

This novel is a work of fiction.
Names and characters are the product of the
author's imagination, other than those clearly in the
public domain, and any resemblance to actual
persons, living or dead, is entirely coincidental.

ISBN: 979-8-8621-0025-9
Independently Published

DEDICATION

For those I love and cherish.
You know who you are.

Plus, Aileen and Julie.
Thanks for the encouragement
to carry on writing

IT WASN'T ME!

While attending the glamorous *Ladies' Day* meeting at Yorksbey Racecourse's *Equinox Festival*, Charlotte Tate is found standing over a dead body holding the murder weapon. The game finally looks up for the stunning Femme Fatale. She does, however, know who will help her.

CJ Gray, his enigmatic friend, Eden Songe, and his loyal dog Oscar, are drawn into another adventure of murder, blackmail, greed, corruption, lust, and romance.

CJ Meads' second novel is like the first, an easy read page turner. A light-hearted romantic whodunnit that attempts to please everyone, but maybe not always succeeding. However, if you liked the first novel, you will also more than likely enjoy this one.

There are plenty of twists and turns in this roller coaster story, with the usual red herrings to throw you off the scent.

Set around Edendale, the picturesque North Yorkshire village and nearby Yorksbey, the story takes you from the sunny metropolis of Dubai to the glorious Yorkshire Dales, and finally Cornwall.

The story provides an opportunity for everyone to enjoy the escapism, in a novel with something to please most tastes. Then, just when you think you have it all worked out, the final twist, as all good whodunnits, will have you stunned and again leave you longing for the next adventure in Edendale, with CJ Gray and the gang.

CONTENTS

PROLOGUE - 1919	1
TODAY	3
PART 1 – THREE WEEKS EARLIER	5
CHAPTER 1 – THE RACE	7
CHAPTER 2 – THE MEETING	10
CHAPTER 3 – THE SECRET LOVERS	15
CHAPTER 4 – DINNER DATE	18
CHAPTER 5 – FINANCIAL AFFAIRS	24
CHAPTER 6 – AND FOR AFTERS?	26
CHAPTER 7 – THE ARCHITECT	32
CHAPTER 8 – HOW DID IT GO?	36
CHAPTER 9 – CONTEMPLATING	41
CHAPTER 10 – HOW ARE YOU MAJOR?	47
CHAPTER 11 – A PROPOSITION	49
CHAPTER 12 – WHO'S THAT THEN?	53
CHAPTER 13 – PLAYING AROUND?	57
CHAPTER 14 – SO NICE TO COME HOME	65
CHAPTER 15 – NOT QUITE AS IT SEEMS.	71
CHAPTER 16 – GET IT SORTED	76
CHAPTER 17 – THE PLANS	79
CHAPTER 18 – THE DOCUMENT	84
CHAPTER 19 – LEGAL MATTERS	87

Chapter	Title	Page
Chapter 20	Nice To See You Again	90
Chapter 21	Hello, What's This?	93
Chapter 22	The Arrival	97
Chapter 23	Anything Missing Sir?	102
Chapter 24	The Edendale Project	105
Chapter 25	The Deeds	110
Chapter 26	The Invitation	113
Chapter 27	An Agreement?	115
Chapter 28	Are We Sure?	119
Chapter 29	Another Invite	122
Chapter 30	How Was It?	125
Chapter 31	But What Can We Do?	132
Chapter 32	For Old Times' Sake	135
Chapter 33	Is Everything Okay?	139
Chapter 34	Is It The Right Deed?	142
Chapter 35	There Are Plans Afoot	144
Chapter 36	Can You Trust Kipling?	150
Chapter 37	A Compromising Request	156
Chapter 38	And The Money?	158
Chapter 39	We're Off To The Races	160
Chapter 40	The Heritage Railway	163
Chapter 41	The Dilemma	166
Chapter 42	Ladies' Day	170
Chapter 43	Confrontations	176

Chapter	Title	Page
Chapter 44	Luncheon Is Served	179
Chapter 45	Sorry We're Late	182
Chapter 46	I'm Stuffed	186
Chapter 47	Hargrove Handicap	190
Chapter 48	Winner's Glory	194
Chapter 49	The Body	196
PART 2		197
Chapter 50	What Do We Have Here?	199
Chapter 51	She's Done What?	203
Chapter 52	The Crime Scene	205
Chapter 53	The Interview	209
Chapter 54	So Who Did It?	213
Chapter 55	It's Rather Incriminating	218
Chapter 56	Post Mortem	222
Chapter 57	The Suspects?	228
Chapter 58	You Can Go	234
Chapter 59	Let's Keep An Eye On Him	238
Chapter 60	You Bastard!	242
Chapter 61	Sorry For Your Loss	246
Chapter 62	Let's Go Away?	250
Chapter 63	What Have We Found?	252
Chapter 64	Oh Sienna!	258
Chapter 65	Who's There?!	263

PART 3	271
CHAPTER 66 – A DAWN AWAKENING	273
CHAPTER 67 – DEAD MEN DON'T LIE	276
CHAPTER 68 – WHAT NOW SIR?	281
CHAPTER 69 – NEW HORIZONS	285
CHAPTER 70 – FIRST IMPRESSIONS	287
CHAPTER 71 – AH MRS BROWNLOUGH!	290
CHAPTER 72 – THAT'S GOOD NEWS	295
CHAPTER 73 – RE-EVALUATION	299
CHAPTER 74 – POST MORTEM II	302
CHAPTER 75 – WHAT NOW?	306
CHAPTER 76 – WE'RE OFF WHERE?	311
CHAPTER 77 – A LONG DRIVE!	314
CHAPTER 78 – ANOTHER LONG DRIVE	319
CHAPTER 79 – A SAFE HARBOUR	323
CHAPTER 80 – OXFORD	328
CHAPTER 81 – WAS THIS WHAT HAPPENED?	329
CHAPTER 82 – REVELATIONS?	334
CHAPTER 83 – WHERE WERE YOU?	342
CHAPTER 84 – A DAWN BEACH WALK	345
EPILOGUE	347
ACKNOWLEDGEMENTS	353
THE NEXT CJ GRAY MYSTERY	355

It Wasn't Me!

PROLOGUE - 1919

The meeting at Edendale village hall was drawing to a close, the Minutes had been signed as a true record of the inaugural meeting of *The Edendale Golf Club*. The room wasn't overly crowded, and everyone there was showing a keen interest in the proceedings.

The officers had been elected by those in attendance and the members' book was drafted to reflect the thirty-three members present.

The Four Trustees: Earl Hargrove; Doctor N Spinney MD; Major E Gray MC; and Mr M Warner LLB were each provided with copies of the Deeds, including the covenants in place and the 100-year lease regarding the proposed golf course. Mr Warner, the club's newly appointed solicitor retained the originals for safe keeping.

The course was designated for the playing of golf, by its members and the inhabitants of Edendale Village and the surrounding area. New members were to be proposed and seconded by existing members and voted as to their acceptability by the committee.

It was agreed that renowned architect, Alister MacKenzie, would be commissioned to design the course on the site of the former Yorksbey Racecourse, and following much debate as to whether such an extravagance could be justified, his fee of ten guineas was finally accepted by the meeting.

C J Meads

It was hoped and expected that the course would be open for golf within two years and provide a rewarding and satisfying challenge for its members for years to come.

It Wasn't Me!

TODAY

The air suddenly felt cold despite the sun shining through the stable doorway.

Charlotte Tate looked down at the blood-soaked knife in her hand, and then back at the dead body lying prostrate on the stable floor.

The fine jet-black colt, *Never Say Die,* gave out a chilling whinny, as he looked on indifferently.

'What have you done?' screamed Sarah Brownlough, as she came through the stable door seeing the dead body of the man she loved lying on the floor.

'It wasn't me!' said Charlotte quietly, struggling to come to terms with the unfolding events.

'It Wasn't Me!' she yelled in sudden realisation of how it appeared………

C J Meads

It Wasn't Me!

PART 1 – THREE WEEKS EARLIER

C J Meads

It Wasn't Me!

Chapter 1 – The Race

'Come on, come on *Never Say Die*, come on!'

Charlotte Tate was cheering on the leading horse in the last race at the Jebel Ali Racecourse in Dubai. Alongside her in the grandstand were well-to-do Emiratis and Expats. The sun was just starting to wane as she turned to the prospective buyer of the horse and her latest conquest.

Stuart Brownlough looked her deep in the eyes and smiled, but it was that smug type of smile that is reserved for those perhaps too certain of their own self-importance.

'He's going to do it. Come on, come on. Yes!'

The horse held on by a short head to win, and all those in close proximity - and a huge majority of the 12,000 spectators - gave out a loud cheer.

'Well Stuart, are you going to buy him for me?'

'Maybe, if you're a good girl, I might just do that.'

'Me be a good girl? I thought I was always good!' teased the wonderfully bronzed Charlotte.

She had topped up her tan over the last week at her resort of choice, *Atlantis The Palm,* while Stuart had been in many meetings with wealthy businessman *Sheikh Masud Twoammie,* a distant relative of Sheikh Mohammed bin Rashid Al Maktoum, the current ruler of Dubai.

Stuart had been struggling to get the necessary financial backing for his latest development, but he was getting more confident that the seeds he had sown were germinating and Sheikh Twoammie was finally showing more interest.

Stuart was no fool, and he knew that *His Excellency* was a shrewd negotiator, and that finalising any deal would take time and patience, but the goal was well worth it.

Between meetings, Charlotte had satisfied Stuart's extreme sexual desires in the hope of convincing him to divorce his estranged wife.

However, while Stuart liked Charlotte's high sex drive, which was the polar opposite of Sarah's, as twenty years of marriage often sees the glow of youthful love diminish, he still had his business to consider, and also his family. This included his eighteen-year-old, attractive but headstrong daughter, Sienna, whom he felt doted on him.

'Your Excellency, *Never Say Die,* is truly a wonderful colt. I hope you'll consider parting with him. Charlotte, as you can see, is very much taken with him,' said Stuart obsequiously, as he sought to charm the Sheikh.

'I'm always open to offers that match my valuation and expectation. If you come up with a suitable proposal, I'll obviously consider it,' said Sheikh Twoammie graciously.

'I would like to think that if we can conclude a satisfactory deal on the *Edendale Project* Housing Development, then *Never Say Die* could be part of the arrangement.'

'Perhaps,' said a more cautious Shiekh Twoammie. 'Perhaps.'

It Wasn't Me!

'Oh Your Excellency, I do hope you can see your way to letting him go. I think he's wonderful,' said Charlotte, smiling broadly at the Sheikh, and winking provocatively at him.

'My dear, you perhaps presume too much, but maybe we can discuss things further over dinner this evening. How does that sound?'

'We would like that, wouldn't we, darling?' she continued as she sidled up to Stuart.

'Unfortunately, I've another previously arranged business meeting this evening, but please feel free to dine with His Excellency. If he feels that it is appropriate.'

'Oh!' said Charlotte, seemingly taken aback.

'I would welcome your company Ms Tate; shall I send a car at 7 pm?'

'That would be lovely, thank you.'

Chapter 2 – The Meeting

'Well James, Charlotte didn't take long to get over her husband's death,' said Edee, quizzically smiling at CJ.

'Edee, it was never in doubt,' replied CJ, as he looked longingly into his lover's eyes.

The multi-lingual, enigmatic French beauty, and the former respected and decorated army colonel, made an elegant couple as they watched the events of the last race unfold while enjoying the remaining few days of their short visit to Dubai.

Madame Eden Songe, finally had her unrequited love recognised by her charming and ruggedly good-looking man that was her boss. She had been literally swept off her feet by her long-term *friend* and employer, CJ Gray, after they had solved the tragic events surrounding the death of Oliver 'Bart' Tate at Edendale Golf Club.

The two of them had, since that day, been virtually inseparable, and they both at times felt like young lovers, learning things about one another that they had never realised, despite knowing each other for nearly a quarter of a century.

'I think we both know Charlotte well enough, but even for her, she seems to have no shame.'

'True, but I wonder whether Brownlough knows what he's getting involved with,' added CJ.

'Do you know him?' asked a thoughtful Edee.

'I know of him. He's a housing developer, but similar to Bart, he has a reputation for cutting corners

It Wasn't Me!

and sailing close to the wind with his business ventures. Rather, a Machiavellian type character.'

'Sounds like he's right up Charlotte's street, and not so surprising that she's involved with him.'

'I think they are potentially a match, but what's the saying? "similar poles don't attract." So I think they may both need to watch out for one another.'

'Do you think they're both in the relationship for selfish reasons?' asked a smiling Edee.

'I think you may have a valid point. As always, you're very observant,' added CJ, as he took a sip of the sparkling rose water, the popular alcoholic substitute at Islamic sporting events.

'Do you know if Brownlough is married?' enquired Edee.

'I believe he is, so he and Charlotte may have to tread carefully if they don't want to upset his wife and family, but maybe they don't care. I'm sure Charlotte is probably not that bothered. She has a track record for breaking up marriages and coming out smelling of roses.'

'She is stunning though, isn't she?'

'Not as beautiful as you are, my darling,' said CJ with genuine affection as he chinked glasses with the woman of his dreams.

Edee resisted the urge to kiss him, knowing that signs of affection are illegal in public in Dubai, and frowned upon, even by expatriates. She did though, smile and looked longingly back into CJ's deep brown eyes, thinking about what she would do later when they were back at the local home of CJ's only daughter Jemima.

The moment was broken as they were joined by Stuart and Charlotte.

'Hello Gray, I didn't expect to see you here. I didn't know you were a race goer. And who's this wonderful lady? Punching above your weight, aren't you?' said Stuart as he undressed Edee with his eyes.

'Just like Bart, a complete chancer,' thought CJ.

'Hello Brownlough, Charlotte, what a pleasant surprise,' CJ lied as he continued.

'This is Madame Eden Songe; she's my business partner.'

'And lover?' interjected Charlotte, as she offered CJ one of her dazzling smiles, ignoring Edee as she had a way of doing. Charlotte had, despite their age difference, always maintained a crush on CJ, even though he was the father of her old school *friend* Jemima.

'Hi Charlotte, Mr Brownlough. You seem to be enjoying yourselves,' added Edee, in her normal pleasant manner, completely unfazed by Charlotte's mild but obvious flirting with CJ.

'To answer your question, I occasionally like to go to the races, and while we're visiting my daughter and her family, I thought I would share the experience of racing in Dubai with Edee.'

'Yes, it's slightly different to racing in the UK. No betting is a bit of a drag,' added Stuart, rather haughtily, who clearly missed the buzz of gambling, something prohibited in Islamic countries.

'You seemed to be cheering on the winner, *Never Say Die.* Any reason for your close interest?' asked Edee curiously.

It Wasn't Me!

'I'm hoping Stuart will buy him. I do love horses,' said Charlotte, rather too enthusiastically.

'I'm planning to try to charm Sheikh Twoammie into letting him go, but I may have my work cut out,' added Charlotte, who seemed well up for the challenge.

'On that matter Gray, if I do convince His Excellency to sell him, I was hoping you could sort out the importing of the colt into the UK.'

'As you know, we at GGL specialise in solving any worldwide logistic issue, so if or when you want our assistance, please get in touch. I'm sure Edee will provide you with a realistic price for a comprehensive service.'

'Understood. Let's hope we can do business in the near future,' responded Stuart, before adding, rather in a matter-of-fact way, 'Gray, I believe your family has always been trustees of the golf club in Edendale. Is this still the case?'

'Yes, I am. Any reason for you asking?'

'No, not for now, I was just curious,' replied Stuart, rather too condescending for CJ's liking, as he and Charlotte moved off as smartly as they had arrived.

'What was that all about?' asked Edee, rather intrigued.

'I'm not too sure, but knowing Brownlough, I think he's up to something no good,' replied CJ mysteriously.

'And, *business partner*? You hadn't previously mentioned anything?' asked Edee, rather surprised by CJ's earlier response to Stuart.

'I've been thinking about how we take things forward, not only personally but also regarding Gray Group Limited. I mean, when all's said and done, you virtually run the business already, albeit with just a *little* help from me,' toyed CJ.

'Oh,' said a rather amazed, but also pleasantly pleased Edee.

It Wasn't Me!

CHAPTER 3 – THE SECRET LOVERS

'What's so important?' asked a rather confused Sarah Brownlough, as her companion joined her in a quiet luxury hotel lounge in Etongate, the wonderful and charming spa town in North Yorkshire.

'You mean you're not pleased to see me?' replied Andrew Kipling.

She kissed him gently on the lips, as he sat beside her on the leather chesterfield sofa.

'You know I am. But your message seemed urgent.'

He held her hand and continued, 'Not so much urgent, but it is important, and I haven't seen you for a while.'

'I know. But it's been a bit tricky lately. Stuart has been in a rather strange mood, and to be honest, I'm not really sure why.'

'He's always in a mood. *You* don't have to deal with him regarding business. He can be a complete bastard at times.'

Kipling Solicitors in Yorksbey were Brownlough Developments' legal advisors, with Mr Kipling Jnr. responsible in the practice for the account. The relationship had been established when Brownlough Developments was first incorporated, and whether by good fortune, pure luck or necessity, Andrew Kipling had been asked by his father, Mr Kipling Snr, to oversee the forming of the business for a young Stuart Brownlough, and their relationship went from strength to strength.

'You're telling me. You're lucky you haven't had to live with him for the last twenty years.'

'I know, but you have me to soothe your worries, at least periodically,' said Andrew, as he kissed her with more passion than she had him.

Sarah and Andrew's relationship had also been simmering for the same period, and while Sarah had always loved Andrew, Stuart had got in first, and swept her off her feet with a surprising marriage proposal. This was just as Sarah and Andrew had quarrelled and fallen out over a silly thing as young lovers do.

Her parents were not too pleased with her decision to marry Stuart. They would have much preferred her to marry the well-educated son of the most respected solicitor in Edendale, rather than the charming self-obsessed Stuart.

In hindsight, it was possibly Sarah's biggest mistake, but she stuck with the rather self-righteous and opinionated chancer, more because their daughter Sienna was born soon after they were married.

Andrew also married on the re-bound, and they both kept up the pretence of being happily married, despite both soon realising that their love was greater than that with their respective spouses.

Their secret relationship had been difficult at times, but still sexually rewarding, and as their respective children were now both reaching adulthood, they were contemplating their futures.

It Wasn't Me!

'Look Sarah. Stuart's been putting me under pressure to finalise a legal document that's even more unusual even for him. A bit dodgy.'

'That's nothing new. *You,* more than anyone, should know how he operates.'

'Yes, I realise that, but this deal is going to make him very rich. I mean, very, very rich!'

'So, what's the problem? The more for me also,' said a smiling Sarah.

'I'm not sure you'll be seeing any of the money, plus it's potentially going to make him a lot of enemies. And I mean, *a lot of enemies!*' stated a worried-looking Andrew.

'What is this document?' enquired Sarah.

'I think for now it would be better if you didn't know too much. But I thought you should be aware, because when it becomes common knowledge, the shit will well and truly hit the fan!'

'Well, I think tomorrow's shit can take care of itself for now,' said Sarah, with a twinkle in her eye, as she got up and beckoned Andrew to follow.

'I think you're right,' said Andrew as he caught her around the waist and whispered.

'Just don't say you weren't warned.'

C J Meads

Chapter 4 – Dinner Date

'Are you sure you're still okay with this?' asked an intrigued Stuart, as he was lying naked on the bed of the suite in *Atlantis the Palm*. He was watching Charlotte getting ready for her dinner date with Sheikh Twoammie, and she was reinforcing the male understanding that women take hours to get ready.

'It's a bit late now for second thoughts, especially as it was your idea.'

'I know, but can you handle Masud? He has a reputation for being quite a charmer.'

'Look Stuart, do you want the horse and the money he can provide for the development, or not?' said Charlotte, as she turned from looking in the mirror and applying the final touches to her immaculate make-up, with her customary deep red lip gloss. She looked stunning as always, and had decided that a black Basque, sheer black stockings, and killer Christian Louboutin stiletto heels, might prove to be key in her bid to convince the Sheikh to go along with their plans.

'I guess so, but just be careful. There's a lot *riding* on this.'

'Don't you think I know that, or don't you trust me?' said Charlotte, giving Stuart one of her seductive looks.

'I know I can't trust you. You've always been a rebel, but now you have a cause.'

Charlotte got up from her seat and moved gracefully over to the bed and kissed Stuart gently on the lips. He was suddenly aroused, and looked to grab the seductive femme fatale, but she deftly eluded his attention.

'You're not going to spoil my make-up with a quick fumble just to satisfy your desires. Well, not for now. If you're good, though, I'll see what I can do later. Especially if the night goes as we plan.'

'You teaser!' said a thoughtful Stuart, who was already planning in his mind the events for later in the evening.

CJ paid the taxi driver and offered a generous tip, as usual. As he and Edee walked into the villa's front garden, the two of them finally felt confident that they weren't being overlooked, and instinctively embraced and kissed.

'I've been wanting to do that all afternoon,' said CJ.

'So have I,' said Edee. 'I do love you.'

'And I love you, with a deep passion.'

The two of them laughed and CJ knocked on the large front door.

'Hi. We're back,' called out CJ, as he and Edee entered the villa in *The Meadows*, the much sought after and pleasant suburban district of Dubai.

Jemima, her partner Marcus, and their young daughter Emmy, had lived at the two storey, five-bedroom villa for the last couple of years. It was a wonderful home overlooking the lake to the rear, with distant views of Jumeirah Lakes Towers and the Dubai Marina in the far distance.

The striking young woman, who had inherited her late mother's stunning looks, walked into the lobby from the open plan living area.

'Have you had a good day?' she enquired. 'Did Edee enjoy horse racing in Dubai?'

'It was wonderful, thank you, Jemima,' replied a happy Edee.

'Guess who we met?' asked CJ, tantalisingly.

'Now that could be almost anyone. Horse racing is popular in Dubai.'

'Yes, I know, but it was someone you've known from your school days.'

'You're telling me that Charlotte Tate was at the races in Dubai? Who was she with? Knowing her, some rich and prosperous sheikh,' asked a perplexed Jemima.

'Not quite, albeit she had her eye on a local Emirati. However, she was with Stuart Brownlough. I don't know if you know him,' replied CJ.

'No, I don't think I do. Should I?'

'Not really, and perhaps it's better if you don't,' said Edee. 'Especially if what James told me is correct.'

'Now Edee, I thought by now you would have realised that Dad can be rather judgemental. I guess he's good looking though, this Brownlough?' teased Jemima.

'Not as lovely as your dad,' said Edee as she linked arms with CJ.

'Edee, stop it. You sound like a love-struck young girl, rather than the worldly wise and educated woman you really are,' teased a smiling Jemima.

It Wasn't Me!

Just then, Emmy came running towards them with her favourite doll in her arms.

'Hi Grandad James,' she shouted, as CJ swept her up in his arms and hugged her tight.

'Have you been a good girl for mummy today?'

'I'm always a good girl,' she replied earnestly.

'Now, where have I heard that before?' countered CJ, as they all burst out laughing at the cheeky, rather precocious little girl.

The luxury black limousine pulled up outside the entrance to *Atlantis The Palm*. The hotel porter approached the driver, who had lowered the front window.

'Oh, I'm sorry; I didn't realise it was Sheikh Twoammie's car. Do you want the limousine parking?'

'No, I'm collecting Ms Charlotte Tate,' replied the driver. 'Could you please let her know I'm here?'

'Certainly, I'll go and see where she is.'

The porter rushed into the hotel and approached the reception desk.

He was about to ask the smart young woman to ring Ms Tate's room, when suddenly there was a gasp from those in the grand lobby. Charlotte Tate had emerged from one of the many lifts, looking even more gorgeous than usual.

She had slipped into a most elegant long black ball gown, with a side split that reached nearly to the top of her thigh. She had, though, for her, been rather conservative, complementing the dress with a silk shawl draped around her head and shoulders, so as to not offend the locals or the Sheikh.

The sound of her heels echoed around the lobby, as Charlotte moved sexily across the floor, and all the male expats turned in admiration of the elegant and beautiful woman. Many of their partners also looked on in appreciation, or jealousy, as Charlotte was escorted by the porter to the limousine outside.

The heat of the day was subsiding, but there was still a noticeable difference between the coolness of the lobby and the humidity of the dark evening air.

The chauffeur opened the rear door, allowing Charlotte to elegantly slip in beside Sheikh Twoammie. The Emirati was dressed as usual in traditional Muslim robes, a white full length Kandura, with a Ghutrah on his head held in place with a black Agal, all traditional UAE clothing.

The coolness of the interior was most pleasant, and the sheikh's expensive cologne filled the air.

'Massa Alkhayr, Good Evening, Ms Tate, you're looking stunning. Thank you for accepting my invitation.'

'Good Evening, Your Excellency. The pleasure, I can assure you, is all mine,' said a smiling Charlotte, as she allowed her dress to part, showing off her long sexy legs.

'Law samaht. Please, whilst we are alone, call me Masud.'

'And you must call me Charlotte.'

'Or anything else you want,' thought Charlotte as she accepted a cool crystal champagne glass of sparkling rose water from him.

It Wasn't Me!

'Fe Sahatek, Cheers,' said Charlotte, hoping she wasn't offending Masud.

'Fe Sahatek,' he replied, smiling graciously.

'So, where are we going to dine?' enquired an inquisitive Charlotte.

'For you, my dear, only the best. The one and only 7 Star hotel. The world famous, Burj Al Arab.'

'Oh wonderful. That sounds marvellous,' said Charlotte as the car pulled away from the hotel.

C J Meads

Chapter 5 – Financial Affairs

Brownlough's phone rang. It was his accountant.

'Nick, do you know what time it is?' asked a rather disgruntled Stuart.

'Sorry, but it's only 4 pm here in the UK, and this really can't wait.'

'What's so important?'

Nicholas Banker, or as his school *friends* had called him, "Nicky Banker, a right old *Wanker,*" had been Stuart's accountant for as long as he could remember. The nickname was still used by many who dealt with this dubious financial wizard, but he was pretty damn good at finding any loophole, or dodge, especially when it came to high finance.

He had kept Brownlough Developments afloat on numerous occasions, when more legitimate businesses would have ended in administration or filed for bankruptcy.

Most people keep their personal and business finances separate, but not Stuart Brownlough, and not when dealing with this potentially tricky situation. His dealings were often dodgy, possibly corrupt, and more often than not, sailing close to the wind.

His finances were so intrinsically entwined that any genuine auditor would struggle to convince the authorities as to their legitimacy.

'Look Stuart, how's the deal going? And more realistically, when will I see some substantial funds? HMRC are on our case, the VAT bill is overdue and

It Wasn't Me!

if you don't pay it *now*, you're going to be fined. And we sure as hell don't need more unnecessary costs.'

'Nick, I'm aware of the issues. We only spoke about it yesterday. I don't need you ringing me daily seeking an update.'

'Yes, I know, but please answer my question. If I'm going to look after you and keep you out of jail, I need something positive to work with.'

'I'll let you know when I've something meaningful to report.'

'That isn't good enough,' replied an exasperated Nick.

'Maybe not, but it's all I can offer you at the moment. Or perhaps not.'

'What does that mean?' enquired Nick hopefully.

'Charlotte is dining with Sheikh Twoammie this evening. With her subtle charm, I'm hopeful he'll be on board.'

'Well, that's the first bit of good news you've given me for months. Now I know Charlotte Tate is involved. I'll possibly sleep slightly better tonight.'

'Hopefully, I won't be sleeping too much when she gets back with good news. I plan to celebrate with her in style,' stated an enthusiastic Stuart.

'Fingers crossed, but even with a deal agreed in principle, we will need money sooner rather than later. HMRC aren't too keen on accepting vague promises from UAE Sheikhs as reasonable collateral,' joked Nick, but he recognised that the consequences of funds not being forthcoming soon, didn't really bear thinking about.

Chapter 6 – And For Afters?

Sheikh Twoammie walked side by side with Charlotte as they entered the grand hotel reception, rather than what is deemed the convention in Islamic countries, where men traditionally walk in front of women.

'Charlotte, have you visited here before?' asked Masud.

'No, I haven't, and it looks rather grand..... and no doubt, expensive.'

'The Royal Suite costs AED 100,000 or £20,000 a night,' Masud enlightened Charlotte. 'I sometimes stay here, especially when there is a special occasion to celebrate.'

Charlotte already knew that Sheikh Twoammie was wealthy. That was the main reason she was dining with him, but if he was often staying in such expensive hotels, he was definitely the kind of backer they needed.

Even Charlotte was impressed, and though she had stayed at many luxury hotels, this was undoubtedly the most luxurious she had visited.

'There are many extremely good restaurants in the hotel. Al Mahara is a 2-star Michelin underwater restaurant where, as you dine, the glorious underwater world is visible through the wall to ceiling aquarium walls,' continued Masud, providing Charlotte with an insight into the grand hotel.

'Are we dining there this evening?' enquired Charlotte, who was intrigued by the concept.

It Wasn't Me!

'No, and I had considered the luxury Al Iwan, which serves more traditional Arabic cuisine, but I decided that the Michelin starred Al Muntaha, would be more to your liking.'

'Oh, so you think you've established what I like?' said Charlotte, coquettishly, as she looked longingly at Masud.

'It's on the 27th floor and is considered amongst the best of the restaurants, offering fine dining, intricate flavours and a mesmerising vista of the Dubai Skyline.'

'That sounds absolutely marvellous,' gushed Charlotte.

As they waited for the lift, Charlotte's phone vibrated. She looked into her purse at the phone; it was a message from Stuart.

'How's it going? Xxx.'

'Sod off, Stuart, leave this to me. I know what I'm doing,' she thought, as she closed the purse.

'Anything wrong?' enquired Masud.

'No, just one of those annoying, unnecessary notifications,' she politely replied.

The lift ride was fast and short. The two of them stood quietly alone until the lift doors opened.

As Masud beckoned Charlotte to lead the way, she saw on one side of the panoramic view, the dramatic Dubai skyline, and on the other side, ships' lights shining in the distance of the Arabian Gulf, plus a wonderful view of *The Palm* reaching out into the sea.

'Wow! Now that is impressive.'

The many skyscrapers looked extremely inspiring in the dark Dubai night sky, silhouetted by the millions of twinkling stars.

'Good Evening, Your Excellency, Madame,' the Maître d' courteously welcomed them, instantly recognising Masud. 'Please come this way. I have reserved you your usual table.'

He helped Charlotte by pulling back the luxury chair, before bringing it back as she sat down. He then attended to Sheikh Twoammie.

Charlotte provocatively removed her shawl, to reveal her long blonde hair, tied in a perfectly crafted bun, while exposing her wonderfully tanned shoulders. Her arms were covered with black silk gloves that reached up elegantly above her elbows. Her outfit was complete.

As the Maître d' momentarily left them, Charlotte said, 'Masud, you certainly know how to impress a lady.'

'I try to please,' said the charming sheikh. 'And if you don't mind me saying, so do you. You look radiant.'

Having initially looked at the menu and seen the expensive cuisine on offer, with dishes ranging from AED 300, (£60), to AED 1,200 (£250), and Imperial Beluga Caviar at a mouth-watering AED 2,500 for 50g, Charlotte coyly said, 'I think you should choose, I'm intrigued to see if you really know me as well as you think you do.'

'Charlotte, I think you're toying with me,' said an assured Masud. 'But I'll take up the challenge with

It Wasn't Me!

vigour,' as he smiled at her longingly and continued to place the order.

The evening was wonderful. Charlotte worked her charm on the Sheikh, conveying innocence, womanly charm and, more obviously, sex appeal. Masud was clearly impressed.

It was now getting late, and the restaurant was empty of guests, apart from Charlotte and Masud. He had settled what was a rather expensive bill, being in excess of AED 9,000 (£1,800), but for the Sheikh, nowhere near the realms of his most extravagant nights out.

'Masud, you've been a most wonderful host. Thank you again for a memorable evening. The food was exceptional and the company even better.'

'You are most welcome. I'm pleased you've enjoyed yourself.'

'So, have I convinced you to invest in the Housing Development, and more importantly, to part with *Never Say Die?*'

'You have been most persuasive with your arguments, but I'm still not sure. I'm soon to be in the UK, and Yorksbey, for the *Equinox Festival.* I'm sponsoring the meeting. So I suggest Stuart takes the opportunity to make a formal presentation and perhaps show me the site.'

'Oh,' said a slightly deflated Charlotte, who quickly rallied though.

'Shall we take this further?' coaxed Charlotte.

'I'm not sure what you mean. Would you like to join my harem?' taunted Masud, enquiringly.

'A most gracious offer, Your Excellency, but I'm, as you have possibly noticed, not one to play *second fiddle* to anyone.'

'No. I thought not, but if you ever change your mind, then I believe I can keep you in the manner you desire.'

'How about a little nightcap?' asked Charlotte, as she saw the opportunity to convince Masud, potentially slipping from her grasp. 'Shall we get a room? To cap off a most wonderful evening.'

'Charlotte, I've a busy day tomorrow and I have to be up early, so I think I'll just take you back to your hotel and your *business* partner.'

They both walked to the lift in silence. Charlotte was considering how to win back the initiative she had held earlier in the evening. She had at times felt that Masud was on board with the *deal,* but the recent conversations had shown what a shrewd man Sheikh Twoammie was. Stuart had warned her not to take anything for granted, but she had felt that the task was well within her ability. She had hoped that while alone in a hotel room with the rugged Emirati, she could work her sexual charms, but that opportunity had surprisingly been quashed good and proper.

They had transitioned the slightly cooling warmth of the evening air, and were now sitting quietly in the cool rear of the limousine.

'Masud, perhaps I have one last thing that may convince you as to the suitability of our proposed adventure,' enticed Charlotte, as she pulled her dress to one side again, revealing her long slender legs wrapped sexily in the sheer stockings.

It Wasn't Me!

She initially gently touched his hand with her own gloved hand, and then gracefully slipped it beneath his robe and caressed his manhood.

He quickly became aroused.

'Charlotte! that is wonderful.'

'Your Excellency, please come to our party and finance the deal,' said Charlotte, in her most tantalising way, before going down on his now fully erect penis.

'Yes,' gasped Masud as Charlotte gave head, and expertly performed fellatio, while gently caressing and then squeezing his firm scrotum.

'Yes, Yes!'

The chauffeur momentarily looked in the rear-view mirror, and smiled, before he swiftly ensured his eyes were back on the road. He had not seen that before, well, not in the back of the Sheikh's car.

'Charlotte! I'm convinced!' gasped Masud, as he ejaculated. 'I think we have a *deal*!' he panted, seeking to regain his breath, while gracefully kissing the top of her head in appreciation.

Chapter 7 – The Architect

Harry Tovaine was overseeing the final drawings and specifications for the *Edendale Project* that he had drawn up for Brownlough Developments.

It was possibly the best work he had produced to date, and he was confident that this development would be the springboard to launch his fledgling company, *Tovaine Architects,* into the wider architectural world.

The initial five years of studying, and the following two years to get his postgraduate Master of Architecture, had been a significant drain on his meagre resources. His parents were unable to offer him any financial support, being from humble hard-working stock, but he had worked hard to get where he was, and now had his small company up and running.

His mum and dad, though, were extremely proud of their only child and his achievements. No one from either side of the family had ever been to college, let alone university, or had gained a master's degree.

The small practice in Yorksbey, comprised of Harry, an architectural technician, and an office manager, as she liked to be called, but realistically, she was a glorified secretary.

Harry had taken a very unusual route into the highly competitive world of architecture. It was normal to *serve your time,* with a larger architectural practice, before venturing forth into your own business. However, Harry was far from conventional.

It Wasn't Me!

He had seen a rare opportunity when Stuart Brownlough first floated the idea of the *Edendale Project* Housing Development. Harry had also shown an enthusiasm that Stuart had immediately latched onto.

The only downside for Harry, but a shrewd business proposition by Stuart, was that Tovaine Architects would receive a percentage of the Development's profits, rather than a conventional upfront fee, based on the expected development's value.

The pros and cons of this arrangement were clear to both parties. They both went into the deal with their eyes open. Well, Stuart did, that was for certain. For Harry? Possibly, possibly not!

Stuart had no initial costs to consider in the arrangement before properties were sold, and income from the development was forthcoming. He would, however, finally pay out more, especially the more successful the development became.

Harry had to initially keep his new business going with a high interest rate bank loan until the greater rewards were forthcoming. He had accepted the challenge, even though he had struggled for many years to make ends meet, and a short time more was something he just had to accept. The deal though would make him rich, and establish Tovaine Architects, while also proving his critics and doubting peers wrong.

'Peter, I've just completed my latest review of Section B of the specification. Could you please update it for tomorrow?'

'I've the drawings you *red penned* to revise and complete. I don't think I can get them both done for tomorrow.'

'What about a bit of overtime?' suggested Harry.

Rebecca, the young *office manager,* overheard the conversation in the small office, and gave out a small, but noticeable cough.

Harry looked up and shook his head at her. He knew what she was about to say, but he didn't particularly want Peter, the experienced architectural technician, to hear it.

She was concerned, as he most certainly was, about cash flow, and paying out more overtime was an expensive commodity the business could really do without.

'I can only put a couple of hours in, but I'm still not sure I can get both jobs finished,' continued Peter. 'Jane is out tomorrow night, and I'll be looking after the kids.'

'Okay, let's forget the overtime for tomorrow. Peter, let's concentrate on the drawings. Pictures speak a thousand words. To be honest, a few errors in a specification, that only a few people are likely to read, and that runs to several hundred pages, is not the end of the world.'

Peter and Rebecca both acknowledged the sensible proposal, while Harry suddenly looked at Rebecca and made an alternative suggestion.

'Rebecca, could you please perhaps fit in updating the specification?' he smilingly asked.

The unconventionally attractive Rebecca had rather a crush on the more conventionally attractive

It Wasn't Me!

young man, and as always, she looked to please her boss. This was possibly more in hope that he would reciprocate, and show a similar fondness for her, but it was unlikely.

She considered his suggestion and replied.

'I can work a bit later tomorrow if that helps. I can keep you company, and between us I'm sure we can get to grip on things.'

Harry knew what had to be done, and it would at least be another thing ticked off the increasing list of outstanding items that were slowly getting finalised. He would also continue to tolerate Rebecca's obvious mild flirting, but would have to ensure he didn't unnecessarily encourage her.

Tovaine Architects were also on a strict deadline, which Harry knew he had to meet, and upsetting Stuart Brownlough was not something he relished. He had previously seen him in action when he was displeased and did not want to be on the end of a repeat performance.

Chapter 8 – How Did It Go?

Charlotte quietly opened the bedroom door of the hotel suite. She was hoping that maybe Stuart was asleep, as it was getting rather late.

Perhaps unluckily for her, he wasn't. The prize on offer had meant that he was buzzing and wide awake. A half bottle of malt whisky, and the two lines of cocaine, may also have had something to do with it.

'Well, how did it go?' asked a naked Stuart before Charlotte was even through the doorway.

'Well. Good Evening, to you too!' said a clearly indignant Charlotte.

'Oh. Sorry darling, I didn't mean to be so self-obsessed. How are you? Did you enjoy your evening?'

Stuart sought to quickly get back on the good side of Charlotte. She still looked stunningly elegant, and he couldn't wait to get her out of the dress, regardless of the outcome of her best endeavours. He was definitely seeking good news, and to celebrate. But worse case, he would just indulge in wanton sex to overcome any disappointment.

'Unfortunately, things didn't go quite to plan,' said Charlotte, looking downcast.

'Oh, never mind, you tried your best,' said an equally despondent Stuart, who was seeking to hide his obvious displeasure, as he needed the financial backing to make his plan work.

'Pass me a glass of Champagne, I still have a terrible taste in my mouth,' requested Charlotte, who clearly wanted to remove the remaining taste of Masud's semen.

'Here you go.'

'Thanks. That's better,' said Charlotte, as she downed the glass in one.

'Do you want to talk about it?' asked Stuart, who clearly wanted to know what had gone wrong.

'The night was great. Have you been to the Burj Al Arab?'

'No. So he took you there. That must have been a great experience?'

'It was, and I thought I had him all convinced. I conveyed all the things you and I had previously discussed. He was definitely impressed. But as you said earlier, he's a shrewd cookie.'

'I thought as much,' said a deflated Stuart. 'I did kind of warn you of what he's like.'

'I tried my best. He even offered me a place in his harem.'

'No! The cheeky bastard. You did refuse. Didn't you?'

'Of course. What do you take me for? I even suggested a room, but he was having none of it.'

'So it's a no then?'

'Well, not really. He's coming to the UK for the *Equinox Festival. Would* you believe that he's sponsoring the meeting? But I digress. He wants to see your plans and firm proposals. He's definitely still interested, plus he wants to see the site.'

'Mmm. That could be tricky, but we can go the whole way with the proposal. I'll get Harry to build a model that will surely convince Masud,' said a now more enthusiastic Stuart, before adding. 'Well done, Charlotte. You did your best.'

'That's not all of it,' she said, tantalisingly.

'Go on.'

'On the way back, I indulged in a little fellatio. Like all men, he couldn't resist a quick blow job. He was putty in my mouth. Well, perhaps a bit firmer than that,' joked Charlotte.

'And?'

'He's up for it. He said it's a deal. I guess that may not be a legally binding agreement, but I think we have him,' said a smiling Charlotte.

'You resourceful girl. I knew you could do it. Come here,' said Stuart, who was now fully aroused by Charlotte's adventures.

He pulled her to him and kissed her passionately on the lips, before reconsidering what had recently been in her mouth.

He continued to kiss her neck and fondled her firm enhanced breasts and inner thigh, having pulled to one side the slit in her gown.

'You're wonderful,' he continued, as he unzipped the dress, and let it slip to the floor.

She looked stunning in her basque, stockings, heels, and gloves.

He then toyed with her vagina, which had been free of panties all evening. Charlotte gasped in appreciation.

'You now also appear to be aroused,' she said, as she gently caressed his manhood, which was firmly erect and now seeking a target.

It Wasn't Me!

Stuart pushed her onto the end of the bed, while pulling her dangling legs apart. He knelt down on the floor before going down on her and crudely performed cunnilingus.

Charlotte looked up and contemplated a crack in the ceiling. But then closed her eyes and thought of Masud, and then rather surprisingly, momentarily, CJ, as Stuart stimulated her throbbing clitoris, labia, and vulva. His tongue then ventured towards her anus.

'Can I fuck your arse?'

'I thought you would never ask,' whispered an ironic Charlotte, as she grabbed her heels and spreadeagled her legs, before flippantly continuing.

'I do hope you appreciate my recent anal bleaching.'

Stuart pushed his erect manhood into her exposed anus, perhaps for once, rather too forcibly for Charlotte's liking.

'Steady Tiger, we both need to enjoy this,' she said as she gasped under his continued movements.

'Fucking hell!' Easy boy!'

But Stuart was in the moment and was thrusting like his life depended upon it.

Charlotte orgasmed, as she involuntarily wrapped her legs around Stuart's back, and he ejaculated soon after. As he pulled out, he kissed her clitoris and then on the lips.

'Thanks. I needed that,' he said, rather matter-of-factly.

While Charlotte enjoyed most sexual encounters, and the varied roleplay with Stuart, she was mindful that his occasional extreme desires might potentially, at some point, get out of hand.

'Was she already tiring of Stuart?' she idly considered.

But perhaps that thought was for another day, as she again looked up at the ceiling, but this time wondering how the crack had originally occurred.

It Wasn't Me!

Chapter 9 – Contemplating

Edee was woken from a dreamy sleep by the early morning sunlight streaming through a break in the curtains.

'What's the weather doing? Don't tell me, the sun's shining again in Dubai?' she enquired of CJ.

He was standing in only his designer trunks, while idly thinking and looking out over the lake, with its fountain gracefully splashing. His tanned, tall athletic frame silhouetted by the early sunshine.

'Sorry. What did you say?'

'I was saying.... Oh, it doesn't matter,' she laughed. 'You seem to be miles away.'

He turned, smiled, and looked at her in admiration, thinking how lucky he truly was to wake up beside such a beautiful woman.

'I was just thinking about Oscar.'

Oscar was CJ's loyal and obedient golden working Cocker Spaniel. Until recently, other than Jemima and Emmy, he was CJ's soulmate, but with Edee now a part of his life, the dynamic had changed, albeit only slightly.

He now shared his love amongst four, rather than three. Although, he still often said that Oscar was the most special, but how do you choose between those you love? You don't. Life isn't like that.

They all have a special place in your heart and love you, and you also love them in different, but oh so special, and unique, ways.

'That's not surprising. When was the last time you left him for a holiday?'

'Blimey, I can't remember. It must be some while ago. He normally goes everywhere with me, as you know.'

'He'll be fine. I know he'll be missing you like crazy, but Mrs Wembley will look after him.'

'You're right, knowing Mrs W, Oscar will be as fat as a pig when we get home. She won't let him starve, that's for certain.'

Mrs Wembley was the live-in housekeeper at *Overhear Manor,* the grand Georgian House that nestled in the sleepy, but idyllic, North Yorkshire village of Edendale.

It had been in the Gray family since it was built, and CJ Gray was now responsible for its upkeep. That was, until Jemima decided that she was ready to continue the tradition, or so he hoped.

'Look, there's no point worrying about him. You can't do anything from 3,500 miles away.'

'No, I guess not. I think I'll go for a run, blow a few cobwebs away,' said CJ thoughtfully. 'I really need to get out before it gets too hot.'

'Why don't you come back to bed and worry about me instead,' said Edee. 'I'll provide you with a good workout.' She turned on her side and smiled enticingly at CJ, and winked provocatively.

CJ's thoughts of Oscar were, at least for a short while, put on the back burner as he slipped under the duvet at the foot of the bed and ventured north.

'Oh, Mr Gray! I do like that,' whispered Edee. CJ had tenderly started kissing her feet, and he slowly moved up her graceful legs to more intimate and sensual parts of her body.

It Wasn't Me!

'Oh! Don't stop,' she gasped at his gentle touch. 'Yes! I do like that!'

The love making had been, as usual, sensual, and tender. The two lovers seemed to instinctively know what aroused the other's desire, and were duly reciprocated.

'Thank you. I love you,' said CJ affectionately, as he kissed Edee one last time before slipping off the bed.

'I must go for that run. And don't you dare go saying anything more, you temptress.'

'I love you, too. Are you sure I can't encourage you to come back to bed again?' teased a smiling Edee, but she already knew the answer, despite her lying provocatively naked on the bed.

After Edee had showered and slipped into a black bikini and wrap, which extenuated her model curves, she was ready for some sunbathing, and made her way downstairs.

All was quiet inside, but she noticed Jemima idly drinking coffee on the veranda overlooking the pool, seemingly miles away.

'She was like her father in so many ways,' thought Edee, as she joined her.

'Good Morning, Jemima.'

'Morning, Edee, did you sleep well?' asked Jemima, as she was dragged back from her thoughts.

'Yes, once I dropped off, it was fine. I still find the humming of the A/C rather strange, but James's snoring soon drowned that out,' said Edee, as she laughed at her own joke.

'But Dad at least admits he snores like an elephant, not like some. Marcus still maintains he doesn't snore. But by crikey he sure can.'

Edee sat down next to Jemima and looked out at the wonderful vista of the lake and the surrounding palm trees. 'It's a wonderful place to live, and bring up a young family,' she idly thought.

'Do you fancy a coffee?' asked Jemima.

'Oh, that would be nice. Could I please have a cappuccino, like yesterday?'

'Coming right up.'

Jemima walked into the kitchen, seemingly lost again in her thoughts.

'Did Emmy get off to school, okay?' called out Edee.

'Yes, I'll be picking her up about 3 pm. She's really enjoying now, being full time.'

Jemima re-joined Edee and placed the coffee on the table and sat down, still looking thoughtful.

'Is everything okay? I can't help but notice that you seem a little pre-occupied this morning,' asked Edee, slightly concerned.

'No. Yes. I don't know. It's just that......'

'Come on, you can tell me. A problem shared is a problem halved, and if you don't want me to, I won't say anything to your dad,' said a reassuring Edee.

'Thanks Edee, but it's probably me just being a bit sensitive.'

'Go on.'

'It's just that Marcus has suddenly had to go off on another *business trip*.'

It Wasn't Me!

'Is that so strange? He's often away. It's one of the downsides of being a partner in an architectural firm,' said Edee, seeking to further reassure Jemima.

'Yes, I know, but usually he likes to plan things, a bit like dad. That's probably why I love him.'

Jemima smiled weakly, but clearly didn't reassure herself.

'And the last couple of trips have apparently been sprung on him at the last minute.'

'So what are you saying?' asked Edee, not quite sure where the conversation was leading, but fearing the worst.

'I don't know Edee. It's just that... it's just not like Marcus.'

'Jem, I think you're overreacting. I suggest you talk about your concerns with him. Marcus will understand. I'm sure it's nothing to worry about,' said Edee calmly.

'You're right. Once he gets back, I'll suggest we go out for dinner and chat about it.'

'At least he's not having an affair,' joked Edee, but suddenly realising she had touched a nerve.

'So, just like me, you think he might be?' asked Jemima, who couldn't believe what she had said out loud.

'No. Don't be silly! I was joking. It'll be something innocent, and to do with work. He loves you and Emmy too much, to do anything stupid like that,' said Edee, while thinking, if Marcus was stupid enough to have an affair, then CJ would probably kill him. Well, more likely he would get his *Fixer,* former

RSM Cliff Ledger MC, to do it. She had no doubt about that.

Cliff would do absolutely anything for the *Governor,* Lt. Col. CJ Gray DSO, who had saved his career, and by so doing, symbolically saved his life.

While CJ was also eternally grateful to Cliff for actually saving his life while they were serving in war torn Afghanistan.

It Wasn't Me!

Chapter 10 – How Are You Major?

Earl Hargrove swirled his expensive vintage cognac in the large bowl brandy glass, as he sat in the high-backed leather armchair in the golf club Lounge Bar. He was happy and contemplating.

'How are things, Major?' he asked his companion, who had just sat down beside him, looking smugly satisfied.

'To be honest, My Lord, I feel rather content. Things appear to be going along smoothly at the club.'

Major Mortimer Montgomery was secretary of the prestigious and popular Edendale Golf Club, which was set in picturesque North Yorkshire surroundings.

Things were evidently back to normal, especially after the solving of the mystery of the dead body found on the Fourth green of the course, earlier that spring.

Events surrounding the death had plunged his normal smooth running of the club into turmoil. The dead man was attempting to become the chairman of his beloved club, totally against the Major's wishes, and would have succeeded, if not for his demise as he had won the ballot.

His candidate of choice, and also that of the President, who sat beside him, was Mr Graham Brook JP, who was now reinstated as Chairman of the club for his last allowable elected period of two years.

The Major liked him, not surprisingly, because Graham was smart enough to chair the meetings in a manner that suited the Major, and by so doing, the club ran like clockwork; something that would have been unlikely if Bart Tate had been elected. He had proposed controversial plans for change, but they were thwarted when he died.

'Yes, you're right. I think things are back to normal. I like it when things are just so,' agreed Earl Hargrove, as he polished off the last of his Louis Tres.

'Nancy? Sorry! Rachel, another please?' he continued as he beckoned over the young waitress.

Behind the bar, Jarvis, the silver haired long-term club steward, overheard the faux pas, but was already pouring a fresh glass.

'Don't you mind Earl Hargrove; but you do look very similar to the waitress you replaced,' said Jarvis, as he placed the fresh glass on Rachel's tray. 'You've probably heard of her.'

'Yes, I have, and it's okay. I'm sure he'll get it right eventually,' said Rachel, with a smile on her face.

'Your drink, My Lord.'

'Thank you Rachel. I'm sorry about that,' he said apologetically. Something not often heard, especially coming from his mouth.

'That's okay, we all make mistakes, don't we?' she teased in reply.

'Mmm, I suppose so.'

Things seemed to be fine, people were relaxed, and all appeared well at the club, well, at least for now!

It Wasn't Me!

Chapter 11 – A Proposition

'Good Morning. Could I please speak to Sheikh Twoammie?' asked Stuart, who was phoning the Sheikh's office.

'Who may I say is calling?' asked the efficient receptionist whose office was on the Ground Floor of a skyscraper in Downtown Dubai. The business centre of the *Twoammie Empire*.

'It's Stuart Brownlough. I was with him yesterday, at the horse racing.'

'Okay sir, I'll just check if he's available.'

Music played as usual while Stuart was put on hold, but this was traditional Islamic music, and not something Stuart found particularly endearing. Especially as he was disappointingly on hold for longer than he hoped or expected.

'Sabah Alkhayr. Good Morning, Mr Brownlough,' came the sound of another charming female voice. This time, though, from a large office on the 54th floor of the building. 'I'm His Excellency's personal assistant. How may I help you?'

'Oh! Good Morning. As I was saying to the other young lady. I was with the sheikh yesterday, at the races, and I was hoping to discuss further the development we are proposing together.'

'Mr Brownlough, perhaps you're getting slightly ahead of yourself. My understanding was that His Excellency was only in the early stages of considering your idea.'

'That maybe so,' thought Stuart, who was now slightly on the back foot.

'I was hoping to discuss a further proposal with him. I thought he would accept my call. Especially after my business partner had a most pleasant dinner *encounter* with him yesterday evening.'

'I'll see if he's available. But I must warn you, he's very busy. Please hold.'

After a further period of Islamic music, the PA again spoke.

'I'll put you through now.'

'Sabah Alkhayr. Good Morning, Mr Brownlough. I'm sorry you had to wait,' lied a most gracious Masud.

'Good Morning, Your Excellency. Thank you for taking my call. I know you're a very busy man,' replied a more obsequious Stuart.

'The consequences of success. I gather you have a further proposal?'

'I understand Charlotte had a really wonderful evening with you, and I'm sure would like to thank you personally in the near future. She indicated that you were now *up* for a deal regarding the *Edendale Project.*'

'Shall we say, she has a charm about her that has encouraged me to look further, and in more detail, at your plans.'

'Excellent, just what she said, and I gather you'll shortly be in the UK, and more importantly, in Yorksbey?'

It Wasn't Me!

'I'll be in the UK for a couple of weeks on business, and I'm sponsoring the *Equinox Festival* as well as a few races, including the *Twoammie Stakes*.'

'I thought that I would invite you to a presentation of the planned development. It would demonstrate our plans in greater detail and give you an opportunity to perhaps add your own personal touch to some of the proposals.'

'I think that is a sensible idea,' said the cautious sheikh. 'If your plans are as good as you say they are, and the returns are as you described, then I'm sure we can finalise a deal.'

'That's marvellous. Shall we put a date in the diary?' continued Stuart, sensing his plan was finally coming together.

'I'll get my PA to call you and confirm when I'll be free.'

'Wonderful, I'll ensure that my architect and other financial backer are also available.'

'Ah! you have other interested parties with funds invested?'

'Yes, of course I do. Nicholas Banker has already committed finances to the project,' lied Stuart.

Nick would only be at the meeting to spell out the financial benefits, and expected investment sought from Sheikh Twoammie.

'That's encouraging. It sounds like we will also need to discuss how the profits of this adventure will be divided.'

'That's the spirit,' said Stuart enthusiastically. 'I can assure you, the rewards will be significant, and provide a high yield on your investment.'

'Very Good! And perhaps I'll see Ms Tate again while I'm in the UK?'

'I'm sure that she would be very pleased to meet up with you again.'

'Excellent. Now, unfortunately, I have another meeting. Mae Alsalama. Goodbye Mr Brownlough.'

'Thank you, Your Excellency. Goodbye.'

'Well, that went as well as it could have done,' thought Stuart, as he ended the call.

'All I need to do now is get back to the UK, and get Harry and Nick to make sure the presentation is First Class, and the arrangement will be done,' said Stuart smugly.

'Plus, I still have *you* in reserve, in case there's any issue, just to ensure the deal finally gets over the line,' continued Stuart as he smiled at Charlotte, who had listened in intently on the telephone call, while lounging provocatively on the bed.

It Wasn't Me!

Chapter 12 – Who's That Then?

Harry pulled the door closed and then turned the key to the deadlock of the office door.

It was later than anticipated. The changes took longer than he had hoped, but things were definitely reaching a conclusion, and the work had been worthwhile. Rebecca had been a great help.

'Thanks again Rebecca,' he said pleasantly. 'It was a good job out of the way.'

'No problem, I'm pleased I could be of service,' replied Rebecca, clearly attempting to flirt with Harry, as she smiled, and coyly swept back her mousey coloured hair, which had fallen forward.

'Well, I'll see you tomorrow,' said Harry, seeking to get away as soon as possible from her unwanted advances.

'Do you fancy a drink in the New Inn? It's my local, and it's only around the corner.'

'That's kind of you,' lied Harry, 'but I've another meeting to go to.'

'This late?' asked Rebecca, clearly suspicious.

'Ah. Yes, it's with Stuart Brownlough's accountant. He's asked me to go through some of the financial proposals,' he lied again.

'No rest for the wicked. You know how important this project is for the business,' continued Harry, hoping Rebecca would see the sense in him refusing her offer.

She clearly did, and answered, 'I understand Harry, business before pleasure. Perhaps another time?'

'Perhaps. That sounds lovely,' he lied for the third time, within a matter of minutes.

He suddenly felt cold, and he shuddered. His superstitious nature made him hope that breaking one of his *rules* wouldn't lead to bad luck. He didn't need any, that was for certain.

'I'll look forward to that. Goodnight Harry.'

'Goodnight Rebecca.'

Harry quickly turned and missed Rebecca's clumsy attempt at a peck on the cheek, and he strolled off meaningfully towards the Renault Clio that was parked in the Market Place carpark.

Rebecca, slightly crestfallen, but still full of hope, walked off the other way, towards her parents' home on the other side of town.

Harry opened the passenger door and slipped in beside the driver, Sienna Brownlough.

'Hi there,' said Harry, as he kissed her gently on the cheek.

'Hi. I see Rebecca still has a crush on you?' said the observant Sienna, as she started the engine.

'You noticed? She's, at times, like a little love-struck puppy. I just don't know how to let her down gently.'

'Harry, if you don't do something soon, she might become a *bunny boiler*,' joked Sienna.

'Don't be silly. She's not like that.'

'Are you sure?'

'Of course, I'm sure. Anyhow, I don't want to upset her. She's a real asset to the business. I don't think I would get anyone else to do what she does. Well, not for the money she's on.'

It Wasn't Me!

'Well, where shall we go for a drink and a bite, then? How about the New Inn?' asked Sienna, innocently.

'I don't think that would be a very good idea,' replied Harry. 'I can't afford to run into Rebecca, not with you for company.'

'Okay, let's go to the Watermill Arms in Edendale instead. It's really nice there.'

Harry and Sienna were in the early stages of a relationship. He was unsure how it would develop, and the seven-year age gap, while not ridiculous, was possibly larger than some parents would believe was acceptable. Especially for their precious eighteen-year-old daughter, who was also uncertain if university was her thing, and was taking an unscheduled *gap year*.

Sienna, on the other hand, quite liked the idea of being involved with a slightly older man. She also felt her *friends* might somewhat envy her.

Her relationships with *boys* of her own age had been rather predictable, and uninspiring. So she hoped that Harry would prove to be a catch worth pursuing, at least for the time being, and provide her with the satisfaction she was currently seeking.

Harry was also hoping that Sienna might prove to be an asset, especially when he was dealing with her father. He felt that he might need all the help he could get, particularly when dealing with the older, shrewd businessman who was his client.

'You're again working very late?' said Sienna. 'I hope Daddy isn't treating you like he does his other associates.'

'I think he's the same with everyone. I don't think he's singling me out in his demands.'

'Well, don't let him take advantage of your good nature,' suggested Sienna, as she drove the tiny car her parents had bought her for her 18th birthday out of the carpark.

In the shadows of the adjacent street, a pair of envious eyes looked on, definitely none too pleased with what they had just witnessed.

It Wasn't Me!

Chapter 13 – Playing Around?

'What a wonderful office you have, Jemima,' joked Edee.

She was standing next to the first tee of the Montgomerie Golf Club, Dubai. Beside her for today's 4 Ball were CJ and Marcus, who were watching Jemima take a couple of practice swings as she prepared to tee off.

'Yes. I think many people would be envious of my working environment.'

Jemima was the part time pro for lady golfers at the club, but today she was playing golf with those she loved, rather than teaching her skills to others, not so fortunate.

'I must admit at times I wish I could swap my office for this, but to be honest, my golf is not up to Jem's standard,' said Marcus, who was more a bogey golfer, playing off a handicap of twenty. 'And I'm so busy at work at the moment, I don't have the time.'

'It's good to get out on the course, though. I haven't played *around* with Jem for a while,' he continued.

The stunning, links style championship course, designed in a collaboration between Colin Montgomerie and Desmond Muirhead, was in the heart of Emirates Hills. Set in 200 acres, the 7,446-yard course, featuring 14 lakes and 81 bunkers, was a challenge for golfers of all levels.

CJ and Edee had finally got to play a round of golf on the last day of their short holiday. They were both keen golfers, albeit they had both been better players in their youth. Playing then off single figures, they were now playing to a similar standard with handicaps of 12 and 13 respectfully. However, neither of them was a match for Jemima.

All four of them looked ever the consummate golfer, wearing attire that was appropriate for the surroundings. Edee had adopted her familiar all-red outfit, of golf top and short skirt, embraced by most lady golfers of her stature, complemented with a red visor and her long ebony hair tied in a neat ponytail. Jemima was identical, other than adopting her all-white colour of choice. The men were in shorts because of the Dubai heat. CJ in all black, as was his way, while Marcus wore a mixture of royal blue golf shirt and navy shorts.

'Damn,' said Jemima. Her tee shot was not up to her normal high standard. She drove it slightly to the right, with it landing just off the fairway, but still a good 250 yards from the tee.

'Edee, I think we might just be in luck today. It looks like my little girl is not at her best,' teased a smiling CJ.

'Don't get too cocky, too soon Pops,' retorted Jem jovially in return.

CJ placed his tee and ball, and having earlier warmed up with some stretches, he addressed the ball with his driver without any further practice swings and hit a pretty good drive. Like Jem, it was over to the right, but still on the fairway.

'I'll take that,' said CJ, thankful it was a reasonable drive.

It Wasn't Me!

Edee was up next, and having taken a couple of smooth practice swings with her driver, she addressed the ball and ping. The ball went straight as an arrow down the fairway about 220 yards, just missing the fairway bunker on the left. A near perfect shot.

'Good shot Edee,' said Jemima. 'Marcus, it looks like we might well have our work cut out today.'

Marcus completed the quartet, and was pleased to hit a pretty good drive for him, similar to Edee's distance, but just on the left fringe of the fairway.

'Game on,' said Jemima, recognising that the varied handicaps of the players today might just provide for an interesting game.

Edee and Marcus got into one of the two buggies, which are commonplace because of the Dubai heat, and drove off towards the left-hand side of the fairway. CJ and Jem took the other buggy and made their way down the right, stopping just short of their respective balls.

'Is everything okay, Jem?' he pointedly asked his daughter, as the two of them watched Marcus take his second shot.

They both knew each other so well and had similar traits. They also had an understanding that they both subconsciously recognised. Born out of love and mutual respect, possibly as they had become dependent upon each other, when Jemima's mother, Eve, had died so young. If they had an issue, they would always raise it. Life was, as they both acknowledged, too short to let things lie.

'What do you mean?' she defensively replied. 'Has Edee been speaking with you?'

'No, she hasn't. It's just that you've seemed a little distant and pre-occupied at times?' he intimated, before continuing. 'Plus for you. That drive was crap!' he teased.

'There's no fooling you, is there?' she earnestly replied.

'It's probably something and nothing.'

'Go on?' said CJ, now slightly concerned.

'It's as I said to Edee.'

'Oh! So you've been talking with Edee, have you?'

'Yes. But only because she asked. I think you have a similar intuition.'

'I've also noticed that. I'm not sure if that's a good thing or a bad thing?' said CJ, thoughtfully, before adding. 'But go on.'

'It's just that Marcus suddenly went off on another *business trip,* and it's so unlike him. It wasn't planned.'

'So, here's a man who loves you, worships the ground you walk on, and who's clearly busy at work. He goes and does something unusual, and suddenly you're getting your knickers in a twist?'

'I guess when you put it like that, it does sound rather an overreaction.'

'I suggest you talk through your concerns with Marcus. He'll understand. I'm sure it's nothing to worry about,' said CJ matter-of-factly.

'That's just what Edee suggested.'

'I'm sure we can't both be wrong.'

It Wasn't Me!

'Good shot Edee,' said CJ, as her second shot to the green landed within 5 feet of the pin, rather better than Marcus' effort, which had come up 10 yards short of the green.

'No. I'm planning to take Marcus out to dinner. We haven't had a night out for a while,' said a more relaxed Jemima.

She then pulled out her 5 iron and hit an absolutely stunning shot that ended inches from the hole.

'There you go. Sorted,' said a smiling CJ, who kissed his daughter on the cheek and briefly hugged her. He remained so proud of his daughter, just like when he first taught her the basics of golf.

'Unless I get this in the hole,' he continued, 'I think you have probably done enough to at least square this hole, as Edee and I don't get any shots here.'

CJ also took a 5 iron, but his shot ran on and ended a good 15 feet past the pin.

Marcus' chip ended on the fringe, and he two putted for a net 4, while CJ, also two putted for his par.

'Edee you need to hole that putt, to square the hole, as Jem has a certain 3.'

'Thanks for the added pressure, Mr Gray.'

Edee's putt was good, it had the line, it looked to have the length, but it just lipped out at the death.

'That was unlucky,' said Jemima. 'It deserved better.'

'One up to Marcus and Jem!'

The round continued in a similar manner to the first hole. Each new hole provided a challenge with a slightly different result, but the scores remained tight throughout the match.

The wonderful course, set amongst the many luxury villas, was in great condition, and the sun shone gloriously in the clear blue sky of the early September day.

Having all teed off for the last hole, the tie surprisingly was hanging nicely balanced, at all square.

Once again, the two pairs found themselves on opposite sides of the last fairway, not in too dissimilar positions from the first.

'Jem. I need to ask you something else.'

'Go on,' said Jemima, the one now sounding slightly concerned, but also intrigued.

'It affects you, well, just a little bit really, but I wanted you to hear it from me.'

Jemima was now definitely curious. 'Go on.'

'Well, you know Edee has been with the Business for over 25 years, ever since your Great Aunty Betty took her on?'

'Of course. You couldn't manage without her; she virtually runs the day-to-day stuff single-handedly?'

'Exactly. Well, I'm considering making her a partner and fellow director of GGL,' said CJ, unsure how Jemima would react.

'What a good idea! No more than she deserves. Perhaps you should have done it sooner?'

'That's great. I wasn't sure how you would react, but I should have known you would be okay with it,' said a relieved CJ.

'It's your business, so it's really up to you.'

It Wasn't Me!

'I know that, but it does have an effect on your inheritance.'

'Dad, let's concentrate on living, rather than dying, shall we?' said a smiling Jemima.

'Okay, but I'll now have to update the information at Companies House, and revise my Will. You'll now initially only inherit half the business, but I'm sure that Emmy will still eventually end up with it all,' said CJ, rather ironically, with a smile on his face.

Having unburdened his soul, CJ hit a 6 Iron into the heart of the green, while Jemima, who was 10 yards further on, hit a majestic 7 Iron, to within 3 feet of the flag.

'Great shot. That might just be the difference,' said a now calmer CJ.

Marcus, though, had unfortunately again come up short, and his approach chip was too strong, and ran through the green.

'Sorry Jem, you're on your own.' He knew his influence on the outcome was over, but he had, at times with the highest handicap, kept his pairing in the match.

Edee had played a sweet 5 wood and was also on the green, but a good 30 feet from the hole.

'Well, this is tense,' said Jem, who was used to the nip and tuck variances of golf.

Edee studied the subtle contours of the green, and having taken her stance, hit a reasonable putt, but it ran past by a good five feet. No *gimme*, especially not in the circumstances.

CJ, as usual, walked up to his ball, having studied the layout as he approached, and with the minimum of fuss, addressed the ball with his putter and hit an excellent shot to within a foot of the pin, a certain 4.

'Well done partner,' said Edee. 'Pressure putt now for the professional,' as she gently teased Jemima.

Jemima, being the accomplished professional she was, approached the shot as she always did, and having considered everything, hit a confident, firm putt into the heart of the hole.

'Well done! A fine birdie to win the round,' said Edee, recognising Jemima's skill.

'Well done partner,' said a celebrating Marcus as he embraced Jemima and kissed her fondly.

'Hang on a goddamn minute there,' said CJ, laughing. 'Hold your horses. This isn't over by any means.'

'What do you mean? Edee can only get a four if she putts out,' said Marcus, rather perplexed.

'Exactly, but she gets a shot on this hole. So if she putts this, it will be a nett 3, and we tie. Pressure on Edee!'

'He's right Marcus. As usual,' said Jemima, laughing. She clearly hadn't been taken in by the moment.

'This is a tricky shot. It could go either way,' replied CJ, not wanting to put any more unnecessary pressure on his partner.

Edee smiled weakly, addressed the ball, hit an assured putt, and off it went, seeking out its target.....

.

It Wasn't Me!

Chapter 14 – So Nice To Come Home

Jemima pulled the Range Rover into the drop off area outside Terminal 3 of Dubai Airport. She had swapped her usual Mini with Marcus' SUV, so she could comfortably drop CJ and Edee at the airport.

All three of them got out of the car and CJ heaved the two suitcases out of the boot.

'Thanks Jemima! You've been a wonderful host; it's a shame Marcus has been so busy. It's been lovely to see you,' said a most grateful Edee, as she and Jemima fondly embraced.

'It's also been great to see you, and to have a few girly chats with someone from the UK. Don't leave it so long before you come out again.'

CJ and Jemima then hugged one another and fondly kissed each other on the cheek.

'You take care of yourself. Thanks for a great time. Love You,' said CJ. When he met or left Jem it was one of the few times that he showed his true inner emotions. 'Look after Emmy. She's growing up so quickly, and I see so many of your mannerisms in her.'

'Take care Dad. I love you so much,' said an emotional Jemima, and unusually for her, tears pricked at her eyes. 'Call when you get home?'

She briefly embraced him again, and then fleetingly waved before getting quickly back into the car and driving off, so her feelings really didn't get the better of her.

CJ and Edee also momentarily waved to Jemima before turning, pulling their luggage behind them, and being pleased to enter the cool atmosphere of the extensive Departures Hall.

'Are you okay?' asked a slightly concerned Edee.

'Yes, I'm fine. It's just that it's been a while since I've seen them. Come on, let's get these bags checked in.'

'Don't look now, but I think that's Brownlough and Charlotte.'

'Quick, I definitely don't want to get stuck with them before we fly back to the UK. I hope they're not on our flight,' said CJ as he put on a spurt. Leaving Edee to catch up, as she momentarily tottered on her customary Christian Louboutin high heels, while he joined the baggage drop off queue.

Fortunately for them, they didn't see Stuart or Charlotte again at the airport. They were going home via Manchester, while CJ and Edee were flying into Newcastle.

The Emirates Boeing 737 made short work of the 3,500-mile, 8-hour journey, as CJ and Edee relaxed in Business Class, watching movies on the excellent ICE system, eating a couple of meals, and in CJ's instance, also having a quick nap.

The plane touched down slightly ahead of schedule, and for once, the transition through customs and baggage claim was rather uneventful. They were soon driving back down the A1, towards Edendale, having collected CJ's car from the medium stay carpark.

'Well, you've had time to consider what we observed at the races. What's your take on things?' asked an enquiring Edee.

It Wasn't Me!

'I'm not sure, but anything to do with Stuart Brownlough is likely to be a bit dodgy. I think we need to do some digging, especially now we're back in the UK, and we should look to use your charm to get some answers,' said CJ, as he smiled, and briefly admired Edee, who as usual, personified elegance.

Meanwhile, Stuart and Charlotte had landed at Manchester Airport. Unfortunately for them, the UK's third busiest airport was operating as normal. Their transition from airside to landside was not going smoothly, and they were still waiting for their luggage nearly two hours after landing.

'What a shit hole!' exclaimed Charlotte, as she continued to wait for her suitcase, with the plethora of other hapless souls, whom she looked down her nose at.

'I said we should have gone via Newcastle. I had no problems when we did that before.'

'Yes. I get it. You were right. I was wrong. Anything else?'

Stuart was also pissed off. Why were UK airports so bloody awful at times? Not a bit like it was when they landed in Dubai.

'If the bags don't come soon, I'm getting the train, and you can drop my suitcase off later,' said an extremely annoyed and frustrated Charlotte.

At that moment there was an announcement over the Tannoy.

'We are sorry to inform you, but there is an issue with the baggage handling equipment. We hope to have this resolved shortly.'

'Bye Stuart. I'll see you sometime. Please drop my suitcase off at Tate House when you finally get home.'

With that, Charlotte abruptly turned and walked off towards the *nothing to declare* exit, with her small carry-on bag in tow, her high heels tapping rhythmically on the tiled floor.

Just over 75 minutes later, CJ turned off Etongate Road into Edendale Lane.

Edendale was that idyllic countryside spot where most people dreamed of living, a wonderful English haven.

They shortly passed the prestigious Golf Club and travelled along *Millionaires' Row*, before passing under the old stone viaduct of the *Edendale Heritage Railway*.

The large village green, with its modest but beautiful homes and gardens overlooking the stream and duck pond, looked as inviting as ever. They continued bearing left onto the five arched stone bridge that straddled the free-flowing river Eden, with the adjacent *Watermill Arms* pub, standing guard as usual, with its carpark packed with the customary satisfied clientele.

CJ turned the Audi RS6, his daily car of choice, into Church Lane, past the 12th century *St John's Church* and nearby rectory. The row of Georgian style houses was set off by the immaculately cut grass verges down both sides of the narrow lane.

The tall black wrought-iron gates between the high Yorkshire stone walls came into view, and they

It Wasn't Me!

slowly opened, as the operating system recognised the approaching vehicle.

'It's nice to be back,' said Edee, opening her eyes from a brief sleep, as she subconsciously recognised she was back at her new residence.

'It's nice to go travelling. But it's oh so nice to come home,' quoted CJ, from the famous Frank Sinatra melody.

They continued up the long gravel drive, and pulled into the yard of old converted stables on the left, which was now home to his numerous motor vehicles, and parked up.

'Did you enjoy your short break?' asked CJ, as he turned and kissed Edee gently. 'I know I did.'

'I did. Thank you. It was great to see Jemima, Marcus, and Emmy, plus I got a bit of a tan, while also seeing Dubai for the first time.'

'Come on, I can't wait to see Oscar,' said CJ as he opened the car door.

Immediately, a golden working Cocker Spaniel leapt onto his lap.

'Hello boy, have you missed me?'

Oscar started profusely licking CJ's ears and making such a fuss. Oscar always hated being parted from his master, but this parting had been longer than most, and he was quite hyper with excitement.

'Don't you mind me' said a jovial Edee, as Oscar totally ignored her, and she got out of the car.

CJ rubbed Oscar's ears and pulled him close.

'I've missed you.'

Oscar leapt from the car and CJ followed, closing the door. Suddenly, Oscar was aware of Edee, and he ran around the car, and momentarily made a fuss of her, before running back to CJ for an obligatory treat.

'There you go, boy. Now! Go find Mrs Wembley.'

Oscar sped off, leading the way, running ahead as always, completely manic, as though CJ and Edee had never seen the charming grounds of *Overhear Manor* before.

Edee linked arms with CJ, and they walked around to the steps leading to the grand entrance.

'I'll get the luggage later. I think a nice cappuccino is the order of the day, with some of Mrs W's fruitcake.'

'That sounds, magnifique,' said Edee, who for once accentuated her French accent that had long ago softened.

CJ opened one of the two large oak doors, and they walked into the grand hallway with its welcoming twin staircases.

'Hello! We're home Mrs Wembley.'

It Wasn't Me!

CHAPTER 15 – NOT QUITE AS IT SEEMS.

Stuart pulled up at the security gate to Tate House in his silver Mercedes S Class, and having lowered the window, pressed the call button.

After a short period, the familiar seductive voice of Charlotte emanated from the speaker.

'Hello. How can I help you?'

'Hi Charlie, it's Stuart. I've got your bag.'

'Come on up.'

The buzzer sounded, and the gate slid aside to let Stuart progress up the sweeping driveway leading to the modern 6-bedroom house. It had been architecturally designed for the late Oliver Tate, located in the much sought after post code area of Edendale Lane.

Stuart, parked adjacent to Charlotte's Black Audi TT, and while surveying the property and grounds, pulled her suitcase from the boot. He then rang the bell to the large, glazed door.

Charlotte duly opened it, and looked stunning as usual, in a figure hugging blouse, tight-fitting jeans, and her usual high heel shoes. It was for her, rather unadventurous, but then again, she was just slumming it at home.

'Thanks lover. You eventually got away then?'

'Yes, after another hour of waiting, then the M62 was like a bloody carpark. How long have you been back?'

'About an hour. I got the train to Etongate, and then a taxi, as I'd missed the last *Heritage Train.*'

The Edendale Heritage Steam Railway was one of the most popular tourist attractions in the area, and was virtually always busy, no matter what the time of year, but only ran four trains daily each way between Etongate and Yorksbey. The railway and its four quaint stations en route (*Edendale; Hargrove Halt; Folly Overblow; and Cannal*) were renowned for being used as TV and Film locations because of the breath-takingly beautiful surroundings.

Charlotte invited Stuart in, and he lifted the suitcase into the large modern tiled hallway.

'Would you like a coffee? Or something stronger, perhaps?'

'No, thank you. I think I should get back home. I don't want Sarah to get any more suspicious than necessary, and knowing her, she will be monitoring the flight number on Google.'

'Understood. Thanks for the trip. You'll have to let me know when you'd like me to again work my charm on Masud.'

'Sure, but I might want you to work on me before then,' teased Stuart, before pryingly continuing.

'Are you planning to sell this pad?'

'We are still waiting on Probate to be finalised. Bart's finances were, shall we say, *complicated,*' replied Charlotte thoughtfully.

'I know the feeling.'

'As his estate is effectively split between Jason and me, at some point, I guess I may have to sell, but I would like to think that Jason would let me keep the house. I do love it, and it's now my home.'

It Wasn't Me!

Jason was Bart's twenty-year-old son from his first marriage to Carol, and he spent a considerable amount of time at his mother's luxury apartment in Etongate, which he now considered his family home. He had despised his father, and lost no sleep over his father's untimely death. He also preferred the more varied nightlife of the town, which suited his lifestyle, rather than the quiet village setting offered in Edendale.

'I quite like the feel of the place, and it has a great view over the golf course and the dale in the distance,' said Stuart enviously.

'It's in a wonderful location,' added Charlotte. 'That's why I hope to hang onto it.'

She did, however recognise, that while she would inherit half of Bart's apparent fortune, it was likely HMRC would be after its pound of flesh when things were finally settled. Plus, she was concerned that the police *Fraud Squad* might just start digging into where Bart had made his money. Therefore, she wasn't overly confident that she wouldn't have to sell, unless, of course, further money was forthcoming, and her dealings with Stuart might just provide the necessary funds she sought.

'Well, if you do think about selling, please give me first refusal,' added Stuart, already thinking about re-decorating.

'Let's hope it doesn't come to that.'

'Right, I'd better be going,' said Stuart as he embraced Charlotte and kissed her on the cheek.'

After a short drive towards Yorksbey, Stuart turned into the driveway of his family's home. A large modern house, built as part of his last development just off Etongate Road, constructed on land which had previously been considered as *green belt*. But after the application of some dubious back handers, he had convinced the planning authorities as to the benefits of this highly profitable development, both for him, and the town in general. Also, certain town councillors clearly saw the financial benefit, while providing Stuart with potential future leverage on any new planning application.

Sarah's green Tesla and Sienna's Clio were parked in the drive.

'Hello Daddy, how was your trip?' asked Sienna vaguely, while she sat at the island in the modern kitchen, her nose in her phone, as all young people seem to do.

'You know, all work and no play,' he replied, as he kissed her absentmindedly on the head. 'Are you okay?'

'I guess so.'

'Oh, you're back then?' said Sarah directly as she joined them. 'I thought I heard a car.'

Stuart kissed her obligatorily on the cheek, before adding falsely, 'How are you, my darling?' I trust you're okay?'

'I'm fine. I hope your business dealings were profitable?' she asked, for purely selfish reasons and without particular feeling.

'I'm confident that things are moving forward, but they are far from finalised. There's still some work

It Wasn't Me!

to be done, so don't be surprised if I have some late nights over the next few weeks.'

Stuart poured a large shot of malt whisky into a crystal glass tumbler.

'Want one?' he asked, as he necked it, before pouring another and walking off towards the lounge.

'No, and I don't think I'll be surprised at any of your escapades, Stuart, plus if you're planning on coming home late, and drunk, could you perhaps consider sleeping in the *guest room*?' said Sarah rather indifferently.

C J Meads

Chapter 16 – Get It Sorted

Andrew Kipling's phone was ringing. He looked down at the Samsung Galaxy S23. Unlike his father, he kept up to date with the latest technology, and always updated his phone with the latest edition.

'Shit!'

He declined the call and put it back down on his desk.

'Something wrong? Aren't you going to answer it?' asked an inquisitive Mr Kipling Snr.

'It's not important.'

'Okay. But it's not good to ignore clients, albeit I know they should really call the office number.'

'No Dad, I'm aware of maintaining good relationships with our clients,' replied a rather agitated Andrew.

The two of them were in the archetypical offices of Kipling Solicitors, which were situated in *The Market Place* of Yorksbey, the small busy North Yorkshire market town of about 10,000 inhabitants. Yorksbey provided many of the day-to-day amenities to the local area that were lacking in some, if not all the small adjacent villages.

'Okay, back to the Accounts. When is Stuart Brownlough going to pay his account? It's been three months since his last payment.'

Andrew's phone rang again. He picked it up, saw who it was, and again declined the call.

'Persistent, aren't they?' said an ironic Mr Kipling Snr.

'Mmm.'

It Wasn't Me!

'Well?'

'Well, what?'

'When will Brownlough be paying his account? I'm not aware we offer free advice? Well, especially not to the likes of Stuart Brownlough.'

'I'll speak to him.'

'Please son,' said an earnest Mr Kipling Snr. 'He's not in financial trouble, is he?' continued the astute lawyer.

'I believe he's in the middle of finalising a significant venture, and it will provide us with more profitable work.'

'Well, let's hope he remembers to pay for it.'

The phone rang yet again

'Dad, I'd better get this. Do you mind?'

With that, the senior partner raised his eyes and whispered, 'Kids!' as he walked out of Andrew's office and into his own next door.

'Hi Stuart! Sorry about that. I was just in a meeting. How are you?' said Andrew, sycophantically.

'Andy, how's it going with the *Document*?' said Stuart forcibly.

He needed the document, and he needed it now. He was desperate. The plan was completely dependent upon it.

'I've finalised it.'

'Brilliant, well done. When can I have a copy?'

'Whenever. Where shall we meet? Your offices?'

'Let me think. How about we meet at the golf club? That seems appropriate in the circumstances,' said Stuart, as he smiled at the irony of his suggestion.

'Fine by me. When then?'

'Let's say 6 pm tomorrow night, in the Lounge Bar.'

'I'll see you then,' agreed Andrew, before he shyly enquired. 'Dad's asking when you'll be settling your account?'

'Andrew! You'll get paid soon enough. Just make sure the old man doesn't go nosing around,' said Stuart, now in a menacing way, that Andrew fully recognised.

'You wouldn't want your little secret getting out now. Would you?' continued Stuart, relishing the hold he had over the solicitor.

'No Stuart. I wouldn't. Goodbye.'

'Hang on a minute, I haven't finished. Have you got the original? We can't afford for that to come to light.'

'No, not yet, but I'll sort it.'

'Well, just make sure you do,' threatened Stuart. 'I'll see you tomorrow at six. Don't be late,' he continued, before abruptly ending the call.

Mr Kipling Snr walked nonchalantly back into Andrew's office.

'Is everything okay? You look a little ashen?'

'It's fine,' lied Andrew. 'But I might just have to leave a little bit earlier tomorrow evening.'

It Wasn't Me!

CHAPTER 17 – THE PLANS

Brownlough Developments' office was situated in a modern brick and glazed building on the Langham Arch Retail Park, to the east of Yorksbey.

The typical two-storey building was constructed by them, as part of a Design & Build development undertaken in collaboration with Langham Arch Estates, who owned and managed the 1,000 acre, 200 building complex.

The estate was originally agricultural land, upon which the Royal Ordnance Factory Langham Arch was constructed during the Second World War. The factory was opened in 1942 by King George VI at a cost of £5.9 m.

Since then, the site had been transformed into the modern thriving business hub it is today, comprising a mixture of businesses, from the very modest one-man band up to the large, instantly recognisable, International Brand warehouses.

Harry and Rebecca were sitting nervously in the reception. They had both rehearsed the planned presentation, but they knew at times what a strict taskmaster Stuart could be.

'Mr Brownlough, will see you now. He's in the conference room. You know where it is?' said the secretary rather condescendingly.

'Thank you. Yes, we do.'

Harry glanced at Rebecca.

'Into the lion's den. Nothing ventured....'

She looked back at him and smiled weakly.

They both strode off down the corridor. Harry knocked on the conference room door and they entered.

The bright airy room with its large oval table and twelve large leather swivel chairs was familiar to Harry. He had been there on numerous occasions since the development was first conceived.

'Good Morning, Harry. How are you?' asked Stuart, rather too friendly for Harry's liking.

'What was he up to?' thought Harry, before realising that Stuart had clearly forgotten who Rebecca was. Why would he? She was only the office secretary.

'Good Morning, Stuart. I'm fine. Nice to see you. You remember Rebecca, my Office Manager?' said Harry as the two briefly shook hands.

'Yes, of course,' lied Stuart. 'Morning. Both of you. Please take a seat.'

Stuart was clearly unimpressed by Rebecca's plain appearance, and more to the point, she was not the kind of person he generally appreciated.

Also in the room was Nick, who was sitting on the other side of the table, busy at his laptop. He briefly looked up rather indifferently. He was more interested in the figures, and what profits could be made from Tovaine's designs.

'You know Nick Banker, my accountant?' said Stuart, not seeking a response, as Harry and Nick nodded to one another in acknowledgement.

'Now then Harry. I take it everything's ready?'

'I do believe it is. We've been working long and hard on the project, and today we'll show you where

It Wasn't Me!

we're at. We have a Power Point Presentation and video to show to you today. Plus, we can go through all the drawings and specifications for the complete project,' said Harry as he sat down and proceeded to remove his laptop from his briefcase.

'You've been busy. Well done,' replied Stuart, rather underwhelmed.

'I think we can dispose of reviewing the drawings and specifications today. They are, when all's said and done, more for the estimating and construction phases,' continued Stuart.

'Oh. We'll concentrate on the presentation then,' replied Harry, rather dejected at the response to all the hard work the team had put in.

'That's the spirit. The visuals will be really important in getting our main financial backer on board, and he's due here in less than a week.'

'Who's that then?' asked a curious Harry.

'I would prefer not to say until the day of the formal presentation, but he's an influential figure in the Middle East.'

'Understood, but if we want the presentation to be designed for him, I'll need to know before then who he is,' stated Harry.

'That's a good point,' said Nick, who realised the importance of tailoring the planned meeting around Masud.

'Okay. It's Sheikh Masud Twoammie, from Dubai. But let's be clear, that *Name* goes no further than this room. Do I make myself clear?'

Stuart intently eyeballed Harry and Rebecca, who fully recognised the consequences of disobeying Stuart's instruction.

Seventy-Five minutes later and the presentation was complete.

'Harry old boy, I have to say you've done us proud. Well done.'

'Not bad,' said Nick, who was similarly impressed, but wasn't going to convey this to Harry, not yet anyhow.

'Thank you,' said a relieved Harry. 'I'll review the few suggestions we have discussed and revise things to suit. I think we'll then be there.'

'Very good.'

'So, when and where are we making the presentation?' asked Harry, who was intrigued as to the planned location.

'I've been giving that some serious consideration. I'll confirm it shortly, but I think I might hire the restaurant at Edendale Golf Club. I think that would be applicable. What say you Nick?'

'I'm not sure it's really appropriate or necessary, but I'll be led by your intuition. You're seldom wrong,' replied Nick, unsure this time as to Stuart's real motives.

'Harry. One last thing. I think a model would be really useful in conveying the extent of the development. The Sheikh has also intimated his desire to see in 3D how the development will look.'

'A model? We hadn't budgeted for one, and I'm not sure we have the time to build it.'

It Wasn't Me!

'Harry. Let's be clear. The Sheikh wants a Model. Nick wants a Model. I also want a Model. Let's make sure we have a Model.'

'But the cost. I haven't got the money to do that,' replied Harry, clearly frustrated. 'Perhaps if you could pay for the model, Stuart? It would really be helpful to me,' pleaded a downcast Harry.

'Harry, Harry. You know what we will all make from this? Surely, quibbling about the cost of a model is rather unnecessary in the circumstances?'

'Yes, I know. But I'm not sure I can get another £10k loan, for what the model is likely to cost.'

'Harry, get it sorted. Order the bloody model and Nick will ensure you get reimbursed. You have my word on it,' said Stuart, clearly losing his temper, but managing to just about control it.

'Okay,' said Harry. 'Thanks, I really appreciate that. It will help enormously.'

'That's the spirit,' said Stuart, reverting to his slimy best.

'You'd both better get going and get the model started. Well done again for today. Great Presentation, both of you,' added Stuart, as he led them out of the room towards the reception, keen to get on with other more important matters.

When he returned, Nick immediately quizzed him.

'Are you really going to pay for the model?'

'Don't be fucking silly. Of course Not!'

Chapter 18 – The Document

'Excuse me sir, are you a member?' asked Jarvis, clearly aware of the answer.

He had been instructed by the Major, to interrogate Stuart, who nonchalantly sat at one of the high back leather armchairs in the Lounge Bar. It was 5.58 pm.

'Jarvis, you know I'm not. We have this conversation every time. The Major has no doubt put you up to it as usual.'

'Sir, you know the club rules. You must be escorted by a club mem....'

'Here's my chaperone now! Sorry to piss on your parade, Jarvis,' said a smiling and very smug Stuart.

At that very moment, Andrew entered the classic golf club Lounge Bar, with a briefcase in hand.

'Mr Kipling, is this gentleman with you?' enquired Jarvis politely.

'Yes he is, and before you ask, I have signed him in the Visitors' Book.'

'Very good. Can I get you any drinks?' the popular steward enquired, now back in the easy mode he preferred when assisting members and guests.

'Why doesn't the Major do his own dirty work?' thought Jarvis.

'I'll just have a pint of lager shandy please, Jarvis, as I'm driving,' replied Andrew. 'Stuart, for you?'

'I'll have a malt whisky. I'm also driving, but worst case I'll walk back. It's not far,' said Stuart, who had no intention of walking anywhere, before adding, 'Go on, make it a double.'

It Wasn't Me!

'Shall I put them on your tab, Andrew?' enquired Jarvis, pretty sure of the reply.

'Yes, please. Thank you.'

'Good to see you're prompt and on time, Andrew. It's always a good sign.'

'Agreed. Punctuality is key, in most walks of life, and especially in the legal world, where time is most definitely money.'

'Too bloody right it is. The rates you charge are extortionate.'

'It would be nice to be paid those rates,' whispered Andrew to himself. He recognised that if the account wasn't soon settled, then his father would definitely be back on his case, and rightly so.

'And it's not us, that are the extortionate ones,' he idly thought.

'Well, have you got it?' asked Stuart, desperate to see the final document.

'Of course. It would be a bit silly meeting if I hadn't,' replied Andrew dryly.

'Let's have a look, then? I've been dying to see this all day.'

Andrew opened his briefcase, carefully pulled out the document, and passed it to Stuart.

'Fantastic. It's just what I would expect a 100-year-old deed document to look like.'

'I thought that was the whole idea,' replied Andrew sardonically.

'Yes, I know that. Well done Andrew, it's bloody marvellous. It's perfect. This is going to make us a lot of money.'

'Talking of money. Now you have the document. I trust you'll be paying your account?'

'Of course. Of course!'

'When?'

'As soon as I know the original is safe, and in my hands, I'll get Nick to transfer the agreed sum. Is that alright?'

'Okay, understood.'

'You do have it don't you?' asked Stuart. 'It's crucial!' he again markedly pointed out to Andrew.

'I know. I'll get it sorted,' replied Andrew, rather less convincing than he hoped.

'Your drinks sirs,' said Jarvis, as he took the glasses from the silver tray and placed them in front of the two businessmen.

Stuart quickly concealed the document, so prying eyes didn't read its title.

'A toast. To the *Edendale Project*!' said Stuart excitedly, chinking his glass with Andrew's.

'The *Edendale Project*,' toasted Andrew, in return, but slightly less enthusiastically. He was still extremely worried at the likely fall out when the document became common knowledge.

'Now. Where's the Major? I need to book the Restaurant for the Presentation.'

It Wasn't Me!

Chapter 19 – Legal Matters

CJ closed the front door of GGL's offices, turned, and bumped into Andrew, just as he was also leaving the offices of Kipling Solicitors, the late autumn afternoon sun momentarily blinding him.

The two businesses had been situated next to each other in central Yorksbey since they were both established in the 1960s.

In the subsequent years, the two original founders, Mr Kipling Snr, and Ms Elizabeth Gray, had established a firm friendship and bond that, even on Aunty Betty's sad passing a few years ago, had seamlessly transferred to CJ.

Despite their close connection, CJ, for some unfathomable reason, had never formed a similar friendship with Andrew. He was always courteous and polite, but there was just something that prevented a closer connection.

This wasn't particularly unusual, as there were few that were allowed into his inner circle. Those that did knew him as James. To everyone else, it was CJ, or Mr Gray, with many older service colleagues, still respecting him by addressing him as Colonel Gray.

'Good Afternoon, CJ, how are things?' enquired Andrew, more out of politeness rather than any particular concern for the wellbeing of others. A seemingly normal, and quite common greeting, often implemented by many in business.

'Afternoon, Andrew. I'm fine, thank you. I trust you're also well?' replied CJ, offering what again is considered a polite response, and definitely not expecting a reply.

'I'm good,' lied Andrew, who remained under pressure from Stuart.

'Is your father in? I have a few legal matters I would like him to address for me.'

'What! Oh No!' said Andrew, looking and sounding rather flustered. 'Dad left earlier today. I'm just off to another meeting myself.'

'That's a shame. I'll try to catch up with him tomorrow. If you see him, please let him know that I'll be in touch.'

'Yes. That's fine, I'll do that,' continued Andrew, clearly in a hurry and wanting to get away, before adding absentmindedly. 'Goodbye.'

With that, he purposely strode off across the square, clearly in a rush towards a bright green Tesla.

'Bye Andrew.'

CJ turned and opened the front door to the office.

'That was quick,' said Edee wryly, who was engrossed in finalising the arrangements for a large shipment from the USA.

'Mmm, it was rather. Apparently Mr Kipling Snr, has left early, and Andrew has also just departed.'

'You seem uneasy. What's up?' enquired a reflective Edee.

'It's probably something and nothing, but I don't know. Andrew seemed agitated.'

'I don't know. There's you, getting all concerned with the wellbeing of others. Definitely not like you at all?'

It Wasn't Me!

'I know, it's strange, isn't it? You must be having a good influence on me, and your good nature must be rubbing off,' laughed CJ, but inwardly sensing something just didn't seem right.

Chapter 20 - Nice To See You Again

Charlotte looked at her watch again for the umpteenth time. Where was Stuart? He said he would pick her up at 7 pm. It was unlike him to be late for any meeting. He prided himself on his punctuality.

Meanwhile, on Edendale Lane, a Ford Focus ST was pulling out of the golf club carpark and making its way towards the village.

The driver was the resident golf professional, Ian Westbank, who had just finished work for the day, and he was en route to a meeting at the Watermill Arms with *The Lads*. It was their weekly get together to catch up on things and discuss all matters male, while in the process, slowly getting drunk.

As he passed Tate House, he suddenly noticed Stuart's Mercedes pulling into the driveway.

'What was Brownlough doing at Charlotte's?' thought an extremely jealous Ian. He needed to have a chat with Charlotte, pronto, to find out what was going on, but for now, it would have to wait. The lads beckoned.

Ian and Charlotte had an on and off *casual* acquaintance, which had developed over the last eighteen months or so, which Ian had always wanted to develop further. Since Bart Tate's demise, he had hoped their relationship would become more open and established, but Charlotte had cooled slightly. He was unsure why, although the occasional sex was no less or rewarding than it had been before Bart's untimely death.

It Wasn't Me!

Charlotte was standing waiting on the steps to the front door, looking radiant as always. She enjoyed fine dining, and she hoped that Stuart had booked somewhere nice for the evening.

Stuart lowered the car window.

'And what time do you call this?' enquired Charlotte, clearly annoyed at being kept waiting. 'I thought you said you were never late.'

'Sorry Charlie, something came up that couldn't wait. You look ravishing, as always.'

Charlotte's displeasure melted at the compliment.

'Well, thank you, kind sir. I wasn't sure what to wear, so I hope I'm not overdressed?'

'Charlotte, you know you could wear anything, and you would still be stunning.'

Fortunately, Charlotte had decided to go slightly OTT, and she had adopted her most recent *LBD,* with customary black high heels and make up to suit.

She graciously walked around the front of the car and slipped in beside Stuart, who kissed her on the cheek. He would have preferred the lips, but Charlotte was never going to spoil her lip gloss this early in the evening.

'Go on then, what kept you?'

'Oh, yes. Masud's PA rang to confirm that he was in the UK, and we now have a firm date for the presentation. It's this coming Sunday.'

'Sunday! That's an odd day for a meeting?' asked a quizzical Charlotte.

'Not for Masud. Don't forget, it's like a Monday for him. Remember, he is a Muslim.'

'I take it you'll want me in attendance?' enquired Charlotte rhetorically.

'Of course!' No show without *Judy*!'

'Okay. Now then, where are we going?' continued Charlotte, looking forward to a good night out.

'We're off to Oak Hall. Masud is apparently staying there, and with a bit of luck we might just inadvertently bump into him,' said a smiling and hopeful Stuart.

Oak Hall Luxury Resort, was the 5-star hotel and Michelin starred restaurant, just four miles from Yorksbey. It was not surprising, with Masud's tastes, that he should be staying there, as it was possibly the finest place to stay and eat in the district.

'Oh, I do like Oak Hall! I hope you have your credit card with you. I fancy something rather extravagant?'

As Stuart and Charlotte turned right out of the driveway, in the other direction, driving to another clandestine meeting, a speeding green Tesla went unnoticed by them, but they were clearly seen by its cunning and far more observant driver.

It Wasn't Me!

Chapter 21 – Hello, What's This?

Market Place appeared full of emergency vehicles, with blue lights flashing randomly.

The small police Fiesta had arrived first, closely followed by the ambulance and paramedics.

It was 8.30 am, and the town was just waking with early shoppers and workers.

Edee who had been at work since 8 am, like she had for the last 25 years - it's difficult to break long-term habits - despite being in a relationship with the boss. She had now been joined by him; CJ having arrived at his customary arrival time of 8.30 am. The two of them were now standing outside the office front door, watching the commotion.

Presently PC Patricia Perfect emerged from the front door of Kipling Solicitors. She looked concerned as she stood next to them.

'Hi Pat. Is everything alright?' asked a similarly concerned Edee, despite recognising things were far from alright. She and PC Perfect were good friends, and she hoped that Pat might just convey what was occurring.

'Good Morning, Edee, CJ,' she replied quietly, so no one else overheard. 'It's Mr Kipling Snr. He's been knocked out. It also looks like there's been a break in.'

'Is he alright?'

'I think he'll be fine, just a slight concussion from what I can gather from the paramedics, but I guess they'll take him into hospital, initially for observation.'

With that, Andrew suddenly appeared from next door, looking ashen and extremely worried.

'Are you okay sir?' enquired Perfect, clearly concerned.

'I'll be fine. It's Dad I'm more worried about. They say he should be okay, but they're going to take him in to be on the safe side. He's getting on a bit when all's said and done.'

'Excuse me sir,' said one of the paramedics as he lifted the front of the wheelchair over the door threshold.

Mr Kipling Snr. looked actually more spritely than his son. Other than a clear bump and bruise on the side of his head, he seemed okay, albeit possibly slightly concussed.

'Are you okay Mr Kipling Snr?' asked Edee, clearly anxious for her old acquaintance.

'I'll live. Thank you, Madame Songe,' he replied, smiling weakly.

'Well, you take care now,' continued Edee. 'If you need anything, please let us know.'

He acknowledged the gesture with a slight wave of the hand, while Edee and CJ turned and went back into the GGL office.

Mr Kipling Snr. was wheeled over to the ambulance and the hydraulic lift manoeuvred him into the emergency vehicle.

Just then, an unmarked police Astra pulled up and out got DS John Jones. He briefly checked in on the ambulance and made a few notes in his little black notebook, before then walking over to PC Perfect.

'Morning, Pat,' said a smiling Jones.

It Wasn't Me!

'Morning,' Jonesy,' replied Perfect.

The two of them had a soft spot for each other, and despite them clearly having feelings, they hadn't developed further. They both probably didn't want to lose a good mate by purely indulging in carnal lust.

They had a conversation; the details of which Jones wrote down in his Little Black Book (LBB).

If one thing was certain, Jones was always thorough. He never relied purely on his memory. Not anymore!

He had learnt the hard way that it's most important to get a full record of events. He had been made a fool of, by defending council, during his very first court appearance as an inexperienced bobby on the beat. Following that unmitigated disaster, where the accused got off, and his sergeant and inspector had torn a right strip off him, he vowed never to make the same mistake again, and he hadn't.

As he finished writing, another unmarked car, a Vauxhall Insignia drove into the Market Place and parked up.

'Look lively Pat, the *Boss* has felt it necessary to join us.'

'DI Simon Smith, a cross between TV's *Barnaby and Morse*, was a well-respected and good copper, plus a good boss to the easy-going detective sergeant, whose manner was like a combination of *Troy and Lewis.*

'Morning, all. What have we got here then?'

'Morning, sir. The station received a 9 9 9 call at 8.10 am this morning, from Andrew Kipling. Mr Kipling reported a break in at their offices and advised that he had found his father unconscious from what looked like an attack. Paramedics have attended, and so has PC Perfect. Forensics and CID were also notified. Forensics are still to arrive.'

'Any evidence of a forced entry?' enquired Smith.

'On initial inspection, the rear door appears to have been jimmied, and Mr Kipling Snr. has received a concussion, probably from a blunt instrument.'

'Is he okay? He's no spring chicken.'

'Having been assessed, he's been taken to Etongate General Hospital for further examination, but by all accounts, will probably be okay with a bit of rest and some strong painkillers.'

'Anything taken?'

'Difficult to say at this stage. PC Perfect has asked Mr Kipling to check and let us know, but nothing was immediately obvious. But we may need Mr Kipling Snr. to also check once he is well enough to do so.'

'Okay, let's have a word with Andrew Kipling, and also get forensics to do a sweep, but my guess is they'll come up with nothing.'

'Okay Sir. I'll report anything further, but I guess this will go down as another burglary that went a bit wrong. Fortunately, no one is seriously injured.'

'You might be right Jones, but check with the locals and also have a word with Mr Kipling Snr. to establish a timeline. For some reason, something doesn't quite smell right.'

It Wasn't Me!

Chapter 22 – The Arrival

CJ and Edee were relaxing in the Lounge Bar of the golf club. They were halfway through a round of golf. At their feet, Oscar was dozing contentedly.

As a trustee of the club, and with the Ninth Hole and Tenth Tee being right outside the rear of Overhear Manor, he often started his round by agreement at the Tenth. Edee had today decided to join him and Oscar, who was allowed on the course as is often the way with prestigious golf clubs.

It was still relatively early for a Sunday, and they had just ordered a couple of cappuccinos and bacon butties to refresh them after the earlier exertions. Edee had been playing well, and was teasing CJ as she led by two holes, predominately because of a wayward drive by CJ on the Eleventh, which landed in the River Eden, and also to a totally misjudged putt on the Eighteenth.

'You're going to have your work cut out if you're going to get back into this match.'

'Edee, my turn will come. You've been playing very well, but I think you'll slip up soon. Or perhaps the round in Dubai is paying dividends?'

'Perhaps. Thank you Jarvis,' said Edee, as the Steward placed their order on the table.

'Not such a good putt, was it CJ?' said a smiling Jarvis. 'Even I couldn't help noticing you totally mis-reading the green, even from here.'

'Thank you Jarvis,' said CJ, sarcastically, but recognising the truth.

Oscar was suddenly awake, his nose in the air, smelling the wonderful aroma of the sandwiches.

'The butties are not for you Oscar,' said Jarvis, who rubbed the dog's ear affectionately. Nonetheless CJ broke a small piece off, and offered it to Oscar, who first had to sit and offer his paw.

'Good Boy. Oh, and by the way Jarvis. I gather the restaurant's closed this morning until noon. What's that all about?'

'Apparently Brownlough Developments' are making a big presentation to a Sheikh from Dubai.'

'Is it Sheikh Twoammie?' enquired Edee.

'That's the fellow. By all accounts, a right big wheel. Loads of money, and also sponsoring the *Equinox Festival* at Yorksbey Races,' said Jarvis before asking. 'Will you be going to the *Ladies' Day* Edee?'

'I'll have to see if the boss will let me have the day off. But I would really like to,' she replied, winking at Jarvis and smiling knowingly at CJ.

'Sounds as though I'll need to get my best bib and tucker out, if we're off again to the races,' said CJ, clearly up for the challenge. 'I must also speak with Earl Hargrove. He normally also sponsors a race and usually has a party in one of the Hospitality Suites.'

'That does sound like fun,' agreed Edee. 'Let's hope the weather holds.'

'Jarvis, is His Lordship here today?'

'I do believe he is. If you're quick, you'll see him before he tees off. He was with the Major earlier.'

'I'll be back in a minute,' said CJ, clearly striking while the iron was hot.

It Wasn't Me!

As he strolled towards the Secretary's office, with Oscar close behind, he couldn't help but notice Harry and Rebecca arriving together in conversation.

'Harry, you do know that Stuart has got to pay for the model, don't you?' advised Rebecca, who clearly had rumbled Stuart's likely intentions.

'I know. But it's really good, *Construction Models* have really pulled out all the stops. It looked marvellous earlier when they set it up. You'll be impressed.'

'I'm sure I will, but I'm just saying. He keeps taking advantage of your good nature.'

She touched his hand gently and whispered, 'Good Luck.'

They entered the restaurant and inside were Stuart, Nick, and Andrew, already strategically placed around the makeshift conference table, resplendent with the model of the development. The overhead screen was also ready for the PPP and video presentations.

'Good Morning, Harry, and ....'

'Rebecca,' prompted Harry, rather annoyed at Stuart.

'Of course, Rebecca. Guys, what a great job you've done! We're most grateful for the extra work you've put in. Aren't we Nick?'

'What? Yes,' replied Nick, who, as before, was more interested in the figures on his laptop than providing fake praise.

'The model is... just right. Well done,' continued Stuart, who was for once extremely impressed.

'Let's hope we get paid for it,' whispered Rebecca. Just loud enough to be heard by Nick, who immediately looked up, and offered a fake smile in acknowledgement.

'Harry, you'd better get set up; His Excellency is due shortly at 10.15 am. We have a tight schedule to meet,' instructed Stuart, who was clearly now in his element and in the zone.

At 10.15 am precisely, Sheikh Twoammie's car pulled up outside the impressive golf club entrance.

Stuart was waiting, and had now been joined by Charlotte, who looked amazing as always. She had chosen a pale grey two-piece suit, that along with her customary high heels, had a hem that showed just enough leg to tease Masud.

Today, though, she had let her long blonde curled locks flow down, rather than tie them in a more practical bun.

The chauffeur opened the BMW 7 Series door, and Masud smartly got out, his PA followed, having got out of the other rear door. He was, as usual, dressed in his customary robes.

'Sabah Alkhayr. Good Morning, Your Excellency. Thank you for honouring us with your presence today,' said Stuart fawningly, as he bowed slightly and offered Masud his hand.

'Sabah Alkhayr. Good Morning, Mr Brownlough,' replied Masud, briefly shaking Stuart's hand.

'Ah, Ms Tate! You look radiant as always. But I'm rather surprised to see you here this morning.'

It Wasn't Me!

'Sabah Alkhayr. Good Morning, Your Excellency,' said Charlotte, before adding. 'I wanted to ensure you kept to our bargain,' while smiling broadly at Masud, clearly not wanting him to forget their night together.

'Of course.'

'Please come this way, our team is ready with the presentation,' said Stuart, leading the four of them through the grand lobby towards the restaurant.

'So that's Sheikh Twoammie?' said the Major who had observed the grand arrival through his office window.

Chapter 23 – Anything Missing Sir?

'Good Morning, Mr Kipling Snr. It's very good of you to see me on a Sunday. I hope you're now feeling better?' asked Jones politely.

The solicitor was back from the hospital, having been discharged after a night in for routine observation, and had invited DS Jones to the office.

'I'm okay. Thank you for asking. I think I was quite lucky in the end. The doctors say they don't think there will be any long-term effects. I was discharged and told to take some paracetamol if I get any mild headaches.'

'I also think you were lucky. It's never good to be taking a blow to the head, no matter what age we are, and if you don't mind me saying, you're no spring chicken.'

'That's true, and I've been called worse things,' replied a smiling Mr Kipling Snr. before adding, 'Come on through. Would you like a drink?'

'No, not for me sir, but thank you for asking. What is of more importance, though, is there anything missing?'

'That's the odd thing. Having done a quick check of things, whoever was here didn't appear to have taken anything.'

'That does seem strange. Why break in, knock you out, and not steal anything?'

'It's rather a conundrum. Now I haven't done a complete inventory review of all the documents we hold. They run to thousands. But as I say, nothing looks to have been stolen.'

It Wasn't Me!

'I assume you hold most of the important documents or valuables in the safe?' asked Jones, pointing at the high security walk in Chubb Safe, that must have been in place since the office was first commissioned.

'That's correct, most of the documents are deeds, etc.'

'Was the safe open when you were attacked?' enquired Jones, who was fishing, as from his inspection on the day of the break in, he had noticed that it had been closed.

'I think the safe was open at the time, but to be honest, everything's a blank that morning. I can't truly recall even coming to the office. It's all rather hazy,' said a rather perplexed Mr Kipling Snr.

'I suggest you undertake a thorough check of everything when you get a chance, but it does seem rather odd,' replied a thoughtful Jones.

'Yes, I will. I'll also get Andrew to check on anything that he may have stored or filed. But I take it you've already spoken to him?'

'Yes, I have, and he hasn't reported anything missing, but I'll perhaps speak with him again at some point.'

'Very good. Is there anything else?'

'No, I don't think there is, and to be honest, especially as there wasn't anything stolen, we won't be taking this any further,' stated a displeased Jones.

'We've also reviewed the Town's CCTV and your own security cameras, and whoever broke in was quite clever, or lucky, as they avoided being observed. So we've no leads to follow up, even for the assault,' added Jones thoughtfully.

'It's strange isn't it?' stated a now reflective Mr Kipling Snr.

'It sure is, sir. It sure is!'

It Wasn't Me!

Chapter 24 - The Edendale Project

The *Edendale Project* Presentation was going splendidly, or as well as Stuart could have planned. Harry was in good form and Masud appeared to be impressed by all the details. The video had set the scene wonderfully, and the PPP added subtle but impressive details of the development.

It was now for the reveal of the model which remained covered but was clearly the *elephant in the room*.

'Your Excellency, I hope you like what you've seen so far?' asked Stuart in an overly flattering manner.

'The development is as you've previously conveyed,' replied an ever cautious Masud. 'But I'm impressed by Mr Tovaine and his colleague's detailed presentation.'

'Excellent, that's what we want to hear. Now the pièce de résistance.'

Stuart grandly swept the cover from the model, and everyone immediately gathered around.

'Impressive!' said Masud, who was not one to overly show any emotion, especially when conducting business.

'I like it!'

'That's the spirit,' replied a clearly relieved Stuart.

Masud stood quietly contemplating every detail of the model, and when Stuart went to speak, he raised his hand and stopped him in his tracks.

Stuart was momentarily taken aback. He was not used to being quietened, but he immediately recognised that Masud needed some thinking time. This was definitely not the moment for any hard sell. The model would do that for him.

Masud then walked fully around the model, and glanced out of the large bay window, towards the eighteenth green, before going back to his seat. He then sat down, reflecting on what he had seen, his hands together touching his lips, as if in prayer.

'I think it is time for you and Mr Banker to perhaps provide the specific financial figures that go with the excellent build detail.'

'Of course, Your Excellency. Nick over to you?'

Nick got straight down to business. He was not one to put on airs and graces, even for Middle Eastern sheikhs.

Nick pressed the button on his laptop and the Power Point Presentation again sprang into life on the video screen.

'The Development comprises approximately 50 Hectares, or 100 Acres in old money.'

'Old money?' interjected Masud.

'Sorry Your Excellency, in the UK we still have a habit of stating land area in acres, rather than the metric equivalent of hectares,' informed Stuart courteously.

Masud smiled, and as Nick was about to continue, the door to the restaurant suddenly started to open.

'Sorry! This is a private meeting, no one is allowed in!' said Stuart, clearly annoyed at the interruption.

It Wasn't Me!

The door continued to open, and a head popped into the room.

'Sorry, but if I'm not mistaken, I hear the dulcet tones of His Excellency Sheikh Twoammie.'

'Get out Gray. This is a private meeting,' continued Stuart, before being interrupted.

'Colonel Gray, James. My Friend. How are you? It has been so long,' replied Masud, who rose from his seat and warmly embraced CJ.

'Sabah Alkhayr. Good Morning, Your Excellency. I'm well. How are you and your family?'

Stuart was clearly furious at the intrusion, but just held his temper in check, while the remaining members of the room were similarly taken aback at the clear affection shown by the two men.

'They're all fine.'

'Wonderful,' continued CJ, before adding. 'I'm sorry, I'm clearly interrupting your meeting. I do apologise. But before you go Masud, please come and see me. I'm in the Lounge Bar, next door.'

'Sawf Alwadae. I will. Goodbye James.'

CJ turned abruptly, having reviewed everything in the room, and made his way out while adding unapologetically. 'Sorry about that Brownlough.'

Stuart looked daggers at him, before smiling at Masud and asking, 'You know Gray?'

'Yes, we are old acquaintances, but it's a long story. Perhaps one for another day.'

With that, Nick continued as if nothing had happened.

'As you can see, we plan to provide 1500 new homes, at the reasonable rate of 30 homes per hectare. The selling price will be between £500k and £750k per detached house, providing a total income of £900 million. The estimated costs of the development, including all labour, materials, fees, and miscellaneous costs, will be £600 million. A profit for the development of £300 million. Split 40/40/20.'

Nick paused for the figures that appeared on the large screen to sink into Masud's subconscious.

'That appears to be in line with current market values,' said Masud, clearly aware of what was achievable in the North of England.

'You've done your homework, Your Excellency,' said a pleased Stuart, who was now feeling happy again, especially as he now didn't really have to sell the project further, other than to let Nick continue with the figures.

'So, more to the point, what are you seeking as an investment from me?' asked a studious Masud. 'And what can I expect in return?'

'We require a total of £125 million up front to get the project going, then after that, the project will be self-financing, and progressively provide the profits noted as houses are sold.'

'You haven't answered my question?' said Masud, looking deeply at Nick, who eyeballed him in return, before adding with a grin.

'Your part of the investment would be £50 million, with a return of £120 million, providing 140% on the investment. Not a bad day's work?'

It Wasn't Me!

'Mmm. That seems reasonable,' said Masud, clearly impressed, but playing his cards close to his chest.

'I told you it would be worthwhile,' said Charlotte, who had up until then remained silent, other than adding reassuring comments when nudged by Stuart.

'Yes, my dear, you're correct,' replied Masud, returning her smile with his own, before adding.

'And the timescale for this venture, is what?'

'We anticipate that from the purchase of the land to the final completion it will be a maximum of 3 years, but with the main contractor we are planning to use, he thinks that with a suitable incentive, he could complete in 24 months,' said Stuart, hoping that this detail would seal the deal.

'And you're confident this can be achieved?'

'Yes. We're extremely confident. Harry has completed everything from a design, specification, and planning perspective. We are good to go if you can immediately provide the balance of the funds.'

'That all sounds very good,' added Masud, who seemed to be warming to the concept.

'Excellent,' said a ginning Stuart.

'Just one thing, though?'

'Yes, Your Excellency. What's that?'

'How are you going to get the golf club to sell you the land?'

C J Meads

Chapter 25 - The Deeds

'That's a perfectly sensible question in the circumstances. I'll ask my solicitor to provide the answer. Andrew, if you don't mind?'

'Thank you Stuart. Your Excellency,' started Andrew, nodding towards Masud. 'When the club was formed back in 1919, there was a clause contained within the Deeds that if an offer in excess of £25 million, or the current value of the land was received, then the club was obliged to accept the offer, or put the deal to its members to decide.

'I've written to the club formally setting out our proposal, but we are confident that the members will endorse the proposal, even if the committee initially decides to object to the proposed sale.'

Masud looked sternly at Andrew and then Stuart, before responding.

'What makes you so sure the members will accept the offer?'

'Stuart, would you like to answer this point, as it's a financial point, rather than a legal one?'

'Of course. There are 400 members, and we've offered £30 million; therefore, each member would receive £75,000 each. I can assure you for the majority of members that's an offer they can't refuse, and they'll gladly accept.'

'What makes you so confident?' asked a thoughtful Masud.

'We've checked on the members plus their home addresses and have also conducted a poll of some of them. Based upon their personal circumstances, they

It Wasn't Me!

are more than likely to accept the offer, while subsequently finding another club in the area to play golf. There are plenty of them around, albeit possibly not quite as grand as Edendale.'

'You seem extremely confident, Mr Brownlough?'

'I am. We do, however, recognise that there will be some members, especially those like Earl Hargrove, for instance, who would see £75,000 as a derisory offer. But based upon our review of the members' circumstances and positions, we believe that those who would object to the offer, number about 125, at most.'

'That sounds like you've considered most things, Mr Brownlough. May I please see the document you refer to?'

'Andrew, would you be so kind as to show His Excellency the Deeds?'

Andrew bent down to one side and pulled an old document from his briefcase, and passed it to Masud.

'If you look at page 3, there's a covenant, which is quite clear.'

Masud looked at the document and read the relevant part.

'You see Your Excellency; Stuart has thought of everything. We wouldn't have asked you all this way if things weren't fully above board,' said Charlotte, smiling broadly at Masud.

He looked up momentarily and nodded back to her, before adding, 'That appears to be satisfactory. I would, however, like my legal team to review it to make sure they are also fully satisfied.'

'Of course. It is only sensible you would take such measures,' replied Stuart. 'Andrew, will you please ensure a copy is sent to Masud?'

'One more thing?' asked Masud, looking somewhat doubtful. 'Why are you in possession of the Deeds to the Golf Club?'

'That's an easy one. Kipling Solicitors hold the Deeds on behalf of Edendale Golf Club.'

It Wasn't Me!

Chapter 26 - The Invitation

'Good Morning. My Lord. How are you today?' greeted CJ earnestly.

'Grand Morning, CJ, good to see you, and Oscar too, as usual,' replied Earl Hargrove in his normal, haughty manner.

Oscar rolled on his back in anticipation of a belly rub, but Earl Hargrove ignored him completely, as was his way.

'Have you got a minute, please?'

'For you CJ, always.'

'My Lord, are you attending the *Equinox Festival* at Yorksbey Races?' enquired CJ politely.

'CJ, you know I will. I'm sponsoring the Hargrove Handicap on *Ladies' Day*. I wouldn't miss it for the world.'

'Very good.'

'Go on, why are you asking?'

'Edee, having seen racing in Dubai, has suddenly taken a liking to all things equine.'

'Well, if Madame Songe wants to go to the races, who am I to stop her? Do you think she would like to join us on *Ladies' Day*? I have a hospitality suite booked, and I'm sure we can fit in an extra two guests. Especially as it's you two.'

Oscar looked up and gave a short bark.

'I'm sorry lad, dogs aren't allowed at the races, not even you,' said Earl Hargrove, this time rubbing Oscar's ear warmly.

'That is most generous. I think she would love that. Thank you.'

'I'll send you an invitation with all the details. Please make sure you are dressed accordingly, but you'll no doubt look the part.'

'Of course we will. Any excuse to get all dressed up.'

Just then, the Major came storming out of his office. He looked incandescent, waving a letter in his hand.

'Major, what is it?' asked CJ.

'I've just received this by Special Delivery,' he shouted before continuing.

'That man. That bloody man Brownlough, and his legal stooge, Kipling Jnr. I'll fucking swing for them.'

'Calm down man!' shouted Earl Hargrove. 'You're making no sense.'

'He thinks he can fucking buy the golf course and build fucking houses on it. Read this!'

He passed the letter to Earl Hargrove, and both he and CJ quickly read its contents.

'That can't be right,' they both said together.

'Too bloody right it can't. I'll fucking swing for him,' repeated the Major, his blood pressure clearly in the danger zone. 'I'll kill him! The Bastard!'

Chapter 27 – An Agreement?

'Now, Your Excellency, as you've seen our proposals, can I take it that you're still prepared to partner us in the *Edendale Project*?' asked Charlotte, who had provocatively moved next to Masud. 'Or is there anything else I can do for you, to convince you as to the benefits of the deal?'

Masud looked deeply at her, and smiled knowingly, understanding what Charlotte was offering, before returning his gaze to Stuart and the rest of his team, who had suddenly looked away from Charlotte's obvious flirting.

'Mr Brownlough. I'm impressed by the presentation today, and also the financial advantages of the proposal.'

'Good. Very Good,' replied an overly keen Stuart, who was seeking to get an agreement.

'I think we can take this to the next stage. We have an agreement in principle. What do you now propose?'

'Excellent. Wonderful,' said Stuart, clearly relieved, but recognising that there was many a slip between *cup and lip.*

'I'll send you and your team a copy of the presentation you have seen today, plus Andrew has already drawn up a proposed contract which we will also forward to you, so your legal team can review.'

'That sounds very reasonable. Please issue everything to my PA. She will ensure my team gets all the information,' replied Masud, nodding towards her, as she courteously passed her business cards to Stuart and the team.

'Very good, but to get things moving, I suggest that Andrew issues a Pre-Contract Agreement to establish both parties' intent, and it will allow you to transfer £35 million to an *escrow* account. This will provide the necessary protection to all parties, but allow us to get things moving, especially with the purchase of the land,' added Stuart.

'You appear to have thought of everything, Mr Brownlough. I like a man who's prepared.'

'Time waits for no man. We should strike while the iron is hot, so to speak. Do we have a deal?' enquired Stuart, who stood up, looking confident, with his hand extended.

'Mr Brownlough. We have a deal!'

The two-wheeler dealers warmly shook hands and smiled broadly at one another, recognising the good business deal for what it was.

'Wonderful. Grand. That's the spirit.'

The rest of the room broke into applause, but the moment was immediately shattered, as the Major suddenly burst into the room - nearly taking the door off its hinges- with Earl Hargrove and CJ close behind.

'What the fuck's this all about, you conniving bastard?' shouted the Major, wildly waving the letter held in his hand.

'Major. Please, we have royal guests from Dubai present. Please show some dignity,' replied a very cool Stuart, who had clearly recognised what

It Wasn't Me!

Andrew's letter would instil in the Major, who'd acted accordingly.

'You smug bastard!? You won't get away with this.'

'Major, I'm unsure of what you are implying. We have purely invoked a clause within the Deeds of the golf club. There is nothing untoward about this whatsoever.'

'How come you've got a copy of the Deeds? They are the club's property and should be under lock and key.'

'Major, how we've come to acquire a copy is rather irrelevant. The issue is that legally you're obliged to accept my offer.'

'Fuck you Brownlough, and fuck you. You, you Judas,' pointing at a rather self-satisfied Andrew who sat at the other end of the table.

'Major, I think we should leave it for now,' interjected Earl Hargrove, who was equally livid, but had over the years recognised that it wasn't the skirmish that required winning, but the war. And that was clearly for another day.

He attempted to cajole the Major to leave, but the Major was clearly determined to have his moment.

'We'll see you in court, you sneaky bastard. And you can all get out of my club now! Along with that monstrosity.'

With that he turned, pushed the model of the *Edendale Project* onto the floor, and stormed out of the room.

'I do apologise Your Excellency, Gentlemen, Ladies,' said Earl Hargrove. 'Please conclude your meeting, but you'll have noticed, the Major is none too pleased.'

It Wasn't Me!

Chapter 28 – Are We Sure?

'Major, calm down. There is no sense in getting upset and angry. We need to deal with this with rational thoughts and clear minds,' said Earl Hargrove, as the three of them and Oscar joined Edee in the Lounge Bar.

'What's happened?' asked Edee, clearly aware that the Major was distressed. 'Major, are you okay?'

'Not really, my dear, but I agree with His Lordship. I'm sorry, I have made a complete fool of myself.'

CJ passed the letter to Edee, who skimmed its contents and got up to speed.

'Jarvis. A brandy for the Major, please, and I'll also have one. CJ, Edee, would you like a drink?'

'No thank you,' they both replied.

'This surely can't be right?' said Edee, having read the letter. 'But the copy of the Deeds implies that it is. What do you plan on doing?'

'Major, you'll need to speak with Mr Kipling Snr. as soon as possible, but be tactful. He's just come out of hospital,' instructed Earl Hargrove.

'Of course. I'll make an appointment tomorrow.'

'Good. We'll then need to consider how we counter this abomination. Hopefully, Mr Kipling Snr. will have a legal strategy.'

'Yes, indeed,' replied the Major, deep in thought.

CJ, who'd been quiet and reflective, then spoke up. 'Are we sure the copy of the Deeds is from the original?'

'What are you implying, CJ?' asked Earl Hargrove.

'I'm not sure, but I wouldn't put anything past Brownlough.'

'You think he's tampered with the Deeds? Surely not! Not even he would stoop to fraud.'

'Not everyone's as honourable as you, My Lord. I think we shouldn't take things at face value. I suggest we investigate further.'

'Yes, you're right. Thinking about it I'm not sure if I have a copy of the Deeds somewhere. I vaguely remember Papa passing something to me shortly before he died, but knowing me, I've probably destroyed it. What about you CJ. You're a Trustee. Do you have a copy?'

'I'm not sure. I'll do some digging at Overhear Manor, but Dad didn't specifically give me anything, not that I recall, but that doesn't mean there isn't a copy somewhere.'

'Well, there's not much more we can do now, but I'll provide some feedback once I have spoken to Mr Kipling Snr,' concluded the Major.

'Your drinks, My Lord, Major.'

'Thank you Jarvis.'

'I couldn't help overhearing the commotion. Is there anything the staff need to be concerned about?' asked Jarvis, sounding rather worried.

'No Jarvis. Not for now. I think everything will be fine,' answered the Major, but not sounding very convincing.

It Wasn't Me!

'Mr Brownlough, what was that all about?' asked a quizzical Masud, undoubtedly aware of the issue.

'Your Excellency, I think it was inevitable that some of those passionate about the club would react in an unseemly manner. I'm sorry you had to witness it,' replied Stuart, trying to placate his prospective backer, while defusing a regrettable and unwelcome incident.

'But I can assure you we've the law on our side and as much as people like the Major, huff and puff, there is nothing they can do about it. Is there Andrew?'

'Stuart is correct, the document is watertight. We have right on our side. You shouldn't be alarmed by incoherent and ranting observers. They will, once they have taken legal advice, realise the situation for themselves.'

'I understand gentlemen, ladies, but if you will, as agreed, forward the details we discussed. My legal team can also independently verify things.'

'Of course. So we still have a deal?' asked Stuart, who was not 100% sure how the recent events had been interpreted by Masud.

'My word is my bond; I have seen nothing at this time to change my opinion. Of course we have a deal,' replied Masud, smiling broadly and again shaking hands with Stuart.

'Wonderful. Great. That's the spirit,' said a totally relieved Stuart, who glared at Andrew in a manner which said. 'You had better be right.'

Chapter 29 – Another Invite

'Masud, now we have a deal, I was wondering, about *Never Say Die,*' enquired a smiling Charlotte, as she linked arms with him.

'Ah, yes. The horse,' replied Masud, clearly now thinking.

'Can we deduct the value of the horse from your £50 million and the horse becomes mine?' suggested Stuart.

'Mmm, I think not,' countered Masud.

'Oh!' said a visibly deflated Charlotte.

'No, my dear, it will not form part of the deal.'

'That's a shame. I thought we had some sort of understanding, after our discussion in Dubai,' said Stuart, who was not overly concerned, but would have really liked to have acquired a leading thoroughbred stallion.

'My dear Charlotte, the horse is yours, a gift from me to you.'

'Oh Masud! How generous. Thank you. You must let me know how I can repay you,' said Charlotte, who embraced Masud and kissed him warmly on the cheek. Even she recognised that in mixed company, she could only show a certain amount of affection, and clearly, anything further would have to wait until another time and place.

'You are welcome, my dear. Now I think I'll be going. My PA will be in touch once we have received the documents, and my team has reviewed them. Once again, thank you all for an excellent presentation and the opportunity to work together.'

It Wasn't Me!

He shook everyone's hand warmly, and then promptly left the meeting, his PA walking close behind. He turned immediately right into the Lounge Bar and instinctively sought out his old friend.

'James, As-salaam 'alykum. Peace be with you.'

'As-salaam 'alykum,' replied James as they again embraced.

Edee stood, smiled warmly, and nodded towards Masud.

'And who is this beautiful woman?'

'Masud, this is Madame Eden Songe.'

'Charmed. As-salaam 'alykum Madame Songe.'

'Please call me Edee.'

'My dear, I could never be so bold. And who is this little chap? He is nearly as magnificent as you, my dear.'

'This is Oscar, my dearest friend in all the world, other than Edee, of course.'

Oscar bowled into Masud's legs and sought an ear rub, to which the Sheikh swiftly obliged.

'James, you choose your friends well, and I should know.'

'Masud, I also count you as a dear friend. Do you have a moment to join us?' asked CJ, clearly hoping his old acquaintance would find the time.

'James, unfortunately I've another pressing appointment that can't wait.'

'Oh, that's a shame,' said a disappointed CJ. He wanted to interrogate his old adversary about his association with Stuart, but it looked like that would have to wait for another day.

'Look, I'm here for a few more days and I'm sponsoring the *Equinox Festival*. Why don't you join me? I have a suite booked in the Grandstand. We can then discuss old times.'

'That would be marvellous,' said a smiling Edee, who looked at CJ and raised her eyes, as much to say, two offers in quick succession. It sure looks like we're definitely going to the races.

It Wasn't Me!

CHAPTER 30 – HOW WAS IT?

'Thanks Rebecca, I think that went really well, other than the Major's outburst,' said Harry, as the two of them left the golf club, leaving Stuart, Nick, and Andrew contemplating the finer points of the deal.

'You're welcome. I agree, I think Stuart was also very pleased. It looks like he now has his backer on board, which is good news for the project and the business. Your business!'

'Yes, it sure is. I think we can take some credit for the presentation, and we can look forward to things progressing. Well, I must get going, and I don't want to take up any more of your weekend.'

'Oh. That's okay,' said Rebecca, who had been hoping that Harry might just suggest going for some lunch to celebrate. But it was now evident this was not the case.

'Well, thanks again, and I'll see you bright and early tomorrow morning.' With that, Harry waved goodbye and climbed into his old Audi A3.

'Bye Harry. See you tomorrow,' said a rather deflated Rebecca. Who was now left with looking forward to either lunch with her mum and dad, or a glass of Chardonnay on her own at the pub, neither of which filled her with much enthusiasm.

She looked on, dreaming of better things with Harry, as she got into her own car.

'Well done Men!' said Stuart, clearly extremely pleased with the outcome of the presentation and the meeting.

'Ahem!' replied Charlotte.

'Sorry. Well done Team. You've also played your part magnificently, Charlie. Thank you all.'

It was a rare show of appreciation for others from Stuart, who was not one to dole out praise willy-nilly.

'Yes, everyone played their part today. It was a good joint effort,' added Nick. 'The best thing, though, was getting Sheikh Twoammie on board, and the promise of funds. When do you think they'll be transferred?'

'Look, let's all keep our side of the bargain, and issue all the information to Masud pronto. I'll then follow up with him, but I'm hopeful we can get the advance into our account within a few days.'

'Brilliant. I can then get HMRC off our backs,' continued Nick, who was desperate for some influx of cash to ease Stuart's current financial position.

'There aren't any issues financially, are there Stuart? I really need your account settling before Dad gets any more suspicious,' said a slightly concerned Andrew.

'Nothing for you to worry about, Andrew. Nick will sort out your account this week. Won't you Nick?'

'If you say so, Boss.'

'And Andrew, you need to set the legal wheels in motion to buy the club.'

It Wasn't Me!

Harry turned left out of the carpark, en route to the Watermill Arms.

He checked the rear-view mirror and absentmindedly noticed a silver Mercedes turning the other way out of the carpark. He then punched a recent number on his phone, and Sienna picked up on the second ring.

'Hi.'

'Hi.'

'How was it?' she enquired, but not particularly bothered.

'Really good. I'm on my way. I'll be at the pub in a few minutes.'

'Okay, I'll see you there. I'm also leaving now.'

'Bye.'

'Bye. Bye.'

Harry parked up in the pubs carpark. He waited patiently for Sienna to arrive, leaning nonchalantly on the boot of his car. It was just starting to get busy with the regular Sunday Lunch trade.

Shortly Sienna's Clio turned into the carpark and pulled up next to Harry. Sienna elegantly got out, looking like she had spent all morning getting ready for the lunch date.

'Hi. You look good enough to eat,' said Harry, as he kissed her.

'Thanks, but I think lunch first,' replied Sienna, before adding. 'So it went well? Was Daddy his usual self?'

'It went really well, and your dad was on top form. He got the backing he needed. Which is good for everyone.'

'Excellent.'

'Hello. What's Mummy doing here?' said Sienna, as she spotted a green Tesla. 'Perhaps she's meeting Daddy.'

'I'm not sure that's the case,' replied a confident Harry.

'What do you mean? How can you be so certain?'

'Well, he left the meeting with Charlotte Tate, and they looked to be going the other way.'

'Oh.'

The two of them walked arm in arm into the pub, Sienna considering what Harry had said, and the likely implications. She was aware that her parents' marriage was becoming one of mere convenience, rather than the one they both persistently strove to convey to others. But her father was normally far more circumspect regarding his dalliances.

Sarah saw them first, and was evidently not expecting to bump into them, well not here, and not in these circumstances.

'Harry, please get me a large glass of white wine. I'm just going to see what Mum is doing here.'

'Is Sauvignon Blanc okay?'

'Fine, whatever, or a Pinot,' replied Sienna, as she wandered over to her mother.

'Hi Mum. What brings you here on a Sunday lunchtime? Is Dad with you?'

Sarah, desperately seeking a plausible reason, blurted out, 'I'm just waiting for Jane, but she seems to be running late.'

It Wasn't Me!

'Oh. Are you out for a girly lunch, then?' replied Sienna, clearly revelling in her mother's discomfort. 'Do you mind if Harry and I join you?'

'Ah. Um. Are you sure you two lovebirds wouldn't prefer to dine alone, without me cramping your style?'

'I'll tell you what. Shall we join you until *Jane* turns up?'

'I guess so, if you must, but if she doesn't turn up soon, I'll have to leave you.'

Sienna sat down next to her mother, and presently Harry joined them with the drinks he'd ordered.

'Hello Mrs Brownlough. I hope you're well? I didn't expect to see you here.' He clearly didn't want to have lunch with his young girlfriend's mother. No matter how attractive and pleasant she was.

'Good day Harry. I'm fine. How are you?'

'I'm good, thank you. I've just left a meeting with your husband. It was very productive.'

'Oh, was it?' responded an indifferent Sarah. Who was plainly not happy with how the day was now suddenly developing.

'I hope Jane has taken as much trouble as you have, mum. You look like you are out on a date,' teased Sienna.

'You look wonderful, Mrs Brownlough. Ignore Sienna. You look more like sisters than mother and daughter,' continued Harry, seeing an opportunity to ingratiate himself with Sarah as he sat down. However, the look from Sienna told a completely different tale.

'Thank you Harry. I find that children tend to be slightly more challenging the older they get.'

At that moment, Andrew walked into the pub. He started to wave towards Sarah, but immediately stopped when he saw the slightest of head shakes from her, something that didn't go unnoticed by Sienna, who immediately looked towards the bar. Andrew, however, had turned his back, and was now speaking with Ted Malone, the jovial landlord.

Sienna glanced back at her mother for any obvious give away sign, but none was forthcoming, and when she looked again towards the bar, Andrew had disappeared. Which similarly did not go undetected.

'It looks like Jane's not coming,' said Sarah, who had looked down at her phone when a message pinged.

'That's a shame Mum!' said Sienna. who seemingly recognised the message was not from Jane. 'But you can still join us for lunch. Can't she Harry?'

Harry, now caught between a rock and a hard place, was unsure how to respond. He knew what he wanted to say, but felt that wasn't the reply expected by Sienna.

Fortunately for him, Sarah solved his conundrum.

'I'll leave you two young things to it. You certainly don't want me ruining your lunch date.'

Harry looked quite relieved, but Sienna was obviously still in a playful mood.

'Are you sure, Mum? You're more than welcome to stay,' she lied.

It Wasn't Me!

'Thank you for the kind invite, but I'll be going.' Sarah stood up and gave her daughter a peck on the cheek. 'Enjoy your lunch. Bye Sienna, Harry,' and she promptly left to seek out Andrew.

'Bye Mum!' said a smiling, mischievous Sienna.

'Goodbye Mrs Brownlough,' said a rather more relieved and courteous Harry.

Chapter 31 – But What Can We Do?

Jarvis had messaged the key staff of the club, and had convened a make shift meeting during a break, when most of them could be available.

The restaurant was still closed, having been booked for the morning, which gave Jarvis the opportunity to get them all together, while the two waitresses were busily returning the room to its normal layout.

'What's the problem?' enquired Ian, clearly perturbed as to why they'd all been summoned.

'Yes. What's so urgent?' asked Tom, the Head Groundsmen, who had Phil, the apprentice Greenkeeper, in tow.

'Brownlough Developments are planning to buy the club, and build new houses on the land!'

'What? You can't be serious?' said Tom. 'The Major won't allow that, nor will Earl Hargrove.'

'Well, the Major has told me not to worry about it, and that everything will be fine. But I'm not totally convinced, and I thought I should give you the heads up, regardless of his reassurances.'

'That's good of you,' replied Rachel, who didn't seem that bothered by the situation, especially as she had only just started her new job.

Ian looked on thoughtfully and then offered his initial judgment.

'It's good of you to let us know, but I suggest we do some more investigating before we get too concerned.' He now perhaps understood why

It Wasn't Me!

Charlotte had been visited by Stuart, but he still needed to check on her *true* involvement.

'I'll tell you one thing though, Brownlough will build houses on this course over my dead body. I'll see him in hell before that happens,' said a resolute Jarvis.

'Hear, hear,' said Tom and Phil together.

'I know the Major is seeing Mr Kipling Snr. tomorrow, and I'm sure we will know more after that meeting. I'll keep you posted. In the meantime, I suggest we play this close to our chests, and let's not set the hare running too soon,' suggested Jarvis, only just realising that he had perhaps done just that.

CJ and Edee were on the Ninth Tee. They were just concluding their round after the rather eventful morning. Oscar sat contentedly looking on as Edee completed her tee shot.

She had hit an easy five iron into the heart of the green, a definite birdie opportunity.

CJ remained one down and needed to win this hole to tie the match. He also chose a five iron, and as normal, addressed the ball without a practice swing. He immediately regretted it as he hit an awful shot that ended in the river.

'Fuck it.'

'James, you've ended the round in a similar way to how you started it,' teased a laughing Edee, before recognising that CJ was definitely pre-occupied.

'Your mind's on other things. Isn't it?'

'Yes Edee, it is. Something's not right with this Brownlough Deed.'

'But what can we do?'

'I think we need to go searching, and if we need to turn Overhear Manor upside down to find something, then so be it. But we must find a copy of the original Golf Club Deeds,' said a resolute CJ. He rammed his club back into his golf bag, and strolled off resolutely over the footbridge to the green, his trolley precariously pulled behind him. He left Edee and Oscar to their thoughts as they trailed in his wake.

It Wasn't Me!

Chapter 32 – For Old Times' Sake

Ian Westbank pulled up to the gate of Tate House in his Ford Focus ST. He lowered the window and pressed the call button on the keypad.

After a short while, a familiar sparkling, but guarded voice emanated from the speaker.

'Good Morning. How can I help you?'

'Hi Charlotte, it's me Ian. Just checking how you are this morning?' he said in a cheery voice. 'I haven't seen you for a while.'

'Oh, it's you? It's not really convenient now,' replied Charlotte, obviously not particularly wanting to see him.

'That's a shame. I've some information that might be to your advantage.'

'Oh! Okay. Come on up. The front doors open.' With that, the intercom went dead and the gate started opening.

Ian parked his car outside the front door, next to the only other car in the driveway, Charlotte's Audi TT.

'At least no silver Mercedes. That's a positive,' thought Ian, somewhat relieved that Stuart was not there.

He opened the front door and sauntered into the hallway, calling out, 'Hi, anyone at home?'

'I'm in the kitchen,' came the cheery reply.

Ian checked there was no one else around and walked in to the kitchen. Charlotte was sitting on a high stool at the breakfast bar, with her back to him. She was cradling a mug of coffee in both hands and looking aimlessly out into the far distance of the extensive garden.

'Hi Charlotte, how are you this morning?'

She turned towards him; she looked stunning as always. Perfect makeup, perfect clothing, perfect high heel shoes! Just like the glamorous woman she always actively sought to impart.

'Hello Ian. It's been a while, but I've been *so* busy, and also trying to sort out Bart's estate. You know, I haven't been at my best.'

Ian gently embraced her and kissed her softly on the cheek, but he was already rather aroused by her sensual charm. He would have liked a more passionate embrace, like it had been only a few months ago, but he sensed that he might have to wait.

'You smell good, Ian. Is that a new cologne?' enquired Charlotte.

'It's the one you bought me for my last birthday.'

'I've always had good taste,' replied a smiling Charlotte, accompanied by an inviting wink, her large false eyelashes nearly taking out Ian's own eye.

Ian was already under her charm. He needed to stay on point, at least until he had the information he was after.

'I was hoping that I could perhaps take you to dinner? It's been such a long time.'

'I'm so busy, Ian, and with sorting out Bart's finances, I'm finding it *hard* to fit things in.'

'Though not too busy to go to Dubai?' Ian struggled to maintain his calm, and the question came out rather more aggressively than he had planned.

It Wasn't Me!

'Ian. That was purely business,' replied Charlotte submissively, although she instantly remembered, with a smile, some of the visit's highlights.

'It's alright for some. Did you pay, or did Brownlough?'

'Ian, I'm not sure what you're implying. But I'm worried Bart's finances may not be as good as I hoped or expected. I'm just seeking to secure my future, nothing more.'

'Is that what you call it?' Ian was now really struggling to hide his jealousy.

'Ian, there's no need to be like that. I do, however, need to keep Stuart onside. With a bit of luck, I can get him to agree to me being his formal business partner.'

'Charlotte, I think you should be careful. Brownlough has quite a reputation for being ruthless in business. He doesn't take prisoners.'

'I know that, but don't forget, I also know how to look after myself. Plus, I need the money, and I'm looking to invest in his latest development. It'll also give me some financial security.'

'Would that be the *Edendale Project*?'

'What! How do you know about that?' asked a rather concerned Charlotte. Who in an instant, looked to go on a more serious charm offensive.

'The events of Sunday and the Major's outburst are the talk of the club. There are now plans afoot to stymie Brownlough's scheme.'

'Ian, I think we should perhaps talk about that later,' said a conniving Charlotte, as she walked sensually towards the hallway, and took his hand, leading him upstairs. 'Let's go to the bedroom. I think we should make up for lost time.'

Ian was immediately captivated by the Femme Fatale, and followed submissively, eager to please her, in any way he could.

Charlotte now knew for certain that she would get the answers to all her questions, plus those she was still to consider.

It Wasn't Me!

Chapter 33 – Is Everything Okay?

Stuart noticed the email pop up on his laptop. It was from Masud's PA, and he was anxious to open it. All the information had now been with Sheikh Twoammie's team for a few days, and he was desperately hoping for a positive response.

He had deliberately not pestered Masud or his team, recognising that it would be counterproductive. In the same way, he despised people that attempted to force him to review things earlier than he planned. Sometimes you just have to let things take their course, but that didn't stop him from wanting to know the outcome of their deliberations.

Despite him knowing he had got everything right, that didn't mean that everything would be okay.

He was initially concerned. There were many attachments, but he quickly recognised that the majority were the documents his own team had issued, with the exception of a couple from Masud.

That was a good sign.

He quickly scanned the lengthy email, and even though there were a few clarifications needing attention, it was reading pretty well.

He finally came to the end and gave a sigh of relief. No deal breakers from the initial reading, and things seemed to be generally acceptable.

He clenched his fist as many tennis players seem to do at the winning of a point, and shouted, 'Yes!'

He sat back in his expensive high back executive swivel chair and momentarily closed his eyes in sheer relief. It looked like he had Masud on board.

'Right, let's have a look at the fine print,' he said out loud, before again starting to read the email, but this time more thoroughly.

His phone rang. He saw it was Nick, and he immediately answered.

'Brilliant news,' said a distinctly relieved Nick.

'It sure looks like it. Have you read everything?' replied Stuart.

'Only quickly, but we have him. The email is most encouraging.'

'It looks that way. It's really positive. I'm just going through all the documents now, but I'm hopeful there's nothing that Andrew can't resolve legally.'

'The good thing is that he plans to transfer the money once we agree to the minor items he's put forward,' added Nick, who still remained desperate for the new funds.

'I'll get Andrew straight on it, but unless there are some *real* deal breakers, I hope to get the documents signed, and back to him pronto.'

'Andrew's not going to be a problem, is he?' enquired Nick thoughtfully.

'No! What do you mean?' replied a rather perplexed Stuart.

'I've just got a feeling that he's having some reservations. He's not going to say anything out of place, is he?'

'Not if he knows what's good for him,' said Stuart. 'I have enough on him to ensure that he will, without a doubt, stay onside.'

It Wasn't Me!

'I hope so, but lawyers have a way of always trying to be honest, even when they're not.'

'Nick, I assure you, Andrew Kipling will not get in our way.'

'Well, he hadn't better. Otherwise he'll be answering to me.'

C J Meads

Chapter 34 – Is It The Right Deed?

The Major sat on the expensive wood and leather armchair in the Solicitor's office. Opposite him at his own desk, was Mr Kipling Snr. who seemed to be showing no ill effects from his recent trip to hospital.

The two old acquaintances were drinking fine filter coffee from *Bone China* cups that had been in the practice for the past fifty years. Many a legal deal had been finalised while drinking from them.

'I'm pleased that you're showing no adverse signs following the break in. You were most fortunate.'

'Not as pleased as I am,' replied the smiling solicitor.

'But down to business. You've obviously got my email with the copy of the Deed, issued by Brownlough Developments.'

'I have.'

'The million dollar question. Does it match the original, in your safe?' asked the Major, hoping that it didn't.

'I'm sorry to have to advise you that it does. It's an exact copy of the original.'

'Damn. I was hoping that it wasn't. Are you sure?'

'The two documents are identical in every way.'

'How did Brownlough get his hands on a copy of the document?' asked a puzzled Major, before adding. 'Not that it makes much difference, as he himself pointed out.'

'From the records we hold, there were four copies made at the initial AGM back in 1919. The Four Trustees: Earl Hargrove; Doctor N Spinney MD;

It Wasn't Me!

Major E Gray MC; and Mr M Warner LLB were each provided with copies of the Deeds. Mr Warner, the club's newly appointed solicitor, retained the originals for safe keeping. As you know, following his death, and the closure of his business, the original document came to Kipling Solicitors for safe keeping. It has been with us ever since.'

'Damn,' repeated the Major. 'Could it have been changed at some point in the last hundred years?' enquired a hopeful Major.

'It's possible, I suppose, but highly unlikely,' replied Mr Kipling Snr. unsure of anything further he could say, to assist the Major.

'So you're definitely sure this copy is legitimate?'

'I am, based upon the document I hold.'

'Is there anything we can do legally to prevent Brownlough from buying the course?'

'The best I can do is to explore bogging down the process in legal red tape. It might buy you some time, but based upon the document, he appears to hold the upper hand.'

'So there's nothing we can do in the end to stop him?' said a very despondent Major.

'It looks that way,' said a similarly disappointed Mr Kipling Snr.

The Major went quiet, in deep thought, before adding to himself, 'Maybe nothing *legally*.'

Chapter 35 – There Are Plans Afoot

'I suggest you get over here quick. I've some information that you should be aware of,' said a worried Charlotte.

'What is it?' replied a now similarly alarmed Stuart.

'I would prefer not to speak about it over the phone. I think it's better if we discuss it face to face.'

'Okay, if we must. I just need to wrap a few things up. Where do you want to meet? At yours?'

'Mmm. I'm not sure that's a good idea. People have been observing us. Let's meet at the Watermill Arms.'

'Okay, I'll see you there shortly.'

CJ and Edee were sitting around the kitchen island of Overhear Manor, with a customary cappuccino and a mid-morning croissant to hand. Oscar was lying at his master's feet, dozing peacefully.

Across from them, Mrs Wembley was making fresh bread, which CJ loved, and despite supermarkets selling value for money varieties, he relished fresh bread and was not stopping Mrs W from doing what she enjoyed. Especially when such wonderful results flowed from the old Aga Range.

Mrs Wembley had been at Overhear Manor since she left school as a young girl with no qualifications, having been employed by Aunty Betty. Because of her, the place ran like clockwork. CJ would never interrupt Mrs Wembley's routine. Well, not normally.

It Wasn't Me!

He looked at Edee, who prompted him by nodding her head sideways, while raising her eyebrows.

'Go on,' she whispered.

'Mrs Wembley?'

'Yes, Master James. What is it? I know something's a foot. You must think I'm a fool, but I've known you from a toddler,' replied a jovial Mrs Wembley.

'There's no fooling you, is there?'

'I don't think so. Well, not today.'

'Well, do you recall if Dad, or Aunty Betty, ever spoke about the Deeds to the golf club?'

'Or if they did, where they were kept?' added Edee, who, like CJ, was keen to find any evidence of the missing documents.

'What makes you ask?'

'I'd rather not say, but do you remember anything?'

'You know I never meddle in business matters, Master James. It's more than my life's worth.'

'There's meddling and there's knowing. Two totally different things,' added CJ, pulling on a thread he felt was figuratively starting to appear.

'I vaguely remember your aunty talking about a copy when your parents died. But I can't recall if, or where, she may have put it.'

'So you think she had a copy?'

'I think so, but don't you recall anything being given to you by Mr Kipling Snr. when your Aunty died? He dealt with Probate on her Will.'

'That's a good point, but I don't remember him mentioning it, or saying he had a copy.'

'But that doesn't mean he doesn't have one,' added Edee.

'No. That's true. I think we'll have to pay him a visit. I still haven't seen him to sort out the changes to my own Will.'

'No time like the present. Let's see if he's available,' suggested a very keen Edee.

'Hello Ted. How are you? You're looking very dapper today,' said a very flirtatious Charlotte, as she sat on a bar stool at the Watermill Arms, crossing her legs seductively, something which didn't go unnoticed by Ted Malone, the well-liked and respected pub owner.

'I'm well, thank you, and it's kind of you to notice. But I have to say you look stunning as always, Charlotte. I trust you're also well?'

'You know me, Ted, always looking on the bright side of life.'

'What can I get you? Are you on your own, or are you meeting someone?' asked an inquisitive, and slightly prying Ted.

'My normal spritzer please Ted, and I'm meeting Stuart Brownlough. We've some prospective business to discuss.'

'Spritzer, coming right up,' said Ted cheerily, before adding seriously.

'Charlotte?'

'Yes, Ted?'

'Be careful with Brownlough,' replied Ted, openly caring and keeping an eye out for Charlotte.

'I can handle him.'

It Wasn't Me!

'I'm sure you can,' said a smiling Ted, who then continued compassionately.

'Just a word to the wise!'

As Ted placed the large glass of spritzer on the bar, in walked Stuart, who kissed Charlotte aimlessly on the cheek.

'Hi Charlie. What's the issue?'

'Let's get a table. What would you like, Stuart?' asked Charlotte.

'Not in here Charlie,' said Stuart laughing.

'Hello sir,' asked Ted politely. 'What can I get you?'

'A pint of your best, Ted,' said Stuart, rather curtly.

'Certainly sir,' replied Ted, now with similar insincerity. He visibly had no time for the arrogant businessman.

'Ted, put the drinks on Stuart's tab. He's paying,' said Charlotte, as she slid graciously off the stool, and made her way to a quiet table in a bay window.

Stuart sat down, obviously not too happy at being dragged away from work, before taking a sip of his beer.

'Go on then, what is it?'

'Stuart, I wouldn't have asked you here if I didn't think it was important.'

'Sorry. It's just we're trying to finalise all the documents so that Masud can transfer the initial payment.'

'I'm aware of that, but this might become an issue, and I don't want anything ruining things,' replied

Charlotte, clearly aware of the importance of the deal.

'Understood. Go on then.'

'It's come to my attention that the golf club staff are likely to try and make matters difficult for you.'

'Who's that then? How do they know about the *Edendale Project*?'

'I have my sources,' replied Charlotte, clearly unwilling to say who had blabbed. 'Apparently the Major's outburst is the talk of the club.'

'Well, there's nothing they can do to stop the development.'

'I wouldn't be so sure.'

'What do you mean?'

'The Major's meeting Mr Kipling Snr. today to check the document is real.'

'Well, we know our copy matches the original held by the old man.'

'Yes, I know that, but that won't stop the Major or Earl Hargrove from getting Old Man Kipling to muddy the legal waters.'

'Mmm. That's a good point. But at worst, it'll still only temporarily hold things up. There's nothing legally they can do. I'll speak with Andrew. I'll get him to put some pressure on his old man to drop it. He'll do that if he knows what's good for him.'

'You seem to have quite a hold over, Andrew. Anything I should know about?' asked a quizzical Charlotte.

'Nothing to worry your pretty little head over, my dear,' said a slightly mocking Stuart.

It Wasn't Me!

'I do worry. We both want this deal to go through without a hitch. We can then look to the future and our life together.'

'I think the future will take care of itself,' said Stuart, pretty convinced he knew how things were going to pan out.

'Something else you should be aware of. The foot soldiers at the club are similarly unhappy with your plans. They see their jobs in jeopardy.'

'Well, there's definitely nothing those plebs can do about it,' replied an overly confident Stuart.

'Maybe. Maybe not, but don't under-estimate a cornered animal, no matter where they're from, or their background,' said Charlotte, a voice of experience in such matters.

'Whatever.'

'A word to the wise, Stuart. All I would say is, watch your back.'

Chapter 36 – Can You Trust Kipling?

'Andy, how's it going?'

Stuart was direct, and straight to the point when he called to get an update on the legal points raised by Masud.

'Good Afternoon, Stuart,' replied a more courteous Andrew. 'I'm just concluding the response to Sheikh Twoammie's PA.'

'Very good. That's what we want to hear. I trust there are no issues?'

'No, not really. His lawyer has raised the points I would have done if I were in their position.'

'Good. Good. So when do you think we'll have an agreement to sign?'

'I expect that once they've read my response and seen our acceptance to their points, we should have a document for signing today. It's then down to you, and Masud when you sign the Agreement.'

'That's marvellous.'

'Andrew?'

'Yes Stuart?' Andrew realised that Stuart was seeking something further from him and was rather dreading the reply.

'Your father isn't going to make things awkward for us. Is he?'

'What do you mean?'

'I gather the Major has been in discussion with him, and I'm concerned that he may look to slow down the buying of the golf club land, by raising unjustified legal issues.'

It Wasn't Me!

'Stuart, I'm not sure what you expected the club to do. Just lie down and accept things? They have been playing golf there for over a hundred years.'

'I know that, but I want this deal moving quickly,' said Stuart, who was starting to get frustrated.

'Your copy of the Deeds matches the original held in our office safe here. So there's very little legally that Dad can do to stop the sale. He might try to get an Injunction, but I'm unsure as to what grounds he would state in any application. It would be a rather pointless process.'

'Can't you have a word with him, and point out how ineffective such a route would be?'

'Of course I will, but I'm sure he will also suggest that the club ballots the members, albeit I don't think that will lead very far. Especially if you're as confident as you say you are of the outcome.'

'Andrew, I need you to put pressure on your father, to recognise that whatever he suggests is futile, and will simply only slightly delay the inevitable.'

'Of course I'll try,' said a rather dejected and uncertain Andrew.

'Andrew. I need and expect you to do more than try. Do I make myself clear?' said Stuart, clearly now threatening Andrew.

'I understand, but you don't know Dad like I do.'

'Andrew, I don't need to. Just sort it. You wouldn't want anything becoming common knowledge that affects you. Would you now?'

'Okay. Understood.'

'That's what I wanted to hear. Goodbye Andrew,' and Stuart ended the call, not waiting for a further reply.

Across from Stuart, Nick had heard the conversation on the office phone loudspeaker. He looked at him doubtfully and shook his head.

'Can you trust him to follow through?'

'I couldn't have made it any clearer for him,' replied a similarly unconvinced Stuart.

'Well, he'd better not let anything get in our way.'

Meanwhile CJ and Edee were sitting in Kipling Solicitors' office, drinking the coffee offered by the senior partner. Oscar was sitting to attention at CJ's feet, also appearing to be listening attentively to the old solicitor.

'So I think I have your instructions for your new Will. The changes are quite straightforward and clear. I'll get the new Will drafted and let you know when it will be ready for signing,' said a jovial Mr Kipling Snr. who was clearly back to his normal self, and showing no ill effects from his recent ordeal.

'You said there was something else?'

'You will recall you dealt with the administration of Aunty Betty's estate and Probate,' stated CJ.

'I do.'

'Do you remember if there was a copy of the Golf Club Deeds with the documents? Also, if there was, do you still retain it with my other legal documents?'

'Well CJ, while my memory used to be quite good, you are clearly testing me now. To be honest, I don't recall seeing a document, but let me check

It Wasn't Me!

what we hold for you. There could be something, but I wouldn't hold your breath. May I enquire as to why you're asking?'

'I understand that you have the original, and that the Major has been in contact regarding its authenticity.'

'I do, and he has, but I'm still unsure as to your request or what you may be implying CJ,' came the stern reply.

'I'm sorry, I didn't mean any offence, or to imply anything. It's just that I, we, would just like to find our copy,' said CJ, as he looked briefly at Edee, and then back to the old solicitor. 'More, for *old times' sake*, and maybe to put to bed any lingering doubts the Major, or Earl Hargrove have, regarding Brownlough's copy.'

'I understand,' came the neutral reply.

'Mr Kipling Snr. you know us both of old. We are, as always, just seeking the truth, as this matter could potentially get nasty. As you will appreciate, there's a lot at stake,' said Edee, smiling, recognising that her feminine charm may be needed to calm things. Which it instantly did.

'Madame Songe, as usual, you get straight to the point, while putting me at ease. Let me go and look in the safe. Can I get you both another coffee?' he enquired as he got up and walked towards the office door.

'Non. Merci. No, not for me,' replied Edee graciously.

'No, nor me,' replied CJ.

As Mr Kipling Snr. left his office, he bumped into Andrew.

'Sorry Son. I nearly took you out then.'

'What do they want?' Andrew asked, rather bluntly, in the circumstances, but obviously still disturbed by Stuart's phone call.

'Not much, Mr Gray is just slightly modifying his Will.'

'Anything else? And why are you going to the safe?'

'He's asked me to check if we hold his copy of the Golf Club Deeds with his other documents.'

'Does he have a copy?' enquired Andrew directly.

'I'm not sure. I can't remember. That's why I'm going to check.'

'Would you like me to check for you?' asked Andrew, suddenly rather more helpful.

'No, it's alright. I'll do it.'

'Are you sure?' continued Andrew, whose keenness didn't go unnoticed by his father. Nor by CJ, who was suddenly leaning on the door frame to the office, listening intently.

Andrew quickly turned and nonchalantly walked back to his office, as if no longer concerned, while CJ returned to Edee.

A few minutes later, Mr Kipling Snr. came back empty-handed, witnessed by a very relieved looking Andrew, who was talking with his secretary in the main office.

'I'm sorry, CJ, Madame Songe. We don't have a copy of the Deeds with your other valuables. If you have one, could it possibly be at Overhear Manor?'

It Wasn't Me!

'Okay, we'll look there. Thanks again for your help,' said CJ. 'Please let me know when the Will is ready for signing.'

'Of course. Is there anything else?'

'Just one thing. Was anything taken during the break in?' CJ nonchalantly enquired.

'No, there wasn't. Which is still a mystery to us all, including the police.'

'Mmm. That's rather odd. Anyhow, thanks again, old friend. Goodbye,' said CJ politely, standing and shaking the solicitor's hand.

'Goodbye CJ, Madame Songe.'

'Au revoir. Goodbye,' said Edee, who briefly embraced the solicitor, and kissed him on both cheeks.

'You're welcome,' said Mr Kipling Snr. blushing slightly as he led CJ and Edee to the front door, with Oscar, who was seeking a brief farewell ear rub.

C J Meads

Chapter 37 – A Compromising Request

Stuart was lying naked, spreadeagled prostrate on the bed.

At his request, Charlotte had bound him tightly to the bed. She was now squatting, steadily riding him, while pouring hot wax over his chest. He was clearly enjoying the domination.

She was also naked apart from wearing PVC stockings and long gloves, plus obviously her patent stiletto shoes.

'Can I ask you to do something else for me?' he pantingly asked.

Charlotte was moving them both slowly towards a climax, and was in the mood for anything within reason. Even though she had limits, they hadn't yet been reached.

'Go on. What now?' she absentmindedly asked.

He gasped as she squeezed his scrotum, possibly harder than she initially intended.

'No! Not that, but that's good.'

'Will you seduce Andrew for me?'

'What!' said an indignant Charlotte. 'I'm not your whore, to do as you demand.'

'No, I know that. That's not quite what I meant.'

Charlotte squeezed his scrotum, this time deliberately hard.

'What do you mean, then?'

'Ahhh,' gasped Stuart, caught between whether this sensation was good, or past the threshold, that even he could endure.

It Wasn't Me!

'I'd like you to just kiss him in a potentially compromising situation, so I can photograph it.'

'And why would I want to do that?' enquired Charlotte, now intrigued by Stuart's request, but continuing to rhythmically drive them both towards a sexual peak.

'I want something further on him, in case he starts to get cold feet.'

'You think that's likely?'

'I don't know, Charlie, but as always, I want a back-up plan. I want to guarantee the deal goes through. We can then both enjoy the fruits of our endeavours.'

'If that's the extent of it, then I'm sure I can accommodate your little plan.'

'That's the spirit Charlie, I knew you would....Arghhh,' he screamed.

Charlotte had increased the pressure on his balls while riding him wildly, and he spontaneously ejaculated.

She then closed her eyes, and continued to steadily move on his Viagra induced erection, while now ardently pleasuring herself to a satisfying orgasm.

'It's good to be in control,' she dreamily thought.

Chapter 38 – And The Money?

Stuart glared at Nick.

'Has the money been paid into the account?' he demanded to know.

'Just hang on. Let me log in and check. You can be so impatient at times,' replied Nick, rather annoyed at being pressured.

'Of course I'm impatient. We are talking about £35 million. Come on!'

'Stuart, calm down! These things can't be rushed. Did you get the photo of Charlotte and Kipling?'

'Of course. She's such a master, or should I say mistress, in such situations. He didn't know what was happening before it was too late.'

'Did he see you?' asked a concerned Nick.

'What do you take me for? Of course he didn't.'

'How did she explain it away?'

'Charlie was brilliant. She just said, she was a bit tipsy, and had always fancied him. But she immediately apologised when her flirtations were clearly not reciprocated.'

'Did he accept her explanation?'

'Of course he did. He even ended up apologising for the encounter.'

'What a fool. But what would have happened if he'd taken up her advances?'

'I dread to think, but knowing Charlotte, he would have had the time of his life.'

Nick laughed, recognising that Charlotte was never likely to do that with him. But you can always dream.

It Wasn't Me!

While he was momentarily daydreaming of such unlikely sexual encounters, his laptop pinged with a notification.

He hit the enter button, and he grinned.

'Yes!'

'Is the Money there?' enquired a desperate Stuart.

'It's there alright. All £35 million of it. Fucking brilliant,' exclaimed a very relieved Nick, now contemplating how to get at the funds and getting the creditors off Stuart's back.

Stuart clenched his fist and shouted, 'YES!'

'Fucking brilliant Nick. We've done it. Now for the next part of The Plan.'

'But before that, let's go to the races and celebrate. Get your glad rags on Nicky boy. We're going to celebrate in style.'

Chapter 39 – We're Off To The Races

CJ looked resplendent in a dark grey morning suit, accompanied by a light grey waistcoat, with a white shirt, and his RLC Regimental tie. To complete his ensemble, he wore a dark grey Top Hat with a black band, and shiny black leather Oxford shoes. He looked the part of a very conventional, but handsome gentleman.

He stood at the bottom of the twin stairways in the hallway of Overhear Manor, looking again at his watch. He had still not quite got used to waiting for the lady of his dreams, and had forgotten how long women can take to get ready for those special occasions.

Oscar sat to attention, a paw raised, one moment looking into CJ's eyes, the next to his right-hand pocket, where he knew the treats were usually kept.

'I'm sorry, Oscar, I'm leaving you again today. I know it's not fair, but sometimes that's how life is.' CJ was talking to Oscar as though he fully understood, despite him knowing that dogs, and Oscar in particular, didn't understand words, purely sounds. But as with many dog owners, CJ persevered as it made him feel better, having explained what was going on. Oscar, though, just wanted another treat.

CJ's attention was suddenly drawn to the top of the right-hand stairway, where Edee's stiletto heels were rhythmically starting to tap on the solid wood stair treads.

She looked more stunning than usual. She took his breath away. She was as beautiful as ever.

It Wasn't Me!

Edee had chosen a crimson red, tight figure hugging knee length dress that emphasised her model curves. The dress covered her shoulders and upper arms, but had a plunging neckline. This accentuated her modest breasts, but remained discreet, and completely appropriate for the occasion. It was, however, set off with a plunging rear neckline, that fully exposed her recently tanned back.

A red belt emphasised her slim waist, and she wore a crimson red fascinator delicately placed on the side of her head. This wonderfully complimented her dark ebony hair, which was tied in a stunning French twist bun - the reason she had probably taken so long to get ready – that, and the exquisite makeup with deep red lip gloss.

To complete the outfit, she wore her customary Christian Louboutin red soled killer heels, this time in deep red patent.

As she moved closer, seemingly gliding down the stairs, CJ became aware of his other senses.

Her expensive French perfume lingered on the air. Not only did she look beautiful, but she also smelt divine.

'My dear Madame Songe, you look exquisite. I love you more with each passing day.'

Oscar gave a short bark, seemingly agreeing with his master.

CJ held out his hand, which she warmly accepted, and he delicately kissed her on both cheeks, ensuring he did not ruin her fabulous makeup.

'Mon Cheri. My darling. You look most handsome. I do love you,' she replied, letting her

French accent slip for once, as she did in moments of pure joy.

'Shall we go to the races? Your car awaits.'
'Let's!'

It Wasn't Me!

CHAPTER 40 – THE HERITAGE RAILWAY

The Edendale Heritage Railway was celebrating in style. They were today formally commemorating the opening of the two-mile extension of the railway from Yorksbey Station to the recently re-built station at *Racecourse Halt.*

The extension had been planned for many years, but until additional funds had been forthcoming, it had remained a pipe dream of the volunteer enthusiasts that ran the railway. Today, though, was definitely a day for celebration, the culmination of the many years of fundraising, including the hard work and toil to build the spur line.

The additional track allowed those travelling to race meetings, especially those from Etongate, to travel in style and enjoy the day without having to drive.

On race days, there were now to be additional train times to suit the starting and ending of the meetings.

The Race Day special had left Etongate at 12 noon with much grandeur. The Etongate Brass Band had played loudly on the Station Platform, with the local mayor and MP on hand for the much publicised event, sending it ceremonially on its way.

It pulled into Yorksbey station on time, exactly 60 minutes later, having stopped at the four stations en route. *Cannal; Folly Overblow; Hargrove Halt; and Edendale.*

Earl and Countess Hargrove had joined the train at Hargrove Halt, which bordered the Lancelot

"Capability" Brown landscaped grounds of Hargrove House. The grand stately home, which was designed by John Carr and Robert Adam in 1771, stood resplendent in the 1,000 acre estate.

Their guests and entourage took up nearly half of a First Class carriage, with everyone looking forward to a wonderful day out, and a glorious afternoon's racing.

Everyone was dressed up to the nines. All Earl Hargrove's male guests were in morning suits, while the ladies had all made a great effort for the *Ladies' Day* meeting.

Some were dressed rather extravagantly, but most were very dignified in their outfits.

The Yorksbey Silver Band played joyously, as the train pulled into the packed station platforms that until that day had been the end of the line. But not today.

Further cheerful glamorous passengers going to the races joined the train, including the band, who set up on board. They then continued playing until the train finally terminated at Racecourse Halt twelve minutes later.

On the platform were local dignitaries, including the Mayor of Yorksbey, Mr Lucas Lowely, the local MP, Ms Davina Dred, and the local vicar, Rev. Rupert Regen. Also in attendance was the Chief Constable of North Yorkshire, along with the Chairman, and CEO of Yorksbey Racecourse, who were likely to benefit most from this additional transport link to the course.

It Wasn't Me!

They welcomed Earl and Countess Hargrove, who were also the patrons of the Heritage Railway, and after he had given a very dignified, but perhaps overly long speech, everyone moved off towards the grandstands in the near distance, keen to enjoy the day's events.

Attendances at the racecourse varied, from about 1,500 for a cold damp February day, to over 12,000 for the more prestigious meeting on Boxing Day, or *Ladies' Day* at the *Equinox Festival*, where a record attendance of 15,734 had been previously recorded.

Today, though, it was hoped and expected that the record attendance would be well and truly broken.

C J Meads

CHAPTER 41 – THE DILEMMA

CJ had chosen the Aston Martin DB9 as the day's mode of transport, the grand tourer seeming more appropriate in the circumstance. He pulled up behind a Bentley that was in the VIP and Executive carpark queue, and lowered his window.

'Are you looking forward to today?' he asked Edee.

'I am actually. The weather is glorious, and it looks like there will be a bumper crowd.'

'I've been thinking about the fact that we have two invites. One from Earl Hargrove, which I touted rather blatantly, and the other one, offered graciously by Masud.'

'And what have you concluded? How are you planning that we don't offend either of them?'

'Mmm. How do you fancy two luncheons?' he laughingly suggested.

'I thought we might end up doing that. But how are we going to keep changing venues without being caught out?'

'That's the challenge. How do you think alternating courses would appear?'

'Strange. If not blatantly obvious.'

'I think we could pull it off. Depending on when the courses arrive and the timing of each race, we might just go unnoticed,' suggested CJ, with a straight face.

'Are you serious?' said a stunned Edee.

'To be honest, it's our best opportunity. Perhaps starter and dessert, with Earl Hargrove's party, and

It Wasn't Me!

the main course with Masud's party. Or vice versa. Which would you prefer?'

'James, I was looking forward to today. I'm not so sure now.'

'You wanted to come to the races,' said a smiling CJ, as he looked across at her and then kissed her tenderly on the cheek.

'Now then sir, we'll have none of that canoodling in the carpark queue, thank you,' said the pleasant carpark steward, who smiled at CJ and Edee. His look at Edee perhaps lingered longer than might have been deemed appropriate, but understandable in the circumstances.

'Which party are you with? We have special guests today, what with the opening of the new railway line.'

'Oh, I'd forgotten about that. Which VIP party is deemed the most special today?' asked CJ, curiously.

'It's a bit of a toss-up, really. Earl Hargrove's possibly, as he's the Heritage Railway Patron, and sponsoring the Hargrove Stakes, but maybe it's Sheikh Twoammie, as he's sponsoring the meeting.'

'Well, we're invited to both,' said CJ, smiling while showing the invites and passes.

'Well, you're the lucky ones,' said the rather surprised steward. 'If you follow the Bentley in front, and look out for the steward over there, he'll guide you to the car parking for VIPs. Enjoy your day,' continued the envious helper.

Having parked appropriately, the two of them made their way towards the Main Grandstand entrance, following the large gathering crowd.

They again joined another very short VIP queue. The attendant smiled warmly and pleasantly advised them where to go.

Many of the others, in the longer queues, looked on rather enviously, wondering who the elegant couple were.

'Well, have you decided?' asked CJ casually, as he observed all that was going on around them.

'What do you mean?' asked a slightly confused Edee.

'Which party are we eating with, and more to the point, when?' added a laughing CJ.

'Oh! Let's check them both out, and then I'll decide,' suggested a calculating Edee.

'A woman's privilege,' replied CJ.

Meanwhile, Stuart had a dilemma of his own. He knew Sarah wouldn't want to be out with him at the races. She wanted to enjoy herself, as did he, but he had to maintain some standards and dignity. Conveying the appearance of a happily married couple, especially for their daughter's benefit, was still a prerequisite.

However, he also wanted to be with Charlotte, and Masud was expecting both of them to be at his function.

'Sarah. I have to attend the invitation from Sheikh Twoammie. It's a business thing, and he has limited numbers allocated to his suite,' said Stuart, hoping Sarah would acknowledge the limitations of business networking.

It Wasn't Me!

'Of course you do,' said Sarah sanctimoniously. 'Don't you worry about me. I'll be fine. I'm sure I can find something to occupy my day at the races. Sienna and I are meeting Jane, and we're having lunch in the banquet restaurant. It is, when all's said and done, *Ladies' Day.*'

'Well, you enjoy yourselves,' said a rather relieved Stuart, who absentmindedly kissed her on the cheek before parting. He hadn't particularly noticed her looking rather elegant in her outfit, which she had picked especially for the day. But why would he? He was seeking out an even more stunning woman.

Chapter 42 – Ladies' Day

CJ and Edee exited the middle of the three lifts with the other numerous hospitality guests. Edee had decided that negotiating the significant flights of stairs in her heels was not for her, well not today.

The lobby to the various hospitality suites and restaurants was thriving with racegoers. All of them were looking most grand in their outfits. Many rather conventional, especially the gentlemen, but others rather unconventional and extravagant, especially those worn by some ladies. They all appeared to be attempting to outdo one another and seeking compliments from all and sundry.

There were selfies being taken at every opportunity. It seemed that virtually everyone - or at least most of the guests - was seeking to get their photos posted ASAP onto their social media platform of choice.

CJ and Edee were one couple that didn't seem to be indulging in such blatant practices, along with other slightly more dignified or refined couples. These generally appeared to be the ones making their way towards the VIP suites.

'Well, my dear, where shall we start?'

'Let's try Sheikh Twoammie's. I think he may be more understanding of our predicament.'

'In to the *valley of death*,' joked CJ, as they showed their passes to the two burly security guards on the entrance doors.

It Wasn't Me!

The one that looked at Edee's pass took the opportunity to take longer than was really necessary, as he clearly admired her radiant beauty.

'Very good, Ma'am,' he said, smiling at her while giving back her pass.

'Merci. Thank you,' replied Edee, while cheekily smiling back at the rather good looking hunk.

'Eyes on the prize, Madame Songe,' joked CJ.

She kissed him tenderly on the cheek, undoubtedly not wanting to ruin her lip-gloss.

'Tu es mon seul vrai amour,' she said, clearly confusing the on-looking security guard.

'You are also *my one true love*,' whispered CJ in reply.

Just inside the door, Masud was greeting the guests as they arrived, but he wasn't in his traditional robes. He was looking rather dashing in a morning suit. He was most guarded and reverent to all of his guests until he spotted CJ and Edee.

'James, As-salaam alykum, peace be with you,' he said as he warmly embraced his old friend.

'As-salaam alykum,' replied James. 'You look rather British today,' he joked.

Thank you for coming, and bringing the beautiful and charming Madame Songe.

'As-salaam alykum Madame Songe. You look very elegant,' said Masud, as he gallantly kissed her hand.

'As-salaam alykum,' replied Edee. 'Merci. Thank you again for the invitation. Are you sure you won't call me Edee?'

'As before, I would never be so bold.'

'Well, my friends. How are you today? Are you looking forward to a wonderful afternoon's racing?'

'We certainly are, Your Excellency,' replied Edee.

Edee ensured that she didn't appear over familiar with Masud, as did CJ, especially while being in the mixed company they found themselves.

'You'll probably know many of my guests, but if not, I'm sure you will introduce yourselves,' said Masud.

'We'll have to catch up later once I've welcomed all my guests. Please help yourselves to a drink,' he continued, as he gestured them towards the waitress, who was holding a tray of drinks. This included Dom Perignon Vintage champagne, non-alcoholic sparkling rose water, orange juice, and chilled water.

CJ and Edee both instinctively took a glass of champagne. They then glided effortlessly through the open bi-folding glazed doors, and out onto the balcony overlooking the finishing line. The racecourse looked wonderful in the Autumn sun.

'Cheers, my dear. Enjoy your day at the races.'

As they started to appreciate their drinks, there was suddenly a gasp from the others inside.

Entering the suite was Stuart, in a conventional morning suite, and with him was Charlotte, who was the reason for the gasp. She was wearing a stunning deep crimson-red dress slightly shorter than that worn by Edee and accentuating her long, tanned legs. It was complemented with a tight buttoned bodice that emphasised her enhanced breasts and bare shoulders.

It Wasn't Me!

She was also wearing matching long red silk gloves that reached to her elbows. Her outfit was completed with red fascinator, and extremely high red stiletto heels.

The outfit, not for the first time on a special occasion, nearly matched exactly that which Edee had chosen.

'She's done it again, just like the Golf Club Masquerade Ball in the spring,' said CJ. 'It certainly appears that you still have similar fashion tastes,' he continued teasing Edee slightly.

At that fancy dress gala event, the two women had both attended as Cat Woman, both looking strikingly tempting, and today they seemed to be following a very similar path.

'I'm not sure she'll be too pleased when she sees me though,' replied a smiling Edee.

Charlotte was flirting outrageously with Masud. She had not really observed anyone else, and certainly not Edee, being too wrapped up in her own little world to notice.

'Stand by for the rapier tongue of the Femme Fatale when she finally spots you darling,' said a joking CJ. 'Charlotte's stare has been known to turn adversaries to stone, even at fifty paces.'

'Here they come. Stand by your beds.'

'Hello Gray, Madame Songe, I didn't expect to see you both here. I thought you would be at Hargrove's party.' As at their last meeting in Dubai, Stuart again undressed Edee with his eyes.

'Hello Brownlough, Charlotte. Another pleasant surprise,' lied CJ.

'Well CJ, it certainly looks like we know how to dress to impress our men,' said Charlotte, as she offered CJ one of her dazzling smiles, ignoring Edee, and flirting with CJ.

'If I wasn't mistaken, I would think you were just copying me again,' said a remarkably restrained Charlotte, as she turned her attention to Edee.

'Hi Charlotte, Mr Brownlough. It certainly would appear our style tastes are similar. I guess we can't both be wrong,' replied Edee, in her normal pleasant manner, completely unfazed as always by Charlotte.

'You seem to be enjoying yourselves. I guess you're looking forward to the racing?' she continued.

'Yes, we are. Especially the Hargrove Stakes. *Never Say Die* is racing, and we have high expectations that he'll win,' said Charlotte.

'So has Sheikh Twoammie brought him over, *especially* for the race?' enquired Edee.

'He has, but he'll now be staying in the UK,' replied an exuberant Charlotte.

'Oh?'

'Yes. He's now mine. Masud has given him to me as a gift, for my part in arranging his partnership with Stuart.'

'Wow. You must have done something special for him to do that?' asked CJ.

'I always seek to please. You should know that CJ,' flirted Charlotte, and offering him one of her trademark winks.

'You should get some money on him, before his odds shorten,' suggested Stuart. 'I think he'll be the favourite, albeit there is some tough competition in

It Wasn't Me!

the race. But I still hope to make a few bob on him today.'

'We might well do that. Thanks for the tip,' replied CJ, before adding rather matter-of-factly. 'I now understand your previous interest in whether I'm a trustee at the golf club, and before you ask, our family does have a copy of the Deeds.'

'Oh. Very good,' lied Stuart, as he stormed back inside, nearly bumping into an ominous-looking Andrew, who was standing in the doorway.

C J Meads

CHAPTER 43 - CONFRONTATIONS

Stuart marched out of the hospitality suite, nearly taking out one of the security guards in the process, and headed towards the main bar. He ordered and paid for a double single malt whisky, which he downed in one.

'Another,' he demanded.

'Please?' said the young bartender politely.

'Just do your job,' replied Stuart, who was clearly upset by CJ's comment.

The bartender obliged begrudgingly and banged the glass onto the bar. 'That's another £10 please.'

'Keep the change,' said Stuart, as he threw him another £10 note.

'Hey, hey, what's up Stuart?' asked Nick, who had seen him hurry to the bar with a face like thunder. 'Calm down, you're making a scene.'

'Gray reckons he has a copy of the Deeds.'

'Are you sure? What did he actually say, word for word?'

Stuart then slowly thought before finally replying, *'Our family does have a copy of the Deeds.'*

'That's it? He's bluffing you,' said Nick assuredly.

'How can you be so certain?'

'We know the Grays had a copy. This was evident from the original AGM Minutes. If he'd found it, or actually had a copy, he wouldn't have just said what he did. He would have said something like *your copy was incorrect.*'

'You reckon?'

It Wasn't Me!

'Think about it, what would you do in his position?' said Nick, now even more certain of his reading of things.

'The sneaky bastard,' said Stuart, similarly coming to the same conclusion.

'Come on, let's get back. It's not like you to get flustered.'

As they walked back in a much better mood, they were suddenly confronted by a stern-looking Earl Hargrove, with the Major closely behind.

'Brownlough. You do know we won't take this lying down.'

'My Lord, let's not make a scene. I suggest you enjoy your day at the races, and we can discuss your concerns at a more appropriate time,' said Stuart, who had regained some of his composure, and was now feeling more confident.

'You're probably right, for once. But I suggest you back off, otherwise, *you* will regret it,' added Earl Hargrove, as he and the Major wandered back to the rest of his party. The Major though turned and looked menacingly at Stuart, who replied with an ingratiating smile.

'That's better,' said Nick. 'He's just all air. Like all small time nobility, he thinks he can get his own way, just because of who he is, but he knows we're in the right.'

'Yes, you're correct. We always knew there would be some minor hiccups on the way to success,' agreed Stuart, now fully recovered.

The two walked back smiling, and having shown their passes to the security guard, who looked none too happy at Stuart, they cheerfully re-joined the guests at Masud's party, passing CJ and Edee on the way.

'Where did you go?' asked Charlotte. 'There was no need to march off like that.'

'I'm sorry, Charlie. You know Gray? I haven't got a lot of time for him,' apologised Stuart, as he kissed her on the cheek.

'Okay, apology accepted. Come on, let's have a glass of bubbly before we sit down for lunch.'

Charlotte stopped a waitress and took a glass of champagne. Stuart and Nick quickly followed suit.

Behind them they were suddenly surprised by a worried sounding Andrew.

'Stuart. I heard what Gray said. If he has a copy, then I'll have to say something. I must.'

All three of them turned and looked rather alarmed at this development.

'Andrew. Don't do anything hasty. Gray is bluffing.'

'How can you be so sure?'

'Trust me. I know,' replied Stuart, in a very confident and assured manner.

'But....'

'Andrew. No buts. Let's just remember not to do anything silly. Otherwise, your little secrets will well and truly come out. Do I make myself clear?' said Stuart, now fully back in control, and in a most threatening way.

'Understood,' said a reluctant sounding Andrew, who left them, and the other guests, seeking out solace in Sarah.

It Wasn't Me!

Chapter 44 – Luncheon Is Served

'CJ, you are a one,' said a smiling Edee.

'I don't know what you mean.'

'You know we don't have a copy of the Deeds.'

'But it made Stuart think, didn't it? An innocent man with right on his side wouldn't have stormed off like that. Would he?' enquired CJ quizzically.

'James, you did it deliberately to test him.'

'I think we need to re-double our efforts in finding a copy of the Deeds. That's for certain.'

'Agreed. But not today. Let's go and see what Earl Hargrove's party holds in store.'

Edee linked arms with CJ, and they quietly slipped out of the room, with Edee winking at the blushing young security guard.

There was no security guard on the door to Earl Hargrove's hospitality suite, but there was still a steward who kindly asked to see their passes.

'Enjoy your afternoon,' said the steward politely, and they entered the room, to be welcomed immediately by the Earl and Countess.

'Good Afternoon, Madame Songe. You look delightful. CJ.'

'Good Afternoon, My Lord, Lady Hargrove,' replied Edee. CJ immediately repeated the greeting to their hosts.

They both nodded slightly as their hosts warmly shook hands with them.

'Please join our party. Everyone else is here, already enjoying themselves. I think luncheon is being served shortly, starting at 1.30 pm,' said the Countess.

'Merci beaucoup,' replied Edee.

'Thank you again for the kind invitation,' replied CJ, before adding. 'I think we are in for a memorable afternoon. What say you My Lord?'

'I think we just might be,' he replied. 'Help yourself to drinks.'

There were 16 guests, of which CJ knew perhaps half. They included members of the Earl's family, plus close friends, and the local dignitaries that had welcomed them earlier at the station.

They both took another glass of champagne, this time a pleasant but more modest Moet & Chandon, to the one provided earlier by Masud.

'At this rate, I'm going to get tipsy rather quickly,' said a smiling Edee.

'We'll need to leave the car here, and get the train or a taxi home,' said CJ, already taking a sip from his glass.

'So, what's the plan? I'm not certain we'll get away with eating at only one party,' enquired Edee.

'I think I'll need to loosen my belt buckle. It looks like two lunches for us. I don't want to offend either of our hosts. The question is, how do we manage to flit between each party, without making it too obvious what we're doing?'

'I think I may have a solution. Just follow my lead, but I suggest you only order something light for each course.'

Fortunately for the pair, the table was round, and they had been seated next to one another. On the

It Wasn't Me!

other side of CJ was the local MP Davina Dred, while next to Edee was the Chief Constable, Martin Shore.

CJ, leant towards Edee, after they had all taken their seats, and whispered.

'I don't know who decided on the seating arrangements, but I think we are in for an eventful afternoon.'

'What do you mean?' replied Edee enquiringly.

'I have the feminist MP next to me, and you have the opinionated chief of police next to you. Good Luck.'

'You still have me, Mon Cheri. I'll look after you,' said a smiling Edee as she gently caressed his thigh.

CJ briefly held her hand and replied.

'I knew I could rely on you.'

Having quickly eaten Melon for their starters, while conducting small talk with their fellow guests, Edee leaned towards Martin.

'James and I are just going to place a little bet on the first race,' as she nudged CJ.

'Please excuse Edee and I My Lord, Lady Hargrove. We are going to check on the horses, and place a bet on the first race.'

'Good idea. That's the spirit. See if you can take some money off the money grabbing bookmakers.'

CJ and Edee left to the other guests' sycophantic laughter to the Earl's feeble joke.

'One down, five to go,' said Edee. 'Just keep following my lead. We ladies can get away with murder.'

C J Meads

Chapter 45 – Sorry We're Late

The burly security guard again eyed up Edee, as she and CJ approached Masud's Hospitality Suite arm in arm.

Edee smiled and asked provocatively.

'Would you like to see our passes? Or are you just pleased to see us again?'

'No. I think we know by now that you're at His Excellency's party. I hope you're enjoying your day.'

'It's different,' replied Edee, winking again at the blushing guard.

He opened the obscured glazed door and invited them both in.

'The missing couple return!' called out Masud from his position at the head of the table. 'Come join us, we are just expecting the first course.'

The space on the table was fortunately between Masud's PA, and the CEO of the Racecourse, while Stuart and Charlotte were placed further down on the opposite side from them.

'I'm sorry. We had to pop out. Edee wanted to see the horses before placing our bet on the first race. I hope we didn't miss much,' said a charming CJ.

As they sat down, Edee whispered. 'First Course. Not the *Starter*. How many courses are there?'

The main enclosures and grandstands were full to capacity. With a crowd that was eagerly cheering on their chosen horse, as the jockeys were seeking to get the most out of their steeds. Six horses were charging

It Wasn't Me!

towards the finishing line of the 6 furlong Maiden Fillies' Stakes.

CJ was beaming as he watched Edee exuberantly cheering on her chosen horse, *Beautiful Love,* which was in a tussle with *Skywoman* for the prize. He did love her, especially when she was obviously enjoying life.

'Oui! Merveilleux,' she exclaimed as she turned, wrapped her arms around his neck, and kissed him passionately on the lips.

'Well done,' said CJ, as he lifted her triumphantly in the air. 'Wow! I must bring you racing more often.'

'How much have I won?'

'£40, including your stake. Not bad, for starters.'

'James, this is wonderful. I do like betting. So much better than in Dubai.'

'Now who does that sound like?' said CJ as he looked to his left. Stuart and Charlotte were both frustratingly ripping up their betting slips before begrudgingly venturing back inside.

'Another drink? Or had we better be getting back to Earl Hargrove? I think the main course was due to be served before the next race.'

'I think a drink to celebrate our winnings first,' said a delighted Edee.

In the main restaurant, Jarvis was showing the first evidence of drinking too much alcohol. He was used to serving, rather than consuming. His Dutch courage, though, was becoming empowered.

'Look at Andrew Kipling and his floozy. Not a care in the world,' he pointed out to Tom and Phil, who had decided to make a boys' day out of it at the *Ladies' Day* meeting. All of them single. Either by divorce, widowhood, timid ambivalence, or sheer bad luck.

'Steady Jarvis. It's not the place to make a scene. You more than anyone should know that,' said an assured and friendly Tom.

'Fuck it,' said an uncharacteristic Jarvis, as he marched purposely towards Andrew.

'If I find out you two had anything to do with Brownlough securing the buying of the golf club....I'll.....I'll....Well, watch yourself. That's all I'll say.'

'Come away Jarvis. Not now,' said Tom as he pulled him away.

'I'm sorry about that. But feelings are running high about this so-called *development*. People will lose their jobs. Their livelihoods,' conveyed a similarly displeased, but rather more controlled Tom.

Andrew held up his hand in acknowledgement and smiled weakly.

'See, I told you it wasn't good,' he whispered to Sarah.

'I understand that, but they can't do anything. It's not *your* fault.'

'Maybe not. But some won't see it that way.'

'What's that all about Mummy?' said a puzzled Sienna, who was looking rather *teenager-ish,* as she joined them. She was similarly starting to show the signs of one too many drinks. Another modern young

It Wasn't Me!

woman who could not restrain herself, when there was too much freely available alcohol.

'Nothing darling. Nothing for you to worry about,' said a slightly worried, but placating Sarah.

Chapter 46 – I'm Stuffed

'I'm not sure how much more of this I can take,' said Edee. She was like other women of her stature. She wasn't used to eating three course lunches, and definitely not two of them.

'You wanted to come to the races. I just arranged two invites,' teased CJ.

'Can't you come clean with Earl Hargrove? Please? For my sake?'

She looked at him dolefully with puppy-dog eyes, like she had seen Oscar use to get to his master.

'Pretty please.'

'Leave it with me. But I'm not promising anything.'

'Go and be your charming self. You know it makes sense.'

Edee kissed him on the cheek, and CJ sauntered over to Earl Hargrove, who was unsurprisingly talking earnestly with the Major.

'Ah, CJ. How are things? Is the delightful Madam Songe enjoying her day at the races?'

'My Lord. Major,' replied CJ, nodding slightly to them both. 'Everything is wonderful. Well almost,' added a now rather concerned looking CJ.

'What is it CJ?'

'I'm still rather worried about this development of Brownlough's.'

'Aren't we all?' replied the Major.

'I'm not sure if you are aware, but Sheikh Twoammie is an old acquaintance of mine. It's a long story.'

It Wasn't Me!

'No, I wasn't. I'm surprised he's got involved with Brownlough. I thought the man had higher morals,' replied a rather displeased Earl Hargrove.

'So am I,' said CJ, shaking his head. 'I was hoping to perhaps have a quiet word with him. You know, to find out what he actually does know. Plus maybe see if he could influence Brownlough to re-consider.'

'Do you think he'll listen to you?'

'I'm not sure, but it's certainly worth a go.'

'Good idea. Go for it.'

'Just one thing though, My Lord.'

'Yes CJ.'

'For my deception to work, Edee and I may have to join him for lunch. He's likely to offer, and I'm not sure Edee can eat *two* rather wonderful luncheons, not if they're both like yours.'

CJ looked over at Edee. Earl Hargrove and the Major both also looked across towards her as she smiled back, seemingly knowing what was being discussed.

'Understood. Say no more,' replied Earl Hargrove knowingly. 'To achieve the goal, it's often worth the odd sacrifice.'

'Precisely. I'll see you both later,' said CJ, as he walked off smiling, while gesturing to Edee to join him.

'How did you manage that? What did you say?' she intriguingly enquired, linking arms with CJ.

'As you said previously, I can be charming, if I put my mind to it.'

The young security guard saw them coming from afar, and already had the door open as they reached him.

'You two will soon make up your minds,' he jokingly stated, as he welcomed them back into Masud's party.

'You're doing a grand job. I'll put in a good word with His Excellency,' said Edee, again making him blush.

Their movements had also not gone unnoticed by Masud, who joined them.

'I don't know what you two are up to, but would you care to tell me?' he smilingly enquired.

'It's a bit of a convoluted story. Best we leave it for another time,' suggested CJ, before adding. 'But I wouldn't mind a quiet word.'

'You definitely now have me intrigued,' said a thoughtful Masud.

They moved to a quiet corner of the room, and Masud asked, 'How is my old adversary, RSM Ledger?'

'Cliff is good. Like me, he's now retired from the army. He still though, works for me. Us. Doing those jobs no one else really wants to do.'

'Ah, yes, Cliff. As I recall, he does have an aptitude for *resolving* tricky situations,' said a knowing Masud.

'Does he work for anyone else?'

'I'm not his keeper, but we both have an understanding.'

It Wasn't Me!

'Mmm. I think I know what you mean,' replied a perceptive Masud. 'Now then. What's on your mind?'

Chapter 47 – Hargrove Handicap

'Charlotte's back where she likes to be, monopolising a rich man,' stated Edee with a broad smile on her face as she, and a pre-occupied CJ, looked on.

The conversation with Masud had not provided much more information than they had already surmised. It was evident though, that unless the *Edendale Project* was illegal, then it was extremely unlikely that Masud would back out. To be honest, why would he? The deal was very profitable for him.

CJ had done his best to persuade his old associate as to the error of his ways. He had warned Masud about the possible issues of going into partnership with Stuart, and maybe the seeds of doubt he had sown might eventually germinate, but CJ was not overly confident.

Their only hope was to find the original Deeds, and that they were not as the version in the Kipling safe, but he was becoming more doubtful of that with each passing day.

'Mmm. Yes.'

'Were you listening?' enquired Edee.

'Sorry. No, not really. I was miles away.'

'No point worrying about tomorrow's dilemma. Let's focus on the here and now.'

'Agreed,' said CJ, before adding, 'I see Charlotte is back where she likes to be, monopolising a mega rich man.'

Edee shook her head and laughed out loud.

It Wasn't Me!

'What is it?' enquired a bewildered CJ. 'What have I said?'

'Come on, let's go. The big race is about to start,' said Edee as she linked arms and encouraged CJ to step out onto the balcony with the rest of Masud's party.

'All the money I've won is now on *Never Say Die.* It's all or nothing,' she continued.

'He has a good chance of winning, looking at the form guide, but it could be close,' advised CJ. 'It's only a one mile race, which is quite short, and he usually finishes strong after a slow start.'

The last horse was just being encouraged into the starting stalls. It had looked nervous throughout the process of being walked around. The other horses were now also getting jittery as they patiently waited for him to be finally pushed and pulled into the stalls by two stall handlers.

Everyone on the balcony was now showing evidence of a glass too many of the free champagne provided by Masud. Obviously, that excluded Masud and the other Muslims in his party, but the fun loving Brits were showing their true colours.

'*He'll do it won't he?*' whispered Charlotte.

'I'm sure he will,' came the assured reply.

Charlotte then linked arms with Masud.

'Thank you again for being so generous.'

'My dear, the pleasure was all mine. I just hope we can remain friends. Very good *friends?*'

'I think I have a new friend for life,' she replied, and for once, she was possibly being quite sincere.

"And They're Off.

The tannoy echoed all around. The capacity crowd was already cheering like there was no tomorrow.

"The one mile Hargrove Handicap is off and running. The going is good to firm, so we should be in for a fast race.

"Run To Freedom has made a good start, closely followed by Happy Romance.

"The field of sixteen is evenly placed except for Never Say Die, who seems to be struggling slightly at the back.

"Run To Freedom is leading the way, followed closely by Happy Romance, followed by Spy Catcher.

"Coming up on the rails is Swingalong, but it's still Run To Freedom and Happy Romance leading the way."

'What's up with *Never Say Die?*' shouted Charlotte, clearly upset at what she was seeing.

'Patience, my dear,' said a reassuring Masud.

"Happy Romance is making a move followed by Spy Catcher on the inside, but Run To Freedom is holding his own.

"What's this? Is Never Say Die making a move on the outside? But is it too late? Only two furlongs to go.

"Happy Romance has taken the lead, but Never Say Die is closing.

"Happy Romance is still leading; Spy Catcher close behind as we hit the final furlong."

The crowd was now virtually incandescent. The noise was deafening.

'Come on, come on *Never Say Die*, come on!'

It Wasn't Me!

Charlotte was now shouting for dear life, along with all the others in the party. Even CJ, with his booming voice, was cheering.

'He's left it very late.'

"Happy Romance from Spy Catcher, Happy Romance from Spy Catcher.

"But here he comes, Never Say Die is closing, they're neck and neck.

"Happy Romance and Never Say Die are stride for stride, but has he left it too late, as we hit the last 50 yds?

"Happy Romance, Never Say Die, Happy Romance, Never Say Die. They're neck and neck.

"Happy Romance is going to hold on.

"It's Never Say Die! by the shortest of heads. What a finish. What a run by Never Say Die. A brilliant run from the back of the field."

The crowd erupted in wild euphoria.

'He's done it. Yes!' shouted Charlotte, as she turned, hugged, and kissed Masud. 'He did It!'

Edee, also wrapped up in the moment, virtually copied Charlotte, but obviously kissed CJ, who lifted her off the ground, and kissed her passionately, unlike Masud when kissed by Charlotte.

'I do love you.'

'I love you too,' replied Edee.

'Come on, Charlotte, my dear. Let's go to the Winners' Enclosure to see your horse, while congratulating the jockey and trainer,' said Masud. 'Stuart, are you going to join us?'

'I'll catch you up. I'm just going to collect my winnings.'

C J Meads

Chapter 48 – Winner's Glory

The perimeter of the Winners' Enclosure was packed with Charlotte centre stage, looking like the cat who'd got the cream. Her smile was wider than that of the Cheshire Cat in *Alice in Wonderland* .

She had congratulated the winning jockey, Frankie Carson, with a kiss on the lips that took him completely by surprise as he dismounted. But he quickly regained his composure and took the opportunity of seconds.

She had also more graciously kissed *Never Say Die's* trainer, the craggy Billy Beer, on the cheek, but he was still suitably pleased to receive it from the horse's new stunning owner.

Even the stable lad hadn't missed out, and was still blushing a bright red, as the presentations were about to be made.

Earl Hargrove gallantly presented the winning trophy to Masud and Charlotte, as she felt that it was only reasonable that the Sheikh should take credit for providing such a wonderful horse.

The reporters and photographers from all the usual racing papers were there, including the *Yorksbey News,* who were also on hand to get their scoop and photo of the winning team. Charlotte ensured that they got the full low down, and also assisted them with orchestrating the photo shoot.

'Well my dear, perhaps the first of many such victories for *Never Say Die* and you in the UK?' stated Masud gallantly.

It Wasn't Me!

'I think it just might be, and you must visit whenever he's racing. For old times' sake?'

The proud, stable lad walked *Never Say Die* back to the course stables, prior to being loaded into the horsebox for his trip to his new home at Billy Beer's stables.

'Time to celebrate Charlotte? Let me escort you back to the hospitality suite. The next race will be starting in about 20 minutes,' said Masud.

'Yes, let's.'

Just then, Charlotte's phone pinged with a message.

She looked down and frowned.

'Masud. I just need to do something. I'll catch you up shortly if that's okay?'

'For you, my dear, anything. Is everything okay?' he enquired, reviewing the vast crowds.

'Yes. I think so,' said a rather thoughtful and puzzled Charlotte, as she wandered off aimlessly towards the stables, still looking at her phone.

CHAPTER 49 – THE BODY

The air suddenly felt cold, despite the sun shining through the stable doorway.

Charlotte looked down at the blood-soaked knife in her hand, and then back at the dead body lying prostrate on the stable floor.

The fine jet-black colt, *Never Say Die,* gave out a chilling whinny, as he looked on indifferently.

'What have you done?' screamed Sarah Brownlough, as she came through the stable door, seeing the dead body of the man she loved lying on the floor.

'It wasn't me!' said Charlotte quietly, struggling to come to terms with the unfolding events.

'It Wasn't Me!' she yelled in sudden realisation of how it appeared………

It Wasn't Me!

PART 2

C J Meads

It Wasn't Me!

Chapter 50 – What Do We Have Here?

DI Smith's mobile rang.

'Jones?'

'Afternoon, sir. Sorry to trouble you so late in the day, but there's been a murder at the *Equinox Festival* at Yorksbey Racecourse.'

'I'll be there shortly,' and with that blunt reply, Smith abruptly hung up.

Fifteen minutes later, Smith pulled up in his unmarked Vauxhall Insignia, and attempted to get into the course while thousands of racegoers were going in the opposite direction trying to exit.

'Can I help you, sir?' asked a weary-looking Marshall, who looked like he didn't need a smart arse swimming against the tide.

'DI Smith. Yorksbey Police.'

'Pull the other one... Oh, sorry sir,' he replied as Smith showed him his warrant card.

'Follow the road up the hill to the next Marshall. He'll direct you to the appropriate carpark.'

Eventually Smith parked next to Jones' unmarked Astra, and the marked Fiesta patrol car of PC Perfect. He also recognised the forensic team's van, and the car of the local pathologist, Dr Steven Stephens.

As he got out of his car, Jones came walking over.

'It looks like the evening may be ruined Sir,' as he pulled out his little black notebook.

'What have we got, Jones?' Smith asked, putting the young sergeant at ease.

'Well, forensics and pathology will need to confirm things, but it appears that a white male in his mid-forties has been fatally stabbed. His body's in the stables over there,' said Jones, pointing.

'Very precise, Jones. How can you be so sure it was a stabbing?' asked an intrigued Smith.

'The culprit was apprehended standing over the body with a bloodstained knife in her hand.'

'A women killer?'

'Yes, and you'll never guess who it is, sir?' said a teasing Jones.

'Jones, this isn't a bloody Who's Who? parlour game. We are talking murder.'

'Sorry, sir.'

'Who is it then?' asked Smith enquiringly.

'Charlotte Tate.'

'Wow. Now I wouldn't have guessed that, not in a million years,' replied an astounded Smith.

'What's more intriguing is that the murder victim is Andrew Kipling.'

'Double Wow,' said an even more stunned Smith.

Charlotte was in handcuffs; her perfect makeup was now not so perfect. She had been crying, and black mascara streaks were flowing down her cheeks.

PC Perfect was escorting her back towards her car.

Suddenly, she saw CJ and Edee walking towards the railway station to pick up the train home. CJ had definitely exceeded the drink drive limit, and Edee was definitely the worse for wear. Expensive free champagne had been extravagantly enjoyed by everyone.

It Wasn't Me!

'CJ. Edee. It wasn't me!' shouted Charlotte. 'I didn't do it. Please believe me. Please help me!'

'Come on Charlotte, please don't make a scene,' pleaded Perfect. 'This is bad enough as it is.'

'What's that all about?' asked a bemused CJ.

'Whatever it is, it looks like Charlotte's in trouble with the law,' replied a similarly confused Edee.

'Come on, let's go and have a look.'

Jones led Smith from the carpark, past the Parade Ring, and Winners' Enclosure, towards the Stable Block. Smith, as usual, was looking intently at everything he felt might help the investigation, observing things that the average man or woman in the street wouldn't even consider. His twenty-odd years in the service had given him a good eye for detail, but he wasn't silly enough to think he knew everything, that premise he left to the fools that thought they did.

Jones continued reading from his notes.

'Uniform received a 9 9 9 call at 4.30 pm, advising that a male about mid-forties had been stabbed in the stables at Yorksbey Racecourse, and was bleeding profusely. Paramedics were immediately on the scene as they were on call for the races. PC Perfect, attended within about ten minutes and on her arrival, she found that the man had died from his injuries.'

'Go on.'

'The dead man - though not yet officially identified, but we all know from the recent break in at the solicitors - is Andrew Kipling.'

'So by all accounts, we have a body, we have a murder weapon, and we have the perpetrator?'

'Yes, sir.'

'So why do you need me?'

'We don't.' Came a readily recognisable deep voice from behind them.

'Sorry,' whispered Jones. 'I forgot to tell you. The Chief Constable was on hand for the arrest.'

'Thanks for nothing Jones,' replied a similarly whispering Smith, who turned and smiled ingratiatingly at the Chief Constable.

'Good Afternoon, sir.'

'DI Smith, I think that Jones can wrap this up,' said a confident Chief Constable. 'It's a clear, open and shut case.'

'From what I'm being told, it sure is. But as I'm here, shall I just have a quick look at the murder scene, and then I'll be going.'

'If you must,' came the curt reply. 'But we have Charlotte Tate bang to rights.'

'Goodbye, sir.'

'Goodbye DI Smith.'

Smith and Jones turned, and continued on their earlier route towards the stables, pleased to have got away from their over-bearing superior.

'Sorry again. I didn't mean to cause you any trouble,' said Jones apologetically.

'A heads-up would have been handy, but what will be, will be,' said a sardonic Smith.

It Wasn't Me!

Chapter 51 – She's Done What?

Masud wandered over to the security guards on the door, and after much whispering, looked for Stuart, who had only just returned to the party, and was now in deep conversation with Nick.

'Do you know what's happened to Charlotte?' asked Masud as he joined them.

'No. I thought she was with you, at the Winners' Enclosure,' replied a startled Stuart.

'I gather from my security team that there has been an incident, and Charlotte has been arrested.'

'Arrested! What for?' enquired a stunned Stuart.

'That, I don't know, but apparently Andrew Kipling has been fatally stabbed.'

'What! Andrew stabbed. Surely not, and not by Charlotte?'

'I'd better go and see if she's all right,' said Stuart, now showing some concern.

'I'll come with you,' said a comforting Nick, as the two of them left a rather perplexed Masud, who was wondering what had just occurred to ruin such a perfect day.

'Let me know what you find out,' replied Masud rather absentmindedly.

As Stuart and Nick exited the lift on the ground floor, they were confronted by an extremely distressed and crying Sarah.

'You bastard! That floozy of yours has gone too far. She's killed Andrew,' shrieked Sarah as she started beating Stuart with her blood-stained fists in pure frustration.

'If you've put her up to this, I'll kill you,' she screamed.

'Calm down Sarah. You're making a scene. It's nothing to do with me.'

'Sarah, please calm down. Stuart had nothing to do with this,' said Nick, trying in vain to placate a clearly enraged Sarah.

'Oh, do shut up. What's it to do with you anyhow? Keep your nose out of our business,' came the stinging reply.

Nick raised his hands in submission and backed off.

Stuart tried to put his arms around Sarah. 'Calm down. Come on, let me take you home.'

'Get your fucking hands off me. I hate you.'

Sienna, seeing her arguing parents, rushed over to find out what was happening.

'Mummy, what's wrong? Are you okay?'

'Sienna, I'm leaving. Will you please come with me?'

'Of course, but what is it?'

'I'll explain on the way.'

'What about Daddy?'

'That bastard can go to hell. And he's not your Father! He's just been killed.'

It Wasn't Me!

Chapter 52 – The Crime Scene

'Let's have a look at the crime scene, and the body, plus I need a quick chat with Stephens pronto,' said Smith, as he and Jones walked towards the stables, the late autumn afternoon sun slowly fading in the west.

A cordon had been set up outside the stable. CJ and Edee were in discussion with Dr Stephens, who, having seen Smith and Jones approaching, quickly went back inside the stable.

'Why am I not surprised you two are involved in this?' said a sarcastic, but smiling Smith, as he and Jones approached the pair.

The two detectives had been thankful for CJ, Edee, and Oscar's assistance in crime solving in the area over the last couple of years. None more so than earlier in the spring, when helping to solve the unusual circumstances surrounding Bart Tate's death.

Smith and CJ were, however, often more alike than they would accept, both in their manner and demeanour, possibly one reason CJ occasionally got to Smith. Begrudgingly though, Smith recognised that CJ was always well meaning and offered another pair of knowledgeable eyes to any investigation.

'Good Afternoon, Edee, Gray,' said Smith. 'You look stunning as always, Edee.'

Smith had previously carried a torch for Edee, but now CJ and Edee had become a couple, he had reluctantly accepted that Edee was out of reach. That didn't, however, prevent him from still admiring her beauty.

'Afternoon, Simon, John,' replied Edee pleasantly.

'Look, you two, we have a job to do, and you both know the score, so please try not to get in the way. I'll try to talk with you shortly.'

Smith and Jones were offered Hazmat suits, overshoes, and masks by a member of the forensic team. As they put them on, Dr Stephens came out of the stable with a blood-stained knife in a sealed evidence bag and walked towards them.

Smith got straight to the point; pleasantries were not really the order of the day in such circumstances. 'Afternoon, Dr Stephens. By all accounts a straightforward, open and shut case. At least according to the Chief.'

'Good day, DI Smith. Well, I'm sure DS Jones has given you the initial synopsis,' replied Stephens, also, in a business-like manner, before continuing. 'And to be honest, until I complete the Post Mortem, I'm reluctant to say too much.'

'Any reason for that?' asked Smith inquisitively.

'Shall I just say. All may not be as it seems,' came the curt reply.

'A more formal response than normal, Steven,' said Smith in a conciliatory tone. 'I'm not going to hold you to anything, but I sense some hesitation.'

'I suggest you have a look yourself. All I'll say is that death was from Exsanguination, caused by a stab wound to the left side of the neck, severing the jugular vein.'

It Wasn't Me!

'Anything else?' asked Smith, hoping Stephens would perhaps be a little more forthcoming.

'No. The team will finish up here, and I'll look to get the Post Mortem completed in the next 24 hours.'

Smith looked down at the entrance to the stable door and the bloodstain on the ground, and when he looked back, he noticed CJ also observing the same spot.

'Right, let's have a look at the body, and then I'll be off,' he said, as he tentatively walked with Jones and Stephens into the stable.

Shortly afterwards, Smith and Jones exited the stable, with the detective inspector in deep thought.

'You know she didn't do it?' stated CJ firmly.

'What?' replied Smith, suddenly broken from his concentration.

'Charlotte. She didn't do it.'

'But she was apprehended at the scene with the murder weapon in her hand?' said an incredulous Jones.

'That doesn't mean she killed him,' retorted CJ.

'And what makes you say that, Gray?' enquired Smith, interested in CJ's thought process.

'Well, for one thing, Charlotte said she didn't do it.'

'Surely that's not the extent of your evidence. The ramblings of a hysterical woman who's been caught red-handed at the crime scene.'

'I'll let you conduct your full investigation, DI Smith, as I trust you and DS Jones to be thorough, not like your Chief Constable.'

'That's very kind and considerate of you,' replied a sarcastic Smith.

'But I'm confident that you'll reach the same conclusion. What's more of a puzzle, is who actually committed the murder?' replied a rather baffled CJ as he and Edee wandered off to get the train.

'Well sir, what do you make of that?' asked a now confused Jones.

'I'm not sure Jones, but one thing's for certain, this is far from an open and shut case.'

It Wasn't Me!

Chapter 53 - The Interview

The interview room at Yorksbey Police Station was like most built in that era, a small plain room with no windows painted a white that had faded over the years. In the centre of the room was a sturdy wooden table with four uncomfortable wooden chairs, two on either side. On the table was the conventional tape-recording machine, that was still being used as Yorksbey, was still a way off going digital. High on the wall were two CCTV cameras used by others to monitor interviews, as necessary.

The room today was starting to feel a little oppressive due to the lack of natural ventilation for the three people sitting in the room, DS Jones, Charlotte Tate, and the young duty solicitor.

'For the tape, I confirm that DI Smith has entered the room,' said a monotone Jones.

'Sorry about that,' said Smith. 'I just had to collect something.'

'Where's Mr Kipling Snr. my usual solicitor?' asked a clearly still upset Charlotte. 'And when can I get my clothes back?'

Charlotte looked totally different, having relinquished her clothes for forensic evidence. She sat in a white Hazmat suit, with her mascara tear-stained face, looking nothing like the normal self-assured woman she normally conveyed.

'Mrs Tate...,' started Smith.

'It's Ms Tate,' replied Charlotte curtly. 'But you can call me Charlotte.'

'Sorry *Ms Tate*! Charlotte, but I don't think Mr Kipling Snr. will want to represent you in the circumstances,' continued Smith dryly.

'I don't see why not; I didn't do it! Have you asked him? He, more than anyone, will surely want to find his son's killer.'

'No, we haven't. Do you want us to?' asked Smith, who was pretty sure he knew the likely reply.

'Let's get on with it. I've nothing to hide. I just hope this lad is up to the job,' replied Charlotte, glancing at the solicitor to her left, who was writing copious notes.

'How long are you going to keep me here? I haven't done anything.'

'Charlotte, this is a murder investigation, and we need to get all the facts. I'm sure you'll appreciate that,' said Smith seriously.

'Of course I do,' she replied in a conciliatory way.

'Charlotte, would you like to tell us what happened this afternoon regarding the death of Mr Andrew Kipling?' continued a stern-looking Smith.

'Of course. I have nothing to hide.'

'That will be most helpful, but I must warn you though, that you are still under caution:-

"You do not have to say anything. But it may harm your defence if you do not mention when questioned something which you later rely on in court. Anything you do say may be given in evidence."

'I received a text message from Stuart at about...'

'Stuart? You mean Stuart Brownlough?' interrupted Smith, seeking clarification.

It Wasn't Me!

'Yes, of course, Stuart Brownlough. We were at the races together, with Sheikh Twoammie. *Never Say Die* had just won the Hargrove Handicap, and we had been presented with the trophy. Masud will confirm that.'

'Masud?' asked Jones.

'Sheikh Twoammie, of course,' continued Charlotte. 'As I said, I got the message from Stuart asking me to meet him at the stables.'

'Was the message clearly from Stuart Brownlough?'

'What do you mean? Of course it was! It was from his phone. It said, "*Meet me at the stables*." So I left Masud and went to meet him.

'The Marshall on the gate will confirm that, he could see I was very happy at having just won the race, and he congratulated me.'

'Jones, make a note to check that out,' said Smith, looking to ensure all things were verified. 'Go on.'

'I got to the stable, and there was a blood-stained knife on the ground outside the stable door. I was worried that someone had attacked and hurt *Never Say Die*.'

'Can anyone corroborate that?' asked a doubting Smith.

'There was no one around that I re-call, so probably not.'

'I picked up the knife, opened the stable door, and then I saw a body on the floor, face down. There was blood everywhere.'

'I went in, and was standing over the body, when behind me I heard Sarah Brownlough scream, 'What have you done?'

'She then knelt down, turned the body over, and I saw it was Andrew. Andrew Kipling. She then started crying.'

'The next thing I remember was the Stable Marshall coming in and asking me not to do anything stupid. Then that big thick copper came in and arrested me.'

'You mean the Chief Constable?' asked Smith wryly.

'If you say so. If he's your boss, then heaven help us.'

Jones had to look away as he was struggling not to laugh out loud. Smith, though, just managed to maintain his cool. Albeit, this was one thing he could agree with Charlotte on, as he looked up at the CCTV camera, contemplating who was watching next door.

'Is there anything else you would like to add?' asked Smith, trying to gauge Charlotte's take on events.

'No, I think that's it. But if you check with Stuart, I'm sure he'll verify the message he sent,' said an assured Charlotte.

'We have checked your phone, and you did receive a message,' said a droll-looking Smith. 'The problem is though Charlotte, the phone that sent you that message, it was in Andrew Kipling's pocket.'

It Wasn't Me!

Chapter 54 – So Who Did It?

'So, if it wasn't Charlotte, who did it?' asked Edee lying on the super king sized bed in the master bedroom of Overhear Manor, her red outfit having earlier been cast around the floor in carefree abandon.

'That certainly is the question,' replied the also naked CJ, as he absentmindedly rubbed Oscar's ear while looking out over the golf course in the distance.

The September morning sunshine was shining brightly, and the emerald green grass looked pristine, set off by the many mature trees, with some just starting to change colour as Autumn slowly advanced.

He turned and looked intensely into Edee's deep brown eyes that matched his own.

Oscar seemed rather put out that his master's attention was now elsewhere, so he jumped off the bed and went energetically downstairs, seeking his breakfast from Mrs Wembley.

'Your thoughts, my dear, on this puzzle?'

'Well, I've been thinking.'

'Always a good starting point, in my opinion,' teased CJ.

'No need for your wry English humour, Mr Gray. Would you like my view or not?'

'Pray continue,' he replied, smiling at her beauty as she suddenly sat up, folding her arms, and slender tanned legs in front of her. She looked like a Buddha in deep thought.

'As we learnt from Dr Stephens, we're pretty sure Charlotte hadn't the stature to attack Andrew from behind and slit his throat.'

'Correct. So who could have done it?'

'Well, to be honest. I don't know!' she declared ruefully.

CJ burst out laughing, 'Well, that makes two of us.'

'What I was wondering though,' she countered, 'it surely has to be someone involved with the *Edendale Project*.'

'My darling, I think you are spot on. My thoughts exactly.'

'You agree?' asked Edee, slightly surprised.

'Of course I agree. It's no coincidence that Andrew Kipling is involved with Brownlough's deal.

'He also heard me talking about our copy of the Deeds with Stuart.'

'We both think the Deeds have been doctored. So do you think Andrew was silenced before he came clean about his involvement?' continued Edee, now further contemplating.

'It's definitely a line of inquiry worth pursuing,' CJ added thoughtfully.

'Do you think Simon and John will do it though?' she asked, not convinced they would. 'Or will they just focus on Charlotte?'

'I think we need to give them a gentle nudge.'

'What do you mean?' asked a perplexed Edee.

'Let's go and pick up the DB9, and while we're there, you can see your friend, Michelle Argyle, the General Manager at the Racecourse. I think the

It Wasn't Me!

CCTV may just be key,' stated CJ, as he kissed her, before sliding off the bed. 'I'll race you for the shower.'

Stuart sat in his office. He looked pretty rough. The excessive champagne had taken its toll, plus the effects of cocaine were wearing off. He had not slept or shaved; he was very weary.

There was a knock at the door and Nick entered.

'Morning, Boss,' he said cheerily. 'Blimey, you look rough. Bad night?'

'Fuck off Nick. Of course I've had a bad night.'

'No need to be like that.'

'Sorry. It's just that I can't get my head around what Charlotte's done.'

'You and me both,' replied a contrite Nick.

'Why do you think she did it?' asked Stuart.

'Women can do strange things. I've never really understood how their minds work,' replied Nick mockingly. 'She was probably on her period.'

'Nick, you can be a complete arse at times.'

'Sorry. It's just my coping mechanism. I was only joking.'

'But it's not a joking matter, is it?'

'No. I guess not,' replied an apologetic Nick.

'The police wouldn't let me see her,' stated a nonplussed Stuart.

'They're unlikely to. She's been arrested for murder,' replied Nick, now back in his normal business-like manner.

'But what are we going to do?' asked Stuart.

'Do? We can't *do* anything, but get on with our lives. If she did it, the police will charge her. If not, they'll no doubt let her go. They have what, 36 hours to make up their minds?'

Edee scrolled down the phone numbers on the head up display and keyed in Michelle Argyle.

She was driving her metallic blue BMW Z4 sports car, perhaps rather too quickly, for the speed limit, but when all's said and done, she was French!

CJ was in the passenger seat, with Oscar precariously sitting on his lap, looking observantly out of the windscreen. He was clearly enjoying what, for him, was a very unusual position in a car, and he was making the most of it.

The phone rang three times before being answered by a pleasant sounding young woman.

'Good Morning. Yorksbey Racecourse. Danielle speaking. How may I help you?'

'Good Morning Danielle, could I please speak with Michelle Argyle? It's Eden Songe.'

'Hi Edee. I'll just put you through.'

'Does everyone know you in Yorksbey?' asked a smiling CJ.

'Bien sûr, je suis français. Of course, I'm French. Everyone knows me,' replied Edee, laughing.

They were interrupted by a very friendly voice.

'Bonjour Edee. How can I be of service? You'd better be quick though. It's a bit hectic here. Especially after yesterday.'

It Wasn't Me!

'Bonjour Michelle. I hope you're well. It's actually about yesterday. Could you please spare us a few minutes?'

'For you Edee, okay. When?'

'In about 5 minutes.'

Chapter 55 – It's Rather Incriminating

'That can't be right! The message came from Stuart,' said a disbelieving Charlotte. 'Ask him?'

'I can assure you the message came from a phone in Andrew Kipling's pocket,' said Jones, referring to his notebook.

'Also, what do you make of this photo?' asked Smith, showing Charlotte a copy of the photo of her kissing Andrew.

'How did you get that?' she answered rather confused.

'It was also on the phone,' replied Jones.

'But...' Charlotte stopped in mid thought, mindful of what she might say, and how incriminating it might be.

'But what?' asked Smith, sensing Charlotte was now on the back foot.

'It was just a playful kiss. I'd had one too many spritzers, and I foolishly kissed him.'

'Is that so?' said an incredulous Smith.

'Yes, it was. More to the point, though, who took the photo?' she determinedly added.

Smith was also pondering that, and he couldn't quite square that away.

'Things don't look too good for you, Charlotte. You're caught red-handed at the scene of the crime with the murder weapon in your hand, plus there's further evidence that you had a liaison with the deceased,' said a pressing Smith. 'Why did you kill him? Was it to shut him up?' quizzed a now even more aggressive Smith.

It Wasn't Me!

'I didn't kill him! You have to believe me!' replied a desperate Charlotte, as she recognised that the evidence didn't show her in a good light.

'Charlotte. Just tell us why you did it. You'll feel better for admitting it,' continued Smith, seeking the required confession to wrap up the case.

'I didn't kill him! Why don't you believe me?

'*You* do something. You useless excuse for a solicitor,' she continued, laying into her hapless looking brief.

'Perhaps we should leave it there for now,' said Smith, standing up.

'What do you mean? Can I go?' asked a distressed but hopeful Charlotte.

'Either charge my client or let her go,' said the nervous young solicitor, who had all of a sudden found his faltering voice.

'We need to do neither for now, as you are fully aware. We will, however, do some further checking. But in the meantime, I suggest you think carefully about what you say next,' said Smith, looking daggers at Charlotte as he left the room.

'Interview terminated at 10.35 am,' said Jones, stopping the tape and following his boss out of the room.

'She sounds convincing. Do you believe her?' asked Jones as he closed the door behind him.

Smith looked desperately up at the ceiling and scratched his chin. A nervous habit he had, especially when under pressure.

'I've witnessed many murderers who were confident of their innocence. She may just be a brilliant liar.'

'I know that. She's cool under pressure. Do you remember when we interviewed her about her husband's death?' added Jones, thinking about their last murder investigation.

'But do you believe her?' continued Jones, pressing his boss.

'I'm not sure,' replied Smith, before adding. 'But we're going to come under extreme pressure from Peel and the Chief to charge her, that's for certain.'

Superintendent Peel was their immediate superior. He had been promoted following the solving of Oliver Tate's death, despite him misinterpreting the evidence, and giving Smith an ultimatum to close the case as a suicide.

But as Smith had learnt in life, it's not always fair, and he had reluctantly accepted Peel's promotion as a backhanded acknowledgment of his and Jones' dogged determination to seek the truth.

'Not for the first time,' said Jones humorously.

PC Perfect approached them with a piece of paper in her hand.

'A couple of messages, sir.'

'Carry on Perfect,' said Smith. 'I hope its something positive.'

'I'm not sure about that. First off, Dr Stephens has asked if you'd like to go and view Andrew Kipling's body. He has some information he feels may be important to your investigation.'

'That sounds ominous, sir,' said Jones.

It Wasn't Me!

'And secondly, a Michelle Argyle, the General Manager at the racecourse, called. She said that you might want to see their CCTV footage. Apparently CJ Gray had said it was important,' said Perfect with a wry smile on her face.

Smith rubbed his face with his hands.

'It had to be Gray, didn't it?'

'Looks like we need to make a couple of trips, sir,' added a smiling Jones.

C J Meads

Chapter 56 – Post Mortem

As Smith and Jones left the police station, they were immediately confronted by a media pack, including the local TV crews from BBC's Look North and ITV's Calendar.

A microphone was thrust under Smith's nose by the confident reporter.

'What can you tell us about the murder at Yorksbey Racecourse? Who was the victim, and is it true you have arrested Charlotte Tate?'

Smith had dealt with many such questions over the years, and answering didn't get any easier, especially when there was some doubt as to the full facts. However, he did what he always did in such circumstances. He sought to play for time.

'I can confirm that the victim's family have been informed of the death, and as you'll appreciate, it is a very distressing time for his family and friends.'

'So it is a man?'

'As you will all appreciate, there are currently reporting restrictions in place until we fully establish the facts,' continued Smith, trying to keep a lid on things.

'But what can you tell us?' persisted the young news reporter, seeking to promote her fledgling career.

'The victim was Andrew Kipling, a local solicitor, but the family has quite rightly asked for some privacy, to reflect, and to come to terms with the tragedy. So I would appreciate it if you didn't pester any of the family at this time,' added Smith, seeking the media's assistance, but not expecting it. 'I can also confirm that a 35-year-old woman has been arrested in connection with the death, and she's currently helping us with our enquiries.'

'Is it Charlotte Tate?'

'No comment,' said Smith dourly. 'If you will forgive me. My colleague and I have further lines of enquiry to pursue. Once we have something further to report, you will be advised,' and with that, the two detectives marched off to his car and drove towards Northallerton, leaving the Media pack still no wiser than they had been before.

Forty minutes later, they entered the Pathology Lab and found Dr Stephens compiling his initial report.

'Good Morning, Dr Stephens. How are you today?' said Smith. 'I gather you wanted to see us? What gems have you got?'

'Good Morning, DI Smith, DS Jones. I'm okay, thank you,' replied Stephens, directly. 'I thought it would be better for you to hear my initial take on things, because I think you may want to ask some questions, and maybe look again at the body.'

'That sounds ominous,' said Smith, wondering what the pathologist was to impart.

'Right, I'll get down to it. Feel free to interrupt if you like, but I'll just crack on. The cause of death, as I advised yesterday, was from Exsanguination, caused by a stab wound to the left side of the neck, severing the jugular vein.'

'So death was pretty quick?' asked Smith.

'From the blood loss, and the area it covered at the stable, I would guess seconds, rather than minutes.

'From the bruising around the mouth and face, I believe the victim was attacked from behind. He was grabbed around the mouth.'

'To keep him quiet?' asked Jones.

'Yes, most likely. His jugular vein was then slashed with the knife found at the scene. It was most probably a strong, right-handed person, and quite tall, by the angle of the cut on the neck.'

'Quite tall! How tall?' asked Smith, as he and Jones looked at the wound on the body, concerned that the current accused may not have done it.

'Based upon the height of the victim, I would say, most likely a man, and at least six feet, maybe slightly more.'

'Shit!' replied Smith. 'So how likely is it that a five foot six, eight stone woman could have done it?'

'In my expert opinion, not a chance,' replied a confident Stephens.

'Are you sure?' asked Jones, writing in his notebook.

'Quite sure DS Jones. Unless the victim was kneeling down.'

'Well, it looks like our current suspect may not have done it. So, can you give us anything else to help us identify the killer?' asked a deflated, but not overly surprised Smith.

'There are apparently some smudged fingerprints on the knife, but it was most likely one that was used by the stable lads for cutting hay bales, so there could be lots of users. Forensics will advise on what they

It Wasn't Me!

find when they check them out,' added Stephens, who couldn't add much more in the circumstances.

'Is there anything else, Dr Stephens?' asked Smith.

'Not really. I'll complete my initial report and issue it shortly, but you have the headlines.'

'Thanks for nothing Doc,' said Smith mockingly. 'I was hoping we might have the suspect in custody, but now I'm not so sure. Jones, I think we still have our work cut out here,' continued Smith, looking and sounding rather perplexed.

'A trip to view the racecourse CCTV might now prove helpful,' said Jones, seeking to aid his boss.

Another forty minute car journey, predominately in silence, as the two detectives were considering the latest developments, saw them pull up outside the Administration Office at the racecourse.

CJ and Edee were sitting on a bench, with Oscar at their feet, taking in the Autumn sunshine. They were overlooking the Parade Ring and Winners' Enclosure, drinking coffee, while in deep discussion, following their review of the CCTV images.

'I hope you're not here to gloat?' said a slightly annoyed Smith.

'Good Morning to you too,' said CJ cheerily. 'We're just seeking the truth. Like I know you are.'

'I suppose so,' added Smith. 'Good Morning Edee. How do you put up with him?'

'Good Morning Simon, John. I've come to accept his traits as rather endearing, albeit I fully understand your perception of James, may not quite be the same as mine,' said a jovial Edee.

'Don't go away. We'll talk to you after we've viewed the CCTV,' added Smith, as he and Jones walked off to meet the Racecourse Manager.

The CCTV images were quite revealing. At 4.15 pm, Andrew was seen entering the stable, shortly after a tall *person* in a morning suit followed him.

This person was very careful to ensure their face was always obscured from any camera, and with a top hat strategically placed, they succeeded.

Two minutes later, they left the stable, dropping a knife by the door. They made their way back to the thronging crowds, again making sure their face was not clearly seen by any camera. Eventually, they couldn't be distinguished from the others in similar morning suits. They had made a suitable exit from the crime scene without being identified.

At 4.20 pm, Charlotte could then be seen approaching the stable, stopping to pick up the knife. She then entered the stable, and shortly after, Sarah Brownlough joined her. Within seconds a Marshall entered the stable.

Smith and Jones viewed all the available footage from the various cameras around the course, going back on numerous occasions to zoom in where required, and seeking to identify the killer.

'Well, that seems to collaborate Charlotte's recollection of events,' said Jones matter-of-factly.

'It sure does,' said a rueful Smith. 'And it doesn't particularly help us to identify the actual culprit.'

'Thank you Michelle. Can you please make a copy of the images and forward them to Jones.'

It Wasn't Me!

'You're welcome. Of course,' she replied, as Jones handed her his card.

Smith and Jones said their goodbyes, and reluctantly wandered back towards CJ and Edee.

'You were right again, Gray. Not for the first time,' said a begrudgingly apologetic Smith.

'We, like you, just want to get to the truth. The issue now, though, is who committed the crime?' replied a pensive CJ.

'Exactly,' said Smith, realising that they were now in the middle of a murder hunt, with few clues to help them.

Chapter 57 – The Suspects?

'Come on, then, you two. Any ideas as to who did it?' asked Smith, as the two officers went to sit with CJ and Edee, for once recognising that the two amateur sleuths might actually be of assistance.

Oscar, suddenly aware of new playmates, ran towards the detectives and bundled into Jones, seeking a belly rub. As always, he recognised that Jones was the more fun loving of the pair.

'You're a good boy, aren't you?' said Jones, as he duly obliged Oscar.

'Well, we're a little like you, I would think,' replied CJ. 'Struggling for clear suspects, now that Charlotte's been exonerated.'

'But we do think it's likely to be someone involved in the *Edendale Project*,' said a confident Edee, who quickly explained to the police officers what it was, and what had been going on.

'Mmm. I think we need to follow up on everyone involved with the development, and by the sound of it, their friends and family. Plus, those that could have their livelihoods thrown into jeopardy if it goes ahead.'

'There are quite a few people now in the frame,' added Jones, as always making a note of everything.

'The list of those people with means, motive and opportunity is longer than a few minutes ago,' added Smith, thankful of Edee's input.

'But don't forget the others, those that aren't involved in the project,' added CJ, throwing everyone a curve ball.

It Wasn't Me!

'What do you mean?' asked Edee.

'As these two know more than anyone, murders are often committed as a result of family differences, or undertaken by disaffected loved ones,' continued CJ.

'Fuck you CJ. I wanted a concise list, not an ever growing one,' said a satirical Smith. 'Come on Jones, it looks like we've a lot of legwork in front of us.'

'Plus, Peel and the Chief aren't going to be too pleased that their prime suspect is about to be released,' added Jones.

'What do you mean, you're letting her go?' said an incredulous Peel. The telephone conversation was going as Smith had expected. 'The Chief is. Was expecting her to be charged today.'

'Well, I could do that, but she's innocent,' said a defiant Smith. 'All the evidence shows Charlotte Tate didn't do it. I'm sure neither you nor the Chief Constable want to see the wrong person charged, with all that that entails.'

'What bloody evidence?' demanded Peel.

'The Pathologist's Report and CCTV footage clearly show that it wasn't her. It was a man that committed the crime.'

'Fuck. How am I to explain that to the Chief?'

'With position comes responsibility,' said a rather too jovial Smith. 'I can let him know, if you like,' he continued, revelling in his superior's discomfort.

'No! That won't be necessary. I'll do it!' responded an annoyed Peel. 'Just get someone charged, pronto. This is turning into a rather higher profile investigation than necessary,' he added before ending the call.

'I gather Peel isn't too happy, sir?'

'No Jones. As expected, he isn't.'

'Right Jones. Let's get down to business.'

Jones pulled out his notebook in readiness of his boss's instructions.

'Based upon what Gray and Edee have advised us and the things mentioned by Charlotte, I think we need to have a little chat with Stuart Brownlough. Where's his office?'

Jones looked at his phone and Googled Brownlough Developments. After a few moments, he confidently declared, 'Langham Arch Retail Park.'

'Jones, are you okay?' asked a quizzical Smith.

'What do you mean?'

'You didn't just refer to your notebook?'

'Mmm. I'm slowly realising that technology does have a place in modern policing, and also my life,' said a smiling Jones.

'Well, I never thought I would see the day,' laughed Smith. 'But I'm for anything that makes you an even better copper,' declared a praising Smith. 'It also reflects me in a better light. But will it ever completely replace your notebook?'

'Ah. Now that *is* the question,' replied a doubting Jones.

Ten minutes later, the two detectives walked into Brownlough Developments' office on the Langham Arch Retail Park.

It Wasn't Me!

'Good Morning. DI Smith and DS Jones from Yorksbey Police,' said Smith, as they both showed their warrant cards to the receptionist. 'Could we please speak with Stuart Brownlough?'

'Oh. Yes. Good Morning,' she replied, rather flustered, but immediately ringing Stuart's phone.

'If you'll come this way,' she continued as she put the phone down.

'Good Morning, DI Smith, DS Jones, welcome to Brownlough Developments. How can I help you?' greeted a confident Stuart as he stood and offered them both a seat in his office next to Nick.

Stuart had taken the opportunity to shave, shower, and change his clothes. He now looked and sounded like his usual confident self.

'It's about the death of Andrew Kipling,' stated Smith evenly.

'Yes, a tragedy. He'll be greatly missed. He and I have been working together for many years,' said Stuart remorsefully. 'Are you aware he's the company solicitor and legal advisor? Sorry. Was,' continued Stuart.

'Mmm. Yes, we are now,' said Smith. 'As you'll appreciate, we're seeking the murderer, and we're looking for the public's assistance in finding the culprit.'

'We'll help with anything. Won't we Nick?' replied a prompting Stuart.

'Yes. We, like you, want to see the killer caught,' said Nick rather nonchalantly.

'We understand Charlotte has been arrested and is helping you with your enquiries. When will she be released?' asked a rather concerned looking Stuart.

'Yes. Regarding that. Charlotte has stated that you messaged her yesterday afternoon - just after *Never Say Die* had won the race – asking to meet her at his stable,' stated a probing Smith.

'Me. Message her?' said a doubtful Stuart, rubbing his temple as if thinking. 'That wasn't me. Here, look at my phone if you like,' as he pulled the mobile out of his pocket and handed it towards Smith.

'That won't be necessary for now. It's just strange that she was clear it was from you.'

'I don't know what further to say,' added Stuart, shrugging his shoulders.

'On another point,' said Jones, handing the photo of Charlotte and Andrew kissing. 'Have you seen this picture before?'

'No, I haven't,' said a defiant Stuart.

'And you, sir?' asked Jones, showing it now to Nick.

'No. But it looks a bit like the sort of thing Charlotte often does,' replied a smiling Nick.

Stuart looked daggers at Nick, and gave the slightest of head shakes, that didn't go entirely unnoticed by the detectives.

'Just a couple of final points before we leave you for now,' continued Smith, clearly now probing Stuart, and looking for any give away signs. 'Where were you yesterday afternoon, between 4.15 pm and 4.25 pm?'

It Wasn't Me!

'I was at the races,' replied a flippant Stuart.

'We know that, sir. But this is a murder investigation,' said a clearly annoyed Smith. 'Where were you actually at that time?'

'He was with me,' said Nick confidently. 'We were collecting our winnings. As you noted earlier, *Never Say Die* had just won the big race.'

Stuart looked incredulously at Nick, and then back poker faced towards Smith and Jones.

'Is that true, sir?' asked Jones, his notebook at the ready.

'Yes. Yes, it is. It was a nice little flutter. It made our day.'

Chapter 58 – You Can Go

'Do you believe him, sir?' asked Jones, as they drove back to the station.

'I'm not sure. He's very confident, a bit like Charlotte,' replied Smith. 'I don't like cocky people. Especially when we're dealing with a murder.'

'But he appears to have an alibi,' added Jones.

'Mmm.'

'So we're still looking for a tall gentleman in a morning suit,' continued Jones. 'But it was *Ladies' Day*, and just like Earl Hargrove and CJ, everyone was dressed up to the nines in morning suits.'

'Exactly,' said Smith. 'Earl Hargrove and Gray also have something to lose if the development progresses.'

'Are you saying they're suspects? Surely not.'

'Jones. You should know more than anyone. Let's not rule anyone out, not until we have the perpetrator in custody.'

'I suppose not. But not CJ. He wouldn't. Would he?'

Their conversation was cut short as they pulled up outside the station, where they were again confronted by the media seeking an update for their supposed desperate viewers and readers.

As Smith got out of the car, he was again immediately faced with a microphone.

'Do you have an update for us?' asked the young reporter, having lost none of her verve. 'Are you charging Charlotte Tate with Andrew Kipling's murder?'

It Wasn't Me!

Smith again sought to maintain some order in this media frenzy.

'Our investigations are ongoing. We'll provide an update shortly, but in the meantime we're seeking any assistance from the general public that attended yesterday's *Equinox Festival*. We're looking for any incriminating mobile phone videos or images between 4 pm and 4.30 pm. Anyone with any information they think may help us with our enquiries should contact Yorksbey Police Station, or please call Crimestoppers on 0800 555 111.'

'But are you charging Charlotte Tate?'

'Ms Tate has been very helpful to our ongoing enquiries, and she's being released shortly, albeit still under caution.'

'So is she innocent, or was she involved in the murder?'

'No comment.'

With that, Smith and Jones marched off towards the station door, where they were met by Edee, who handed them a designer carrier bag.

'Hello Edee, what brings you here?' asked a smiling Smith. As always, he was happy to see her.

'Could you please give this to Charlotte? I guess she might welcome its contents,' said Edee. 'Could you also let her know we're parked over there, if she'd like a lift, or wants to get away from the media.'

'Thanks. We will,' said Jones as he took the bag and continued into the station.

'Did Stuart corroborate my statement?' asked Charlotte, as the two detectives joined her and the young solicitor in the interview room.

'I'm afraid he didn't,' stated a straight-faced Smith.

'Oh,' came the deflated reply.

'But we do have some good news,' said Jones, as he handed her the bag.

'What's this?' asked a quizzical Charlotte.

'A gift from Madame Eden Songe.'

'Edee?'

'Yes. She thought you might need the contents,' said Smith. 'You're free to go.'

'What!'

'Yes. I think you need to thank CJ Gray and Madame Songe; they have assisted us in proving your innocence. Well, at least for now,' continued a stern-looking Smith. 'You are free to go, but please remember, you're still under caution.'

Charlotte looked in the bag and smiled.

'Thank you Edee,' she whispered.

'Charlotte, you may want to go out the side door. Edee is waiting with a car if you'd like a lift. There're a media pack out front,' suggested Jones. 'You might be best placed keeping a low profile, at least for now, or until we apprehend the killer.'

Forty minutes later, Charlotte emerged from the *front* door of the Police Station and was immediately confronted by the media pack.

She had jettisoned the hazmat suit, and was now looking her normal stunning self. Edee had kindly

It Wasn't Me!

provided some of her clothes, make-up, hairbrush, and most importantly some designer stiletto heeled shoes.

The solicitor was still by her side, trying to fend off the media, and advising Charlotte to not say anything, but as was Charlotte's way, she was making the most of the attention. In her world, there was no such thing as bad publicity.

As the paparazzi asked for poses, she graciously agreed, smiling, or pouting to make the most of the attention.

The young reporter seemed less assured, or maybe slightly disinterested, as she was clearly not the centre of attention or the best looking woman now on show.

But she did rally when she was prompted by her soundman.

'Ms Tate. Charlotte. Will you be seeking compensation for wrongful arrest?'

'No comment,' said the solicitor, but recognising that Charlotte would no doubt be calling him shortly, seeking his advice on the matter.

Edee got out of the passenger door of the Audi RS6 and opened the rear door.

'Charlotte. I think it's time to go?'

Reluctantly, Charlotte sashayed over to the car, milking her audience for all it was worth, and slipped into the rear seat next to Oscar as Edee closed the door and jumped back into the car.

CJ floored the accelerator, and the car sped out of the carpark, leaving the media pack, and a rather flabbergasted solicitor in its wake.

Chapter 59 – Let's Keep An Eye On Him

Cliff Ledger looked down at his vibrating phone and immediately pressed the button to answer the call.

'Morning, Governor. How are you?' he cheerily answered.

'Morning, Cliff, I'm good. How are you?' replied CJ.

'You know, another day, same shit.' Cliff's response was a hangover from their military days together, when often that was just how it felt.

'Another day, another dollar. What can I do for you today, sir?' he added.

'How do you fancy a trip to Yorksbey...?'

Retired, RSM Cliff Ledger MC, formerly of the Royal Engineers and Royal Logistic Corps, knew that if the *Governor* called, he was looking for something resolving.

Cliff was CJ's go to *fixer* for anything, especially if it was rather unconventional, or even considered slightly outside the law, but often it might just be something very simple that needed his expertise.

Cliff would though - not to put too fine a point on it - do anything for the *Governor*.

Cliff was therefore back doing what he didn't particularly enjoy, being on a stakeout, but he'd got used to it during his army days, and to be honest, he was pretty good at it. That was why CJ trusted him to do anything that required being resilient and observant.

It Wasn't Me!

Cliff would, however, have preferred Stuart to be out and about more. It would at least have given him the opportunity to be more active. Being in one place for so long was really boring.

Activity today at Brownlough Developments had been pretty ordinary, and like many businessmen, Stuart's days were often rather mundane and scheduled.

The only significant point had been the arrival of Nick Banker.

Edee had given Cliff photos of those people that were likely to visit, and who were also involved with the *Edendale Project*. CJ had wanted Cliff to be as prepared as possible for the job he had earmarked for him.

Cliff sat back on the powerful *Kawasaki Ninja H2* motorbike he had strategically parked, so he could observe the comings and goings, while not being readily observed, and he tuned into his latest podcast of choice. Modern technology had at least slightly improved the lot of the Private Investigator.

'Nick, are you free tomorrow?' asked Stuart, reviewing his diary on his laptop.

'I'm not sure. What's it for?'

'We have the first meeting with the builder. Broadway Construction, the Main Contractor for the *Edendale Project*. Harry is fully briefed. It's predominantly a technical meeting.'

Despite the recent events, Stuart wasn't going to let the grass grow under his feet. Not when such a profitable deal was on the table.

'So why do you need me there?'

'Just in case there are any money issues that need your input.'

Nick searched through his diary on his phone.

'What time?'

'First thing, about 9.00 am. But you can be a bit later if that helps.'

'Mmm. Let me see if I can move my 10 am appointment. It should be okay,' suggested Nick.

'That's the spirit. Great,' added Stuart. 'As I said, I don't think we'll need you, but best to be safe than sorry.'

'On a more pressing subject,' said a stern-looking Nick. 'Who do you propose to get to sort out the legal stuff regarding the Golf Club, now that Andrew...is not here to help?'

'Mmm. I've also been thinking about that,' replied a thoughtful Stuart. 'I think I'll ask Mr Kipling Snr. It would be odd not to. Don't you agree?'

'Do you think he'll want to help?'

'I'm not sure, but I feel we need to at least offer him the gig,' said a smiling Stuart. 'The issue is, how long do I leave it before I raise it with him?'

'Agreed. I'm not sure what the appropriate etiquette is for asking a grieving father to be asked about future work that his son was involved with,' joked Nick.

'Nick. Don't be a complete arse,' said a laughing Stuart.

'Do you think Charlotte will do as you suggested?' asked Edee, as she relaxed with CJ and

It Wasn't Me!

Oscar on one of the large Chesterfield sofas in the Orangery of Overhear Manor.

'I'm just not sure,' replied CJ. 'She is when all's said and done - a law unto herself.'

'She is that. No doubt, time will tell. At least she appreciated our help.'

'But will she learn from it? She has a habit of getting involved with Bad Boy characters.'

'Somehow, I have my doubts. She's not me, is she?'

'She certainly isn't,' said a smiling CJ, kissing her gently while dodging Oscar's licking tongue. 'She certainly isn't.'

'Come on, we still haven't found those Deeds,' continued CJ. 'I'm sure they're key to matters. Let's have a final look around before we finally try looking in the wine cellar.'

The evening light was fading as Cliff mounted his bike and made a quick call.

'He's on the move,' he said, as he slowly and discreetly followed Stuart's Mercedes as it made its way towards Yorksbey.

Chapter 60 – You Bastard!

The Watermill Arms was crowded. All the tables in the restaurant were booked, the bar was heaving, and even outside was busy for an early autumn evening. Ted and his staff were smiling, perhaps too much, as they seemed stretched by how busy they were.

'Why did you want to meet here?' asked a questioning Stuart.

'Because your bloody lawyer's been killed, and despite your best efforts to frame me, you're possibly now the prime suspect?' replied Charlotte with venom. 'And I definitely don't want to be alone with you. Not at the moment.'

The pair had received a number of knowing looks from the pub's clientele, not that Charlotte or Stuart seemed to be particularly bothered, especially as most quickly looked away if eye contact was made.

'What do you mean?' continued an astonished Stuart. 'I didn't frame you.'

'Well, it bloody well felt like it. I get a message from you asking to meet at *Never Say Die's* stable, and the next thing, I'm arrested for murder. And more to the point, you don't say anything to back me up. You Bastard!'

'Wow. It wasn't me that messaged you,' responded a staunch Stuart. 'I couldn't. The phone I use for calling you has gone missing – possibly stolen.'

'You have another phone, just for me?'

It Wasn't Me!

'Of course I do. I didn't want Sarah finding out about us.'

'It's a bit bloody late for that, isn't it?'

'I guess so.'

'Are you ready to order? said the waitress who had crept up on them. 'Can I get you some drinks?' she asked politely, but clearly under pressure.

'Can you give us a few more minutes?' replied Stuart bluntly. 'But I'll have a Malt Whisky. Make it a double.'

'I'll have my normal spritzer please. Ted knows what I like,' added Charlotte, rather more conciliatorily.

'And you are?' asked the blushing young waitress, who was possibly the only one in the pub who didn't recognise the recently arrested Femme Fatale.

'Just say it's for Charlotte. Ted will know.'

'Oh! Okay.'

'So when did the phone go missing, and why didn't you say anything to the police? Do you know what it's like being arrested, accused of murder, and, more importantly, forced to sit in a bloody Hazmat suit for 24 hours?'

'I'm sorry, Charlie,' said Stuart, trying to ingratiate himself with Charlotte, as he reached out to touch her hands.

She immediately pulled them back and nearly knocked the drinks off the waitress's tray.

'Your drinks. Ted says they're on the house.'

Charlotte looked over towards the bar and gave one of her famous smiles. Ted gave the thumbs up and smiled back.

'At least someone doesn't think I did it.'

'Of course you didn't do it. You're too kind and thoughtful for that,' continued Stuart in grovelling mode. He recognised that he had a lot of work to do to get back in Charlotte's good books.

'Well, are you going to answer my question?'

'I don't remember having the phone at the races. I didn't need it, as we were together. It was only later that I couldn't find it. Someone must have taken it.'

'Of course, someone bloody took it. The murderer left it in Andrew Kipling's pocket, with that bloody picture you took of me kissing him. Thanks for that,' said Charlotte, still not totally convinced with Stuart's explanation.

'So why didn't you say anything to the police?' she continued, still seeking some answers.

'When you were arrested, and by the Chief Constable, I initially thought you'd done it.'

'Oh. Thanks for the vote of confidence,' said Charlotte, folding her arms in indignation.

'I just thought it would make it worse if I said anything,' said an apologetic Stuart.

'Mmm. I suppose that makes some sense. So who stole your phone? Who had the opportunity?' asked a thoughtful Charlotte. 'If we find them, we find the killer.'

'I guess we do,' replied a similarly thoughtful and conniving Stuart.

Presently Charlotte looked him in the eye while taking a sip of her drink.

'Did you do it, Stuart?'

'What?'

It Wasn't Me!

'To be honest, I don't really care either way,' said Charlotte matter-of-factly.

'Charlie, you can be so cold-hearted at times.'

C J Meads

Chapter 61 – Sorry For Your Loss

Smith and Jones walked up the large gravel drive leading to Andrew Kipling's mock Tudor house, on one of Stuart's developments. He had bought it as part of a deal with Stuart, and it was worth far more than he would have been able to afford, even for him.

But that was now all rather academic. With the mortgage being paid off by the insurance, Lucy Kipling would be comfortably off for the rest of her life.

Jones rang the doorbell and a well-dressed and pleasant looking woman in her mid-forties answered the door.

'Good Evening, DI Smith and DS Jones of Yorksbey police,' said Smith as usual, as they both showed their warrant cards. 'Are you Mrs Kipling?'

'Yes. Good Evening. What do you want?' replied Lucy, rather bluntly.

'We're sorry for your loss,' said Smith in his most reverent of tones. 'But we thought it only reasonable to check how you were, and give you an update on the investigation.'

'Oh. You'd better come in then.'

She led them through the extensive hallway into a large lounge and they sat down opposite her on a four seater grey sofa.

'So, how are you coping in these tragic circumstances? I hope our liaison officer has been useful to you?' said Smith.

'I'm fine, thank you. PC Perfect has been most helpful.'

It Wasn't Me!

'That's good.'

'I gather from the news on the TV that you don't know who did it?'

'No. But we're pursuing a number of leads. We're looking for a tall man, who was at the races in a morning suit,' added Jones.

'Good luck with that then,' replied Lucy directly. 'Look, I'm not sure what PC Perfect has told you, but be under no illusion. Andrew and I have been leading rather separate lives for a while.'

'Perfect, did mention something along those lines,' said a knowing Smith.

'Now Matthew, our son is older, we were looking to get a divorce. We had only kept together for his sake while he was growing up.'

'Oh. I see. Very adult of you,' added Smith. ' Not everyone is as sensible as you appear to be. Not in such circumstances.'

'He's a solicitor when all's said and done. We both know the score. Well, we did.'

'Quite.'

'I suggest your efforts at placating and supporting Andrew's loved ones should be addressed to others. Maybe his father, albeit their relationship, has become strained over the last few years – work issues I think – and perhaps to his lover, Sarah Brownlough.'

'You know of their affair?' asked a surprised Jones.

'Of course I do. It was the worst kept secret. Both families have kept up the appearance of happy families for the children's sake,' continued Lucy evenly, with no sign of remorse. 'But they're no longer children. So we can all move on. Well, some of us.'

'Indeed,' said a rather surprised Smith.

'Well, who's this?' asked Jones. as they were joined by a strapping young man.

'This is my son, Matthew,' said Lucy. 'I think he inherited my brother's genes. He's also very tall.'

'You must be well over six feet,' added Smith.

'Yes I am,' said a sullen Matthew, who, like many teenagers of his age, had a distrust of authority. 'Who are these men, Mum?'

'They're detectives. They're searching for your father's killer.'

'Oh.'

'Were you close to your father, Matthew?' asked Smith directly.

'We got on,' came the curt reply.

'You'll no doubt miss him,' continued a prying Smith.

'Yes. But Mum's here to help me.'

'A mother's love is forever,' added Jones thoughtfully.

'Will there be anything else?' asked Lucy, sensing that nothing further was to be gained by the detectives' presence.

'Just one thing,' added Smith, 'Were either of you at Yorksbey Racecourse between 4 pm and 4.30 pm yesterday?'

'No. I despise Horse Racing,' said a disgusted-looking Lucy. 'I was here watching *Tipping Point* on the TV.'

It Wasn't Me!

'And you, Matthew?' asked a probing Smith.

'No. I wasn't.'

'He was here. Upstairs. Preparing for University. He starts at Magdalen College, Oxford on Monday,' interrupted Lucy, before Matthew could answer.

'Thank you both. I think we'll be going now,' said a considerate Smith as he and Jones made their way to the front door. 'We'll keep you informed of developments in the investigation.'

'Very well. Goodnight, gentlemen,' said Lucy as she closed the door on the detectives.

'Well, what do you make of that, sir?'

'Mmm.'

'Do you think Matthew killed his father?' asked a searching Jones.

'He definitely has the stature to do it, and possibly a slight desire. But realistically? No,' replied a pensive Smith. 'But let's keep him on our list of suspects. Well, at least for now.'

C J Meads

Chapter 62 – Let's Go Away?

Having finished their meal, Stuart and Charlotte were on the way out, but were clearly being watched in the crowded pub.

'Charlie, this may seem odd, but please hear me out.'

'Go on,' said an intrigued Charlotte.

'Look, I'm going away, and I want you to come with me.'

'What do you mean, going away? What about the *Edendale Project*?'

'That was just a ruse to quickly get £35 million.'

'Quickly?'

'Yes. I make nearly as much money this way, as I do waiting the three years for everyone else to also make their money, and I can't wait.'

'But..,' said a shocked Charlotte.

'I've nothing to stay here for. Sarah despises me, and I'm pretty sure Sienna only wants me for my money.'

'But what about your business?'

'It's bankrupt. Nick's the only one keeping it afloat, and I don't know how much longer the clever bastard can do that.'

'Does he know?'

'No, of course not. I couldn't tell anyone. Not even you. Not until the money came through from Masud.'

'Where are you planning to go?'

'I'm taking my Cruiser from its berth in Padstow, and I'm just going where the fancy takes me. The

It Wasn't Me!

French Riviera, Monaco, Cannes, the Greek Islands. Anywhere that's not here.'

'Wow, it's all a bit of a rush, isn't it?'

'Not really. Not for me,' continued Stuart in a positive mood. 'Please come with me. We make a great team.'

'Why not?' said Charlotte, not one to miss out on an opportunity to top up her tan. 'When do you plan on going?'

'Tomorrow.'

'Tomorrow!'

'Yes, get packed. You won't need much. £35 million buys whatever we want,' said Stuart, as he kissed and hugged her tightly.

'Look. I've got a meeting tomorrow morning with a prospective builder. I'm going to keep that,' said Stuart. 'You can relax on the early train to Cornwall, and I'll meet you later tomorrow night at the boat in Padstow. How does that sound?'

'Sounds good,' replied Charlotte.

'Great,' said Stuart, before whispering to himself. 'But first, maybe some sordid sex.'

In the shadows, at least one pair of devious eyes looked on, definitely none too pleased with what they had just witnessed.

'Hi. I didn't expect to see you here this evening,' said a startled Stuart, as he and a smiling Charlotte left the pub, arm in arm.

'Bye.'

C J Meads

Chapter 63 – What Have We Found?

Despite the two old 150 watt light bulbs, the cellar of Overhear Manor was still pretty dingy. The light was really there, so that those seeking a good bottle of wine could easily make out the type and vintage. It wasn't there to provide lighting for seeking out 100-year-old deeds.

Like all cellars, it was also rather chilly, being a cool 12 degrees centigrade and full of cobwebs. CJ was also contemplating that perhaps he should pay more attention to its cleanliness, but that thought was perhaps for another day.

'It's like looking for a needle in a haystack,' said a rather deflated Edee. 'Are you sure it's likely to be down here?'

'Edee, we've looked in most of the obvious places. This now seems the most likely, based upon our previous searches,' replied CJ, who was also getting frustrated.

'I didn't realise you had so many bottles, and you have some really good French wine vintages.'

'I know. The Gray family has always sought to maintain a good cellar, and I look to keep up the tradition,' said CJ. 'I've always been torn between maintaining the investment and drinking its contents. Such a tricky dilemma.'

'Perhaps I can help you decide,' said Edee as she sidled up to him and grabbed his arm.

'You do know there may not even be a copy here. It may have been lost or destroyed,' added Edee. 'It

It Wasn't Me!

might even have inadvertently been thrown out by anyone not realising its significance.'

CJ was also slowly coming to that conclusion. Perhaps it was a lost cause.

The door of the cellar suddenly opened, and a shaft of light lit up the wooden staircase, followed immediately by Oscar, who bounded down the stairs and sought out his master.

'Hello boy. Are you missing me?'

'Well, as usual, he's not particularly missing me,' said a mocking Edee. As Oscar ran straight past her and bowled into CJ, seeking a customary ear rub, plus perhaps a treat.

'Master James. There's a call for you on the house phone,' called out Mrs Wembley from the open doorway. 'It's a DI Smith. He says he can't get you on your mobile.'

CJ looked down at his phone and realised that there was no signal in the gloomy cellar.

'I'll be right up,' replied CJ. 'Come on Edee, time for a break and a coffee.'

'I'll be with you in a minute.'

CJ climbed the stairs, making his way to the study and trying to make sure he didn't fall over Oscar, who decided to beat him to the top.

'Yes DI Smith. And to what do I owe the pleasure?'

'Hello Gray. Sorry to trouble you. Me and Jones, were just thinking.'

CJ thought about what Edee would have said, if she'd answered the phone, but he let it go, relying on his own caustic response.

'It's often overrated.'

'Sorry?'

'Thinking. It's often overrated,' said CJ, as he sat down in the large swivel chair in the study, and Oscar immediately jumped on his lap.

'Very funny. I don't think,' replied an irritated Smith.

'But you just said you were.'

'What!'

'Thinking. You just said that you and Jones had been thinking. Now you're saying you don't,' teased CJ.

'Gray, stop it. You know you can get to me, and I was in a good mood for once.'

'Okay.'

'Okay what? Okay, you get to me? Or, okay, I'm in a good mood?' asked Smith.

'No. Just okay. I understand. Pray continue,' said CJ, who had decided he'd had enough sport, as Edee joined him, sitting on the corner of the desk crossed legged, tapping her heels against the corner of the Chippendale antique.

'I gather from my sources that you were at the races, and had the pleasure of the hospitality provided by both Earl Hargrove and Sheikh Twoammie.'

'Your sources are accurate. So what? Are you just jealous, and looking to find out what you missed out on?'

'Don't be silly. No, we were *thinking*. Did you or Edee see anyone or anything suspicious? You had the opportunity to be with those with perhaps the greatest

It Wasn't Me!

involvement in the *Edendale Project*. Plus, we agree with you that it's the *Edendale Project* that is possibly key to the murder.'

'Edee and I have been contemplating this since the murder, but currently we are still drawing a blank like you.'

'For once, then, you're not as helpful as we had hoped.'

'It would appear so,' replied CJ.

Suddenly there was a loud click from where Edee had been tapping, and out popped a secret drawer on the side of the desk.

'Hello. What do we have here?' said a surprised CJ.

Edee jumped off the desk and pulled the drawer open.

'Ah, Ha. What have we found?'

'Gray. What is it?' asked an intrigued Smith.

'Maybe the first bit of luck in the case.'

'Go on.'

'It looks like Edee's found the Gray copy of the Deeds. Can I call you back once we've had a look?' asked an excited CJ.

'Of course, but don't keep us waiting. It may be the clue we need,' replied a similarly hopeful Smith.

Edee spread the document out on the desk.

'Open up the page on Covenants,' suggested CJ.

They both quickly scan read the list.

'This is not as the Major's copy,' they both said together.

'Jinx,' they both said, and burst out laughing.

'Wow. So what does it mean?' asked Edee.

'Someone has been fraudulent, and telling porky pies.'

'Porky pies?' asked Edee, who despite living in the UK for 25 years, struggled with some aspects of the English language.

'Cockney rhyming slang for *lies*.'

'Oh. I thought it was slang for *eyes*,' she replied, looking rather confused.

'No. That's *mince pies*,' said a laughing CJ, who kissed her on the cheek. 'I do love your innocence at times,' he added.

Shortly, having re-read the document thoroughly, they called Smith back. They were now all on loud speaker.

'So Brownlough's copy of the Deeds is not as your original copy?' asked Smith, not quite believing what he'd been told.

'Correct,' replied CJ.

'Fuck me. The devious bastard.'

'It also explains or links a number of recent things,' continued CJ. 'The break in at Kipling's solicitors was most likely an inside job.'

'You mean by Andrew?'

'Yes. Having changed the Deed for Brownlough, he needed to get it into the safe and take the original,' added CJ.

'But Mr Kipling Snr. disturbed him,' said Smith realising the connection.

'Yes. So he had to make it look like a robbery. Fortunately, Mr Kipling Snr. wasn't badly hurt.'

'It's strange what people will do for money,' said Edee.

It Wasn't Me!

'I'm not sure it was for money. It was for silence to protect those he loved, and also his reputation,' said Smith.

'So we have fraud, extortion and blackmail on the list of things for Brownlough to explain,' said Jones, as he added to the notes in his book.

'And I guess murder now,' added CJ.

'Brownlough must have thought that Kipling was going to come clean, and he couldn't allow that,' said Smith.

'So he killed him,' added Edee. 'Then looked to frame Charlotte in the process.'

'Well, someone did, that's for certain,' added CJ.

'And from the evidence, I agree Edee, it looks like Stuart Brownlough,' said a convinced Smith.

'I'm sure you'll be visiting him tomorrow,' said a thoughtful CJ. 'He definitely has questions to answer.'

'Jones, I think we need to get our ducks in a row, ready for an early start in the morning,' said Smith, before adding. 'Thanks again, you two. As always, we're grateful for your assistance,' as he ended the call.

C J Meads

CHAPTER 64 – OH SIENNA!

'Sienna, I'm sorry for saying what I did. It was unforgivable as a mother,' said an extremely apologetic and remorseful Sarah.

Mother and daughter had finally sat down together in the family home, having dealt with the aftermath of Andrew's murder, and Sarah's revelation, in their own ways.

They were together on the sofa, and finally Sarah had stopped crying, but she was still coming to terms with the loss of her lover and best friend. But perhaps, more importantly, the loss of the father of her precious daughter.

'I understand Mum. I really do. If I had lost the love of my life, I think I might just have reacted the same way,' said an extremely considerate Sienna, who for once showed a maturity well beyond her years.

'Thank you, my darling. But it was still wrong of me. To say what I did, in that manner, and in public, it was totally unwarranted. Please forgive me.'

'You have nothing to be forgiven for.'

'But to find out like that. That your dad isn't your biological father, and Andrew was..... Well, it was wrong of me. Sorry.'

They momentarily hugged, and Sarah started crying again.

'It's alright Mum. Let it out.'

Sienna had even taken her mother by surprise. How had her daughter suddenly become this understanding young woman, with empathy,

It Wasn't Me!

something she had seldom shown before that day. Perhaps the only other time was when the family pet cat had been run over.

'But your dad isn't your real father. Aren't you upset?'

'Mum, why would I be upset? I've suspected for years, and last year I did a DNA test.'

'What! You did what? Without saying anything?'

'I needed to know. You already knew. What would it have achieved if I'd told you?'

'But why?'

'Mum, it was obvious you loved Andrew, despite your best efforts to hide it from me.'

'Oh Sienna!'

'Oh, Mum.'

'But, what, how...' Sarah was totally lost for words, so Sienna sought to help her mother out.

'Mum, you only have to look at me, Dad and Andrew to know who my father actually was.'

Sarah bowed her head in shame, wondering how she had let her daughter down for all those years.

'Of course you knew. We all suspected, even your dad, but we didn't say anything, mainly for your sake.'

'It's okay Mum, I've had time to reflect on it. I've come to terms with it. I guess the only regret I now have is not getting to know my real father when I had a chance, but such is life.'

Sarah started crying again.

'Oh Sienna. He would have loved to have known you better, I'm sure of that.'

'We'll never know now. Will we?' said a sardonic Sienna.

'I always loved Andrew. I shouldn't have married your Dad. Andrew, and I had a lovers' tiff, and your Dad proposed. I foolishly accepted. Possibly to get back at Andrew,' said a thoughtful Sarah. 'But I always loved Andrew. Not Stuart.'

The long silence was eventually broken by Sienna.

'If Dad killed Andrew. I'll.....'

'If he did, you'll have to get in the queue,' said a resolute and revengeful Sarah. 'I can't believe it wasn't Charlotte Tate. I mean, I caught her red-handed at the scene. Standing over Andrew, so, so, threateningly.'

'But it can't have been her. They've let her go. The police are now looking for a tall man who was wearing a morning suit,' countered Sienna.

'The police don't always get it right. Do they?' posed Sarah menacingly.

'Mum. Please don't do anything silly. Let the police deal with it. I can't afford to lose both my real parents.'

The deathly silence this time was broken by the sound of the front doorbell.

'Who can that be at this time?' asked Sarah. 'I'll get it.'

She dried her eyes and brushed her hair in the hallway mirror before opening the door.

'Oh, it's you Nick. Stuart's not here.'

'No, I know that. He asked me to pick up some papers from his study for a meeting tomorrow. I think

It Wasn't Me!

he recognises he's not particularly welcome here at the moment.'

'Well, at least he's got that right. You know where it is. Second on the right, down the hallway.'

'Thanks. Sarah, I'm sorry. I know you were close to Andrew. It's such a tragedy.'

'Thank you, Nick,' said Sarah rather robotically, not particularly seeking her husband's accountant's condolences. 'Just let yourself out when you're finished.'

Nick quickly collected the necessary documents and made his way out.

'Goodnight Sarah. You take care now,' he called out as he shut the front door behind him.

A few minutes later, the doorbell rang again.

'Who can it be now?' said an annoyed Sarah, as she got up and answered the door.

'Oh. It's you Matthew, come on in. Sienna, it's for you,' Sarah called out as she left Matthew in the hallway.

'Hi Matt. How are you?' said a more jovial Sienna.

'I'm good. I thought I'd better come and say goodbye. I'm off to Uni tomorrow. It's *Freshers' week.*'

'That sounds like fun,' said Sienna. 'Make sure you keep in touch on Facebook or Instagram.'

'Of course, but I think I'm going to be busy. Studying law is a bit full on.'

'Yeah. I think I'll enjoy my gap year, before deciding what to do.'

The two hugged.

'You take care, sis.'
'You too, Matt,' said Sienna, as she waved him goodbye and closed the front door.

It Wasn't Me!

CHAPTER 65 – WHO'S THERE?!

'Good Evening, sir. It's...'

'I know who it is, Smith. What do you want this late in the evening?' asked an irritated Peel.

He had settled in for the evening, was now about to join his wife in bed, and didn't need a subordinate calling.

'Sorry sir. I know it's late, but I felt I should give you an update on the Kipling murder.'

'Couldn't it wait until tomorrow?'

'Not really.'

'Why not?' continued Peel, whose mood wasn't improving.

'We have evidence that shows Stuart Brownlough has committed fraud, has more than likely blackmailed Andrew Kipling, and when his extortion didn't work, he now has a clear motive for his murder.'

'Evidence?'

'A copy of the original deeds relating to the Golf Club have come to light. They're different from those presented by Brownlough.'

'Are you confident of their authenticity?'

'Yes sir. They're from a reputable source.'

'Who might that be?'

'CJ Gray. One of the Golf Club Trustees. He's found the family copy that originates from the inaugural AGM, back in 1919.'

'Okay. So what's the plan?' asked Peel, now sensing a breakthrough was likely, and that he could perhaps take the credit for solving another suspicious death.

'We're planning a bit of a dawn raid. To arrest him and bring him in for questioning,' advised Smith.

'Good. Keep me informed. I'll brief the press.'

'Sir. I think that may be a little bit premature,' stated a cautious Smith. 'Perhaps wait until we have him under arrest.'

'Maybe so,' said Peel as he abruptly ended the call.

Cliff had discreetly followed Stuart's Mercedes from the Watermill Arms and had seen him drop Charlotte off at Tate House. He was now parked up outside Brownlough Developments' office, the halogen streetlights brightening the clear dark night.

He keyed in a message on his phone:

Brownlough alone at his office
Looks like he's going to stop over again
All quiet and lights off
It's midnight, I'm calling it a day
Will resume surveillance in the morning

He pressed *send*, and then started his bike before slowly moving off, looking forward to a good night's rest.

In the other direction a green, unlit car was slowly making its way apparently unobserved down the road.

It Wasn't Me!

'Where are you going David?' asked Countess Hargrove, lying in the stately home's large fourposter bed.

'I thought I heard the dogs. I'm just going to check that all's secure,' replied a rather flustered Earl Hargrove.

'Well, don't disturb me when you come back,' she haughtily replied.

The Major quietly closed the back door to his home on the outskirts of Edendale. It was not like him to be up so late. Especially not today. But he was contemplating and scheming. The events of the last few days were playing on his mind.

'No one was going to turn his beloved golf club into a bloody housing development. And definitely not Stuart Brownlough.'

'You're up late dear,' said Rebecca's mother as she walked back across the landing, having just got up to pay a visit to the bathroom.

Rebecca looked back up the stairs of the council house the family rented on the east side of Yorksbey.

'Maggie's called. She's having one of her melt downs. She's asked if I'll go and keep her company.'

'I thought Maggie was away,' replied her mother absentmindedly.

'No, she came back earlier today,' said Rebecca, thinking on her feet.

'Okay. Take care. It's late. When will you be back?'

'I'm not really sure. Don't worry though. I'll be alright.'

Jarvis was counting up the last of the day's takings. Everyone else was away for the night. All was quiet at the golf club.

It seemed strangely eery this evening, but perhaps that was just Jarvis' interpretation, maybe because of what he had planned.

Having made a final note of everything, and balancing the till takings with the sales and the float, he finally put the money in the safe and locked it.

He then put on his coat and made his way out, locking the staff door. He slowly walked down the gravel path towards the first tee, and onto the steel cable stayed footbridge over the River Eden on his route towards town.

Mr Kipling Snr. sat in his office, contemplating how life can be so cruel. Why had his son been murdered in the prime of his life?

Life was a bitch at times.

He would trade his long and happy life in a heartbeat to just see his son again. But that wasn't going to happen.

Life and death weren't things that could be traded.

Or could they?

It Wasn't Me!

He downed the dregs of his glass and filled it again from the bottle of malt whisky, that was now half full. Or, as he contemplated, it was now half empty.

He finally made his decision. Time for action.

Sheikh Twoammie looked down at his phone. A new message had just pinged.

He smiled. The sort of contented smile that someone in power readily conveys.

He knew what needed to be done.

No one double crosses Sheikh Twoammie, and gets away with it. No one.

He typed a reply and pressed send.

'Revenge is sweet,' he wryly thought.

'Mum, Harry's just called. I'm going to stay at his,' called out Sienna as she opened the front door. 'He has a big meeting in the morning. I think he needs someone to keep him company.'

'Oh, to be young and carefree,' thought Sarah, before replying.

'Enjoy yourselves. Life is too short.'

'Bye,' said Sienna as she closed the door behind her.

Sarah looked at the time.

Midnight.

The witching hour.

Her sleep since her lover's murder had been restless. Haunted by dreams that wouldn't go away. She felt lost. Alone. Desperate for…..

Desperate for retribution.

She walked down the stairs, pleased that Sienna had left. It saved her from making a feeble excuse.

She was alone. With all that it conveyed.

Time to think. Time to plan. Time to…..

Ian Westbank had left the lads following a good night out at the pub. He was fuelled with drink and a line of cocaine. He thought jealously about Stuart's involvement with Charlotte the envy rising.

Charlotte's affection for him had subsided since her involvement with Stuart.

He was annoyed. No. He was pissed off. He wasn't happy. He knew what was required.

'I'm just going to give Oscar a late night walk. It's a clear moonlit night. Would you care to join us?'

Edee was sitting up in bed, her reading glasses gracefully resting on the end of her nose. She was reading a book.

She looked up, over the top of the glasses, in a very sexy and provocative manner. 'Are you sure you really want to go out?' she teased.

'Yes. Oscar wants a walk. Just look at him.'

It Wasn't Me!

Oscar was scratching at the bedroom door one moment. The next, he was back at his master's feet, playfully jumping up and down.

'Well, you have a nice walk; I'm enjoying this book.'

'What is it?' asked CJ, not really bothered, but slightly surprised that Edee had taken up late night reading.

'It's a whodunnit, by a new novelist, CJ Meads. *Murder comes to Wetherby*? It has so many familiar type characters in it. I'm quite into it,' said Edee, as she waved her hand at CJ.

'À bientôt. See you soon.'

'À plus tard. See you later.'

C J Meads

It Wasn't Me!

PART 3

C J Meads

It Wasn't Me!

Chapter 66 – A Dawn Awakening

It was early. Not excessively early, but still early as Smith and Jones walked purposefully up the large, tarmacked drive leading to Stuart Brownlough's house.

Jones rang the doorbell and was immediately confronted by a rather annoyed Sarah.

'What do you want!?'

'Good Morning, Mrs Brownlough, DI Smith and DS Jones of Yorksbey Police,' said Smith, as they both showed their warrant cards. 'Is your husband Stuart Brownlough at home? We would like to ask him a few questions.'

'Do you know what time it is?'

'Yes, we do, Mrs Brownlough, but this is a serious matter,' replied Smith sarcastically.

'Oh. I'm sorry, but he's not here. He hasn't been home since the....'

'Murder,' added Jones enigmatically.

'Quite.'

'Do you know where he is?' asked Smith directly.

'No, and to be honest, I don't bloody care. If I never see that bastard again, it will be too soon.'

'Oh,' replied a taken back Smith.

'So you have no idea where he's been staying, or where he is?' asked Jones expectantly, with his notebook at the ready.

'You're more than likely to find him at the office later. Nick was here last night picking up some documents for him. Apparently, they have a meeting this morning.'

'Thank you. I'm sorry we troubled you,' added an apologetic Smith, this time rather more genuinely. 'If he contacts you, will you please get in touch and let us know?'

Jones handed her a card, which she took without really looking at it, as she suddenly looked up the driveway.

'Where's my car?'

'Sorry Mrs Brownlough?'

'My car's gone. It was there last night. It's now gone.'

'I'm sorry Mrs Brownlough, you'll have to ring the station, or Crimestoppers' if you want to report a stolen vehicle,' said Jones. 'The numbers are on the card.'

With that, the two detectives turned and strolled back to Jones' car, leaving a rather perplexed and angry Sarah to her thoughts.

'What now?' asked Jones.

'Brownlough's office, I guess,' replied Smith.

Ten minutes later, they pulled up outside Brownlough Developments' Offices, to what could only be described as a media circus.

'What the Fuck!' said an exasperated Smith. 'If Peel has tipped off the media.... I'll swing for the Twat.'

It was carnage. The TV crews were back, including the press reporters. But something didn't seem right.

'What's Pat..... I mean, what's PC Perfect doing here?' said a confused Jones. 'Shit, I've turned the

It Wasn't Me!

police radio off by mistake,' he added, realising his error.

As they got out of the car, Perfect came over, followed immediately by the media scrum. The young correspondent was leading the way, with her microphone at the ready.

'Sir?' said a worried Perfect.

'Say nothing Perfect. Just follow us into the reception,' replied a decisive Smith.

'But sir. I think...,' but Smith raised his hand and silenced her with a stare that said, 'Shut Up, and be quiet.'

'DI Smith, is it true you were planning to arrest Stuart Brownlough for Andrew Kipling's murder?' shouted out the correspondent, with what now seems to be accepted behaviour for news reporters.

'No comment,' replied an agitated Smith.

'But you now can't, because he's *dead*!' she added rather smugly.

'What!?' said a disbelieving Smith, as he turned and looked steely at the smiling young reporter.

'I guess that's a *No Comment*!' she arrogantly continued.

Chapter 67 – Dead Men Don't Lie

'Perfect, you could have said something.'

'But sir, I did try to warn you,' replied a now downcast Perfect.

'She did actually,' said Jones, seeking to support the young police officer.

'Okay. It's just that bloody reporter. She's getting to me,' acknowledged a suddenly weary looking Smith. 'What have we got Perfect?' he continued as they were welcomed by the quiet of the Reception to Brownlough Developments' Offices.

'We received a 9 9 9 call at 8.15 am from Ms Audrey Templeton, the Receptionist and Brownlough's secretary. She's over there,' said Perfect, pointing to a well-dressed, but clearly distressed woman, who was being attended to by paramedics. 'She'd opened up the offices and had found a dead Stuart Brownlough in his *private* room.'

'So what time had he got here?' asked Jones.

'It looks like he's been here all night, and by all accounts has been stopping here for the last few days,' continued Perfect. 'The media turned up just before you arrived, and to be honest, I've not had a chance to do much more.'

'Okay. Show us the body, and then make sure no one enters or leaves the building until I say so,' instructed Smith. 'Understood?'

'Yes, sir.'

'I'll speak with Ms Templeton shortly. She looks rather distressed at the moment.'

It Wasn't Me!

Perfect led them along the hallway and up the stairs to the First Floor landing. Next to Stuart's large dual aspect office was a door slightly ajar and labelled, *Private. Keep Out.*

'He's in here,' said Perfect. 'I take it you're broad minded sir.'

Smith pushed the door open with his elbow, to minimise disturbing any evidence, and looked in, with Jones looking over his shoulder.

He was not expecting this to be a natural death scene, but what he saw even took him by surprise, despite Perfect's warning.

The subdued lighting revealed what could only be described as a *sex dungeon.*

All the windows were blacked out. There were numerous sex toys, whips, chains, and other bondage devices hanging from one wall. On another wall - carefully hung on hangers - were numerous readily recognisable leather and pvc erotic sex clothing for both sexes.

There was a large fourposter bed against the other wall, covered with black satin sheets.

Wooden medieval stocks were positioned strategically on one side of the room, whilst a leather *sex* table/bench mirrored it.

On the bench was the dead body of Stuart Brownlough, naked except for a leather gimp mask and blindfold.

He was chained down, spreadeagled on his back, with a large ball gag tightly placed in his mouth.

'Ah. I think we need to let Dr Stephens and the Forensic team do their stuff,' said Smith wryly.

'Not your everyday office storage room, is it sir?' replied Jones, who suddenly had rather depraved thoughts, as he looked and smiled at a blushing Perfect.

'Thank you Perfect, that will be all for now,' said Smith, and she made her way back to the reception.

Following a quick check, it was apparent the rest of the floor was just a combination of normal offices, rooms and facilities which were awaiting the staff to start their normal working day.

They cordoned off the top floor with blue and white police crime scene tape and they made their way back down the stairs.

'Have you seen anything like that before?' asked a probing but unrepentant Jones.

Smith considered the question before responding, recognising that whatever he said could quickly find its way around the force.

'I'm aware of such *rooms,* but it's the first one I've seen, and therefore the first one also where a dead body was found. What about you Jones?'

'The same,' he lied, but similarly, he knew any other response might be misconstrued.

'Fuck it,' said Smith. 'Just when we were potentially getting somewhere.'

As they reached the bottom of the stairs, it was evident that Audrey Templeton had regained some of her composure. She appeared to be a woman of the world, and over the years working for Stuart, had heard rumours about his sexual deviances. What she had witnessed today had just confirmed the rumours.

It Wasn't Me!

'Ms Templeton, I'm DI Smith. That must have been quite a shock, finding Stuart Brownlough like that. Are you okay?' asked a sympathetic Smith.

'I am now. Thank you.'

'Were you aware of the contents of the room?'

'No. Mr Brownlough kept that *room* very secure. No one was ever allowed in it.'

'I gather you arrived about 8.15 am. Did you notice anything else that was unusual?' asked Jones, with his pen and notebook at the ready.

'Not really. The only odd thing was, along with Mr Brownlough's Mercedes, there was a green car in the carpark. When I get here in the morning, the carpark is normally empty.'

'Mmm. We'll check that out,' said a thoughtful Smith. 'But if you think of anything else, please let us know.'

'I certainly will.'

'Oh, and by the way, could you give a list of who has keys and access to the office, to DS Jones, including a list of employees, for, say, the last two or three years? We may need to question everyone.'

'DI Smith, are you aware there is an important meeting at 9 am regarding the *Edendale Project*? What shall we do?'

'Right,' said a thoughtful Smith. 'Who's in charge when Mr Brownlough is not here?'

'Mmm. He runs a tight ship,' said Audrey, colouring up slightly before correcting herself. '*Ran* a tight ship, and only a small team of people, with a flat structure, that ran itself really.'

'That's rather unusual,' said Smith.

'Mr Brownlough liked to know about everything. He was a bit of a control.....'

'Freak,' added Smith.

'I guess many would describe it that way,' she replied reflectively.

'I'm afraid that the offices will be off limits today and I would ask all the staff to work from home. We'll be in touch with them all individually.'

'Okay. I'm sure I can do that. Just let me know if there is anything else I can do to help,' replied Audrey, who had now fully regained her poise, and was working as Stuart had always demanded of her and his team.

'There is something. When those attending the planned meeting arrive, could they be asked to go to a meeting room, and DS Jones and I will interview them.'

'I'll put them in the conference room as planned. It's down the corridor, on the left.'

'Just a couple of points. Are there any other external doors?' asked a curious Smith.

'Just the Fire Exits. They're clearly marked.'

'And finally, do you have CCTV?'

'We do,' said Audrey, looking rather bewildered. 'But when I got in this morning, I noticed that it had been switched off last night. That's a first.'

It Wasn't Me!

Chapter 68 – What Now Sir?

'What now, sir?' asked a bewildered-looking Jones.

Smith, not for the first time in this case, was also looking rather confused. The breakthrough they'd hoped for with the finding of the original deeds was now a closed opportunity. Similarly, the potential suspect they wanted to question was now also dead, in rather unusual circumstances. But with every occurrence, there is also an opportunity to reflect.

'One door closes, and another possibly opens,' answered Smith. 'Well, we need to hope that's the case, but I'm not totally convinced.'

'I guess so,' agreed Jones, still none the wiser. 'What's your take on Brownlough's death, sir?'

'Well, it certainly looks like he had a fetish for the erotic. The question is, was it purely a sex act that got out of hand, resulting in a tragic death? Or is there something more sinister afoot?'

'It's rather a coincidence when we were due to interview him,' posed Jones. 'The question is who was the sex act with? And where are they now?'

'Exactly,' agreed Smith. 'Well, let's allow Stephens and his team to do their initial investigation, while we interview the attendees of the *Edendale Project* meeting.'

The two detectives walked along the glazed corridor to the conference room, and Smith looked through the windows, considering the green Tesla parked outside.

'The green Tesla. Check it out Jones.'

'I have, sir. It's registered to Mrs Sarah Brownlough.'

'Now, why am I not surprised?' said Smith as he entered the conference room.

Sitting around the large table were three men and a woman, all looking rather nonplussed by the events. Smith only recognised Nick from the previous meeting with Stuart, who was the one to initially speak up.

'What's going on, DI Smith? Where's Stuart?'

'Good Morning, everyone,' replied Smith, who deliberately ignored the question, eager to establish control of the meeting. 'I'm sorry to inform you, but Stuart Brownlough will not be attending the meeting this morning.'

Smith looked for any glimmer of acknowledgement from the attendees, but nothing was really forthcoming, other than Nick's further question.

'What do you mean?'

'Sorry Mr Banker, I'll come to that in a moment. For the rest of you, as Mr Banker has pointed out, I'm DI Smith, and this is DS Jones. We are investigating the sudden death of Stuart Brownlough.'

All of them gasped at the news, and appeared completely shocked at the revelation.

'Could you please confirm your names, contact details, and the reason why you're at the meeting scheduled with Mr Brownlough?'

Jones, efficient as usual, wrote down all their details, including those of Jack Broad, the owner of

It Wasn't Me!

Broadway Construction Ltd, the planned builder, who joined Nick, Harry, and Rebecca in his notebook.

'If you don't mind, I would just like you to confirm where you were last night, and to advise you that we may wish to interview you all again once we've established the events surrounding Mr Brownlough's death.'

'So is the death suspicious?' asked a concerned Harry, who was desperately considering the fallout the recent events would have on the development, and more importantly, his business.

'All I can say for now is that the death does not appear to be from natural causes,' answered a straight-faced Smith.

'I was at home in Etongate all night, with my wife Jill,' answered the builder. 'I then drove here to the meeting this morning.'

'I picked up some documents from Stuart's home yesterday evening. Sarah can confirm that,' said Nick. 'I then spent the night at home, like Jack did.'

'Very good sir,' said Jones, making his normal detailed entries. 'And you Rebecca?'

'I was initially at my parents' home in Yorksbey. I then went to see Maggie, my friend. I stopped there all night, before I came to the meeting.'

'Very good, and you sir?' enquired Jones, nodding at Harry, who appeared to momentarily hesitate.

'I was at home in my apartment in Yorksbey.'

'Can anyone verify that?' asked Smith pointedly.

'Sienna Brownlough,' said a reluctant and blushing Harry, who recognised how this would appear to Rebecca, who jealously turned and looked at him with utter disdain.

'Thank you, that will be all for now,' said Smith. 'I'm afraid the office will be off limits until we've concluded our investigations. So I suggest you decide amongst yourselves if and how the meeting can be re-scheduled.'

'Are you saying that Stuart was found here, in the offices?' asked a rather surprised Nick.

'We are, sir. Strange, wouldn't you agree?'

It Wasn't Me!

Chapter 69 – New Horizons

Charlotte tottered on the extremely high heels of her over-the-knee boots, as she tentatively pulled her wheely suitcase behind her along the platform at Yorksbey Station.

As always, she looked stunning.

The conductor, ignoring a frumpy-looking pensioner in a similar predicament, on her way to a Second Class carriage, smiled at Charlotte, and asked if he could help her with her luggage.

'Well, that's kind of you. I've a reservation in First Class,' replied Charlotte, with one of her own infamous smiles.

The day had an autumnal feel to it, and Charlotte had an elegant white leather raincoat on, to keep out the slightly chilly wind.

'There you go, miss,' said the conductor, as he heaved her suitcase into the overhead storage. 'Have a safe journey.'

'Thank you. You have a nice day,' replied Charlotte, offering him a generous tip.

She settled down in the compartment, putting her earbuds in place, and setting her iPhone to shuffle, as her choice of music took her briefly to another place.

She checked her tickets again on her phone app, to ensure she would pick up the connection at Etongate, for the Cross-Country Train to her destination at Bodmin Parkway station.

She was planning to then get a taxi for the drive to her final port of call at Padstow, where she had arranged to meet Stuart later that evening, at his cruiser.

She had reflected on her discussions with Stuart, and while she'd been initially taken aback by his revelations, she was now content to travel with him to the French Riviera.

Well, at least for now.

It meant that she would be well away from any likely fallout from his sudden departure.

She absentmindedly considered how long the relationship might last. She wasn't sure, but for now it offered her what she often craved: sun, sea, sex, and loads of money.

It was an easy choice in the end to make, albeit she still had her doubts about his rather extreme sex demands, but for now, she was okay with it.

The resolution of Probate for Bart's Estate was also still a while off, and the prospect of some autumn and winter sun would prove a welcome distraction to the likely hum drum life at Edendale.

She closed her eyes as the train suddenly jolted into action, but she immediately opened them as a handsome hunk of a young man slid open the compartment door.

'Would you mind if I joined you?' he gallantly enquired. 'My name's Matthew.'

'Matthew. You certainly can! I'm Charlotte,' she replied. All thoughts of Stuart left her mind, while she hoped and prayed the young man was going *all the way*.

It Wasn't Me!

Chapter 70 – First Impressions

Cliff was slowly riding his Kawasaki along Street Five before turning into Avenue C of the Langham Arch Retail Park, and suddenly saw that the media circus had been forced to re-camp outside the perimeter of Brownlough Developments. PC Perfect had done a good job of ensuring the press and media were now at least conducting themselves in a more reasonable manner.

Cliff nonchalantly pulled up and lifted his visor as he enquired of one of the reporters what was *going down*. Having established what he wanted, he moved off and parked up where he could monitor anything that developed. He pulled out his mobile and dialled CJ.

'Morning, Cliff. How are you?' CJ cheerily answered. Expecting the normal response of, *'You know, another day, same shit.'*

But to his surprise, he didn't get that retort.

'I'm okay Governor, but something's occurred at Brownlough's office.'

Cliff quickly explained to CJ what he had learnt and sought further instructions.

'I don't think you can do much more. See if you can use your charm to get Pat - PC Perfect - to provide anything further and let me know. But otherwise, I guess you can stand down.'

'Well, sir. What do you make of those four?' asked Jones, as he and Smith left the conference room to seek out Dr Stephens for an update, following his arrival.

'They all looked rather taken aback by events. I guess their immediate business plans have been totally thrown into disarray.'

As they made their way back through the reception, Smith was pleased with Perfect's initiative and her apparent crowd control skills.

'Pat has at least given us some wiggle room for when we want to leave,' said a complimentary Jones.

'Yeah. I don't really want to be talking with the media. Well, not just yet.'

As the pair reached the top of the stairs, they saw Dr Stephens come out of the *sex dungeon,* and make his way towards them.

'We must stop meeting like this,' said a grim Stephens.

'I couldn't agree more,' replied an equally ominous Smith. 'Go on then, give us the heads up.'

'To be honest, until I complete the Post Mortem, I'm reluctant to say too much,' said an unhelpful Stephens.

'That's taken as read. As always,' said an ironic Smith. 'But give me something.'

'Looks like a BDSM sex act that got out of hand,' replied a thoughtful Stephens.

'Do you have experience of such matters?' asked an inquisitive and smirking Jones.

Stephens gave him a look that said, '*Don't be a complete fool*,' before actually saying, 'Not as much as you might have, DS Jones.'

It Wasn't Me!

'Come on, boys, less frivolity. Let's get back to the matter in hand,' said Smith, intervening.

'Don't hold me to this, but cause of death appears to be from Asphyxiation.'

'Deliberate or accidental?' asked a probing Smith.

'Now that is definitely the question,' replied a deeply thoughtful Stephens.

'I would prefer to conduct the PM before committing further, but I think for now, if I were you, I would perhaps, *err on the side of caution.*'

'So we'll continue as a suspicious death for now,' added Smith. 'Steven, could you please conclude your PM as soon as possible, and let us know if you find anything that may help us?'

'That goes without saying, Smith.'

'Anything else we should be aware of in the meantime?' asked Jones, with his notebook at the ready.

'Nothing you haven't already witnessed and considered when you observed the body,' replied Stephens.

'Any clues as to who may have been with him?' asked Smith.

'No, but she must be quite a dominatrix,' said Stephens wryly, as he walked back towards the crime scene, leaving the two detectives rather dumfounded.

Chapter 71 – Ah Mrs Brownlough!

'DI Smith. Was Stuart Brownlough murdered?' called out the young reporter as Smith and Jones walked to the car.

Smith looked at her with complete disdain.

'Where does this leave your investigation into the murder of Andrew Kipling?' she continued loudly, to the amusement of the rest of the media scrum.

'Why don't you fuck off and pester someone more worthy of your reporting skills,' whispered Smith to himself as he got in the car.

Perfect came over for instructions, as Smith lowered the car window.

'Perfect, you're doing a good job. Keep them back as you have done. I'll look to get a replacement officer shortly,' said a thankful Smith. 'I'll also get Jones to give you an update if things change. With a bit of luck, the reporters will move on once *Forensics* have finished their business, and they realise they're getting nothing more here.'

'Understood sir,' replied Perfect, as the two detectives drove off in a blaze of camera flashlights from the photographers.

'Where to, Sir?'

'You know where. Mrs Sarah Brownlough's.'

The ten-minute return journey to Stuart Brownlough's home was, as usual, conducted in silence as the two detectives contemplated their next move.

It Wasn't Me!

It was difficult to believe that only a short time ago they were making the same purposeful walk up the large, tarmacked drive.

Jones rang the doorbell and was again confronted by a rather annoyed Sarah.

'What do you want now? Have you found my car?'

'Good Morning, again Mrs Brownlough. I'm afraid we have some rather bad news. May we please come in?' said a severe-looking Smith.

'I guess, if you must,' said Sarah, as she led them into the lounge, where they sat on opposite large sofas.

'It's your husband. He's been found dead,' said Smith, pausing before adding, 'I'm sorry for your loss.' Realising when based upon their earlier conversation, the normal police response to this type of situation was probably inappropriate, but choosing to see how Sarah responded.

She was, however, rather nonplussed.

'Dead! What do you mean, dead?'

'Your husband has been found dead at his *office*,' said Smith evenly. 'In what can only be described as rather suspicious circumstances.'

'Oh.'

'Mrs Brownlough, would you like a Family Liaison Officer to stay with you? I'll allocate PC Patricia Perfect in case you need any assistance at this difficult time,' added Smith, as sympathetically as he could, considering he could see that Sarah appeared rather indifferent to the tragic news, while Jones handed her a card with the details.

'Thank you. Perhaps not for me, but my daughter, Sienna, may require some support.'

'Mrs Brownlough, we understand this is a difficult time for you and your family, especially as your husband, and your..... close *friend* have both died so tragically,' said Smith, now in full police mode. 'Are you aware of a *private room* next to his office?'

'Oh. You mean the sex room?' said a slightly blushing but surprisingly self-assured Sarah. 'Yes, of course I am. There was a time when...'

'A time when, what?' enquired an intrigued Jones.

'A time when we were close, and both enjoyed that sort of thing. But that was long ago. Why do you ask?'

'Mr Brownlough was found there,' replied Smith.

'That'll teach the bastard to act out his sordid BDSM fantasies. I warned him it would be the death of him.'

'Quite,' said Smith, not sure where to look.

'Regarding that, I must ask you something about last night,' continued a persistent Smith.

Suddenly, there was a noise from the kitchen as the back door to the house appeared to open and close.

'Mum, are you there? Where's your car?'

'Sienna, we're through here,' said Sarah calmly.

'Oh. Who's this?'

'Darling, this is DI Smith and DS Jones. I'm afraid they have some sad news.'

'Sad news?' said a rather confused looking Sienna.

It Wasn't Me!

'It's about Daddy. He's been found dead at his office,' said Sarah rather evenly and without much feeling.

'Dead! Daddy's dead?'

'Yes. I'm sorry, Sienna,' said a remorseful Sarah.

'Well, as he wasn't my real father, we won't be shedding too many tears, will we?' added a resolute Sienna, taking Smith and Jones completely by surprise.

'Oh,' said Smith, momentarily unsure how to progress the interview.

'You're already investigating the death of my real father. Andrew Kipling,' added a purposeful and unrepentant Sienna. 'And by all accounts, not getting very far.'

'Oh,' said Smith again. Having not been this lost for words for many a year.

'Well, if there's nothing else?' said Sarah, with confidence, now riding on her daughter's coat tails.

'Just one thing,' said Smith, suddenly regaining some composure. 'Where were you last night, Mrs Brownlough?'

'I was here all night,' replied Sarah. 'You saw me here earlier when you woke me. Why are you asking?'

'It's just to rule you out of our ongoing enquiries.'

'Are you implying I was involved in the death?'

'Not yet. But can anyone corroborate that?' asked Jones.

'I can!' said Sienna. 'We were both here all night. Weren't we Mum?'

Sarah, Smith, and Jones all looked incredulously at Sienna.

'Yes. We were,' said Sarah, recognising that they possibly needed to back one another up, especially in the current circumstances.

'Is that right, Sienna?' asked a probing and doubtful Smith.

'Yes. It is,' said Sienna reassuringly.

'Mmm. If that's the case, Mrs Brownlough, could you please explain why your car is parked outside Brownlough Developments' office?' asked Smith.

'I don't know,' said Sarah honestly. 'I told you earlier it had been stolen.'

'Rather a coincidence, wouldn't you say?' added Jones.

'It might be, but perhaps if you did your job properly, you would find who stole the car, and then maybe someone actually involved in Stuart's death,' said a resolute and increasingly confident Sarah.

'Well, that's all for now,' said Smith, standing up, which took Jones a little by surprise. 'But I think we may well have to ask you *both* some further questions, when we have the results of the Post Mortem.'

Smith eyeballed both women, who were suddenly unable to hold his gaze.

He recognised things were not as they were being portrayed, but he would let them stew for now. He and Jones left Mother and Daughter to console one another, and to consider the validity of their alibis.

It Wasn't Me!

Chapter 72 – That's Good News

CJ and Edee were sitting in the Lounge Bar of the Golf Club – Oscar at their feet - drinking coffee, and discussing their recent find with Earl Hargrove.

'It's great news that you found your copy of the Deeds,' said a thrilled Earl Hargrove. 'The Major will be very relieved.'

'I'll be relieved about what?' asked the Major as he joined them.

'Edee and CJ have found the Deeds, and as CJ suspected, Brownlough's copy was not as it appeared.'

'What do you mean?' asked the Major, looking rather confused.

'There is no right to buy the Golf Club. It was all a hoax. A con by Brownlough.'

'Oh. So we didn't have to worry about anything?' said a relieved, but anxious looking Major.

'Major, I thought you would have been happier?' asked Edee.

'I am, it's just I've been so worried,' replied the Major, now looking more like his old self. 'It's really good news.'

'Can I get you all anything? You're looking very pleased with yourselves,' said Jarvis, as he came over to see what was going on.

'Jarvis. We've some great news. The Golf Club is not going to be built on with houses, and I'll have my usual to celebrate,' said a happy Earl Hargrove.

'Wow. That is good news,' said Jarvis, as he eventually looked and sounded rather pleased. 'Anyone else for a drink to celebrate?'

'No. Edee and I are fine,' said CJ, sensing that the news wasn't received quite as he'd expected.

'Go on then, I'll have a brandy, like his Lordship. Let's celebrate,' said the Major, now seemingly recognising that his club was back in safe hands.

On the large wall mounted TV, a young female news reporter was making an announcement with the subtitle.

Local business man found dead in Yorksbey.

'Quick Jarvis. Turn it up.'

"The police have not confirmed anything, but it would appear local building developer Stuart Brownlough has been found dead at Brownlough Developments' offices in Yorksbey. The events surrounding the death appear to be a mystery, but it comes shortly after the death of local solicitor Andrew Kipling, at the Equinox Festival at Yorksbey Races. There is much speculation, and there are rumours the deaths may be linked. Felicity Feelgood for BBC Look North."

'By Jove, that's a bit of a shock,' exclaimed Earl Hargrove.

'No great loss,' said Jarvis as he wandered off to get the drinks, while turning the sound down on the TV.

'That's odd. What say you, Major?' asked a provocative CJ.

It Wasn't Me!

'What do you mean?'

'Brownlough is found dead just as we find evidence his planned development was nothing more than a scam.'

'I think life will go on as usual. His death will not be mourned by many,' replied a resolute Major. 'I'm just happy we can get back to normal. I wonder if Mr Kipling Snr. is aware of events? I'll have to let him know that CJ has found the original deeds.'

'Edee, I think we should perhaps see what Smith and Jones have found out,' said CJ, about to get up. Suddenly, Masud came through the door to the Lounge.

'Ah, my friends. I hoped I would catch you here,' said a smiling Masud. 'Sabah Alkhayr. Good Morning, to you all.'

'Good Morning, Your Excellency,' replied the gathered throng, who stood in unison as Oscar ran towards the Sheikh before rolling on his back seeking a belly rub.

'James, Madame Songe, and Oscar, I couldn't leave the UK without saying goodbye,' said Masud, as he obliged Oscar, stroking him warmly.

'You're leaving?' asked CJ, curiously.

'Yes, my stay for the Races was most rewarding and enjoyable, but I have pressing business elsewhere.'

'Well, I hope it's not so long before we meet again,' added CJ.

'I agree,' said Masud, as he embraced CJ, before then warmly shaking hands with Edee, Earl Hargrove and then finally the Major.

'Have you heard about Brownlough?' asked a probing CJ.

'A most unfortunate series of events,' added a cool-looking Masud.

'Edee has also found an original copy of the Deeds, and they don't match the copy provided by Brownlough,' stated Earl Hargrove.

'Oh,' said a surprised Masud. 'Another reason for me moving on, then. I no longer have any reason to remain. I'm also sure you're all pleased that the Golf Club will remain, just that, a Golf Club?'

'We certainly are,' replied a smiling and pleased Earl Hargrove.

'Well, I must be going. My private jet awaits me at Leeds Bradford Airport,' said Masud, before adding as he left the club. 'Mae Alsalama. Tashabuk Alsalama. Goodbye. Peace be with you.'

'Goodbye Your Excellency.'

Oscar followed him out of the door before swiftly returning to CJ's side.

'Right Edee, Oscar, are we now going?' asked CJ.

'I think we are,' replied Edee. 'Let's see what Simon and John have got to tell us.'

It Wasn't Me!

Chapter 73 – Re-Evaluation

Smith and Jones were reviewing the large whiteboard on the wall of their office in Yorksbey Police Station.

Jones had added a second column of information for Stuart Brownlough, alongside the one for Andrew Kipling. He had included all the things that he felt were relevant to both cases. Smith was rubbing his chin, which was not a good sign.

'Have you got everything on the board, Jones?'

'I'd like to think so, sir.'

'Are the deaths linked or not?'

'On the face of it you would possibly say not,' said a positive Jones. 'But realistically, they must be linked in some way. Mustn't they?'

'Jones, as is often the case, I agree with you. The problem is that our prime suspect for Kipling's death is now dead himself.'

'Agreed. Plus, we're looking for a man for Kipling's murder, while it would appear that we need to find a woman who last saw Brownlough alive.'

'So Brownlough killed Kipling?'

'Probably,' replied Jones.

'And we're now looking for a woman scorned who sought revenge, by killing Brownlough?'

'Looks like it.'

'But what if Brownlough's death is purely a tragic accident?' posed a thoughtful Smith.

'You mean there's nothing else to find? Brownlough killed Kipling to ensure he didn't say anything about the Deeds, and Brownlough's death was a sordid sex act that just went, accidentally, a bit too far.'

'I'm pretty convinced Peel would like to see it that way,' said Smith wryly.

'So we're looking for a Dominatrix, who last saw Brownlough alive?'

'Could be.'

As the two detectives continued to review the board, Smith's phone rang. It was CJ.

He reluctantly answered, just hoping that the amateur investigator might have a nugget of an idea to assist with the investigation.

'Yes Gray. I gather you've heard?'

'Yes. Felicity Feelgood seemed to sum it up quite well,' replied a smirking CJ.

'Who?'

'The young lass reporting for BBC Look North.'

'Oh. Her!' said a cutting Smith. 'What's she been saying?'

'Like all budding news reporters seeking to gain a reputation, she's looking for a story when perhaps there isn't one.'

'Mmm. She does come across like that.'

'Hi Simon, Edee here, you're on speaker.'

'Hi Edee,' replied a suddenly more cheerful Smith. 'How are you?'

'I'm good. I trust you and John are okay, considering the recent events.? What's your take on things?'

Smith continued to update CJ and Edee about where he and Jones were in their deliberations.

It Wasn't Me!

'Well, you seem to have considered most things,' added CJ. 'Just one observation. You seem to have settled on the suspect's gender for each of the deaths.'

'Yes. What are you driving at?' asked a slightly bewildered Smith.

'Well, sometimes things don't always appear as they seem,' continued CJ.

'Simon, you should always keep an open mind on things,' added Edee. 'Women have been known to dress in morning suits.'

'And are you convinced Brownlough was a straight heterosexual?' said a quizzical CJ.

Smith and Jones suddenly looked at one another, realising the sleuths might have a point.

'Just a thought, Smith. Something for you to consider, and perhaps, as Edee suggested, you should keep an open mind,' said a reflective CJ. 'Keep in touch,' and he ended the call.

'Well, what do you make of that?' asked Jones.

'They're right, and not for the first time. We need to consider all aspects, and not get too focussed on the obvious.'

'But that doesn't mean our thoughts are wrong?'

'No. But we're not much closer to solving things, that's for certain,' added Smith.

Chapter 74 – Post Mortem II

DS Jones put down the phone and turned to his superior.

'Sir. Dr Stephens has asked if we could go and view the body of Stuart Brownlough. He has some more information he feels might be helpful to our enquiries.'

'As always with Stephens, it sounds intriguing,' said Smith. 'I wonder what he's found? Come on then, I guess we should do this as soon as possible; I envisage Peel will also be seeking an update today, so we can also see him while we are in Northallerton.'

With that, the two officers left and headed north. Forty minutes later they entered the Pathology Lab where they found Dr Stephens crudely sewing back the chest cavity of Stuart Brownlough, having concluded his investigation.

'Hello Dr Stephens. Thank you for undertaking such a speedy examination,' said Smith. 'What have you got for us?'

'Hello DI Smith, DS Jones. I thought it best that I struck while the iron was hot. I got the feeling this morning you were under a bit of pressure.'

Smith nodded, acknowledging the pathologist's desire to help, which wasn't always the case.

'It wasn't just that. Peel also put me under a bit of pressure. Apparently, the Chief Constable wants a speedy resolution of the case,' said a downbeat and annoyed Stephens.

'Why am I not surprised?' said a sarcastic Smith.

It Wasn't Me!

'Well, I still have a lot to write up, and the final report won't be finished until tomorrow, but here are the headlines.'

Stephens finished the last of the stitches to Stuart's chest, cut the nylon thread, and took a deep breath.

'As I first thought, the deceased died from Asphyxiation.'

'No surprises there,' replied Jones, already making notes.

'No, not really.'

'Time of death?' asked Smith, seeking to verify any alibis from the likely suspects.

'Between Midnight and 2 am,' replied Stephens. 'The deceased was 10 times over the drink drive limit, but based on the near empty bottle of whisky you saw at the crime scene, that isn't really surprising,' continued Stephens. 'Also, he had large quantities of cocaine in his blood. Enough to nearly kill him.'

'So, was it accidental or a deliberate overdose of booze and drugs?' asked Smith.

'Possibly either, but he did die from asphyxiation, which may or may not have been as a result of the excessive drugs and alcohol. The ball gag obviously restricted breathing through his mouth, and there's some evidence that his nostrils had possibly been held tightly together at some point. But I can't be certain as to when.'

'So it could be an accident, or a premeditated act,' added Smith.

'Correct. There's also evidence of whip marks on the buttocks, the abdomen, and to the penis.'

'Were they before or after death?' asked Jones.

'He was still alive. He was, as you saw, also fully restrained, and by the abrasions to the wrists and ankles, he appeared to have struggled at some point.'

'So in your opinion was it deliberate or accidental suffocation?' asked a searching Smith, having already made up his own mind.

'I deal in facts as you know, but while I can't be 100% sure, if I was pushed on an answer, I would guess he was possibly murdered. But knowing certain coroners' they may prefer to record a verdict of misadventure.'

'You might also like to know that there was semen on his lower abdomen and also smothered over his mask.'

'Was that due to him being masturbated by a female accomplice?' asked a smirking Jones.

Stephens looked over his glasses, with one of his searching stares.

'No Jones. I somehow doubt it.'

'Why are you so sure?' asked a now more serious Jones.

'Because it wasn't *his* semen!'

'Fucking hell!' replied Smith, rubbing his head in his hands.

Just then the double swing doors burst open, and not standing on ceremony, in walked a grumpy-looking Peel,

'From what I can gather from the current evidence, it would appear that Brownlough killed

It Wasn't Me!

Kipling to ensure he didn't blab about the fraudulent copy of the Deeds,' said a confident Peel.

'It appears that way,' said Smith, before being quickly dismissed by Peel.

'It wasn't a question, Smith.'

Peel raised his hand in a condescending manner, to stop any further reply from Smith before he continued.

'It also appears that Brownlough has choked to death during a BDSM sex act that got out of hand, while he was under the influence of excessive alcohol and an overdose of drugs.'

'Possibly,' said Smith.

'Smith, that wasn't a question either,' said an annoyed Peel. 'Based upon my findings, I'm planning to release a statement to the media along those lines in the morning.'

'But sir?'

'No *buts* Smith. The Chief wants these deaths putting to bed, and my evaluation provides a suitable closure to the recent events.'

Smith, Jones, and Stephens all looked at one another rather dumfounded, but recognised that - currently - saying anything else would be futile.

'Kipling's family will have some closure. Plus, I'm pretty convinced, no one really cares about Brownlough's death, other than perhaps the media,' said a determined Peel, as he turned on his heels and marched back out, not waiting for, nor expecting, any response.

C J Meads

Chapter 75 – What Now?

The drive back to Yorksbey gave the two detectives time to reflect on what had occurred.

The pressure was clearly off them with Peel's declaration, but it didn't sit well with Smith. While the hypothesis stated by Peel was plausible, he wasn't convinced it was true.

Gray's suggestion to keep an open mind had been proven correct. It was most likely that the last person to see Brownlough alive or the person that killed him was a man. But maybe there were two people involved. Had Gray considered that?

The two detectives sat predominately in silence. Occasionally Jones was about to speak, but he recognised that his boss wasn't quite ready for listening or talking, despite him having things he felt were worth bouncing off his superior.

As they pulled into the police station carpark, Smith finally spoke up.

'If you want to get off Jones, then please feel free. I'm just going to go over a few things in the office.'

'About the case?'

'Yes.'

'Do you mind if I join you? I'd like to talk over a few thoughts I have.'

'Come on then, let's get a large coffee and have a brainstorming session,' replied Smith, who welcomed the opportunity to clear his head of the numerous thoughts that were swimming around in his mind.

It Wasn't Me!

At Overhear Manor, CJ and Edee were in the master bedroom, also reflecting on recent events. CJ was relaxing, lying back on the white leather chaise longue, which was positioned by the window overlooking the Long Drive. Oscar was at his feet, sleeping soundly. Edee was in the En-Suite, taking a shower and getting ready for bed.

'Do you think the deaths are linked?' called out Edee.

'It would be rather a coincidence if they weren't,' replied a thoughtful CJ.

'I've been thinking,' said Edee, as she looked around the door frame, expecting a cryptic comment from CJ, who only offered a wry smile in return. 'What if there's only one killer, and like with Charlotte, they're setting up another female?'

'I think that's highly likely,' replied CJ. 'The green Tesla being stolen and left at the crime scene to implicate Sarah has all the hallmarks of the original killer.'

'It would seem a strategic move by the killer, especially if they knew that Andrew and Sarah were lovers.'

'Yes. By again seeking to throw the police off the scent, while getting them to look in the wrong direction.'

'So we have someone,' stated CJ.

'A man most likely,' interrupted a mocking Edee.

'A man,' continued CJ. 'A tall man, that has set up women on two occasions, who is closely involved with the *Edendale Project*.'

'There can't be that many with a motive,' added Edee.

'Ah. Motive. You're right Edee, establishing the motive is key to solving this mystery,' acknowledged CJ. 'But I once read there are supposedly four reasons for killing. Fear, Anger, Envy and Desire.'

Smith and Jones were again sitting, looking at the whiteboard. Jones had strategically moved a few things around to allow them to re-focus.

'Aren't we pissing in the wind, sir? I mean, the Super has made it pretty clear what he believed happened.'

'Maybe. But let's do a final review before Peel formally instructs us to close the case,' said an invigorated Smith.

'Okay. If you say so,' said a resigned Jones.

'Let's eliminate the women from our list for the moment,' said Smith. 'But let's not forget about them completely. Passion is often a key emotion when considering murder.'

'I've listed some of the likely suspects who had the opportunity. The *means* for both killings are already established,' stated Jones.

'Okay. As we go through them, let's consider their likely *motive*, as this may be key.'

'So Jones, how many suspects do we have?'

'Eight.'

'Eight!' replied an astonished Smith.

'At least eight. But knowing you, you'll want CJ Gray on the list, which would make nine,' said a smiling Jones.

It Wasn't Me!

'Okay, let's eliminate Gray. Well, for now. Who else have we? Let's be realistic.'

'The Major. We know he threatened Stuart, after the *Edendale Project* was launched at the golf club.'

'We need to check him out. Next,' said Smith, thinking that they possibly needed more coffee, as this was likely to go on for a while. 'Who else involved with the golf club is on the list?'

'Earl Hargrove, and Jarvis would both lose out if the development progressed.'

'What about those involved with the *Edendale Project*? Is there anyone who might benefit from Brownlough's death?' asked Smith.

'Not really, sir. They all want the project to go ahead, so they don't really have any real motive. If anything, they wanted him to be alive.'

'So we can eliminate Harry Tovaine, Nick Banker and Sheikh Twoammie from the list straight away,' confirmed an assured Smith.

'I think so,' agreed Jones. 'Now what about the close family of Andrew Kipling?'

'Mmm. Revenge. That could be a strong motive for killing Brownlough.'

'We need to check on Mr Kipling Snr, to see where he was on the night of the murder. But to be honest, I'm not sure he's a murderer.'

'No. I agree with you, Jones,' said a thoughtful Smith.

'What is it, sir?' asked Jones, who recognised when his boss was about to say something profound.

'What about young Matthew Kipling? His father's been killed. We definitely need to check where he was on the night of Brownlough's murder. That's for certain.'

'Isn't he a bit young to be killing?' asked a rather doubtful Jones.

'The youth of today have rather different agendas, to that in our day,' replied Smith, who was seemingly more convinced this was a suspect worth pursuing. 'I suggest another early start tomorrow may be the order of the day.'

It Wasn't Me!

Chapter 76 – We're Off Where?

'So, who's in the frame, my darling?' asked Edee.

'We both agree, it has to be someone involved with the *Edendale Project*,' replied CJ, who was still considering the potential suspects.

'What about Harry Tovaine then?' asked Edee as she again called out from the shower.

'Nah. I don't think so,' said a dismissive CJ. 'Shall I wash your back?..... or maybe something else?'

'No, thank you. What about Sheikh Twoammie? Surely he must be a possibility?' she added, as she turned off the shower, and again poked her head around the door frame.

'Don't call me Shirley. You know it offends me,' joked CJ. 'But you do look rather sexy, so I'll forgive you this time. Are you sure I can't be of service?'

'Actually, you can. Please pass me the thong on the bed.'

Oscar suddenly jumped up and grabbed the black lacy underwear, looking to play a game.

'Looks like I'm now Knickerless,' said a joking Edee.

'Or more to the point,' said CJ, realising that maybe Oscar had an idea. *Nicholas*.

'Oh,' said Edee, as the penny dropped. 'You mean Nicholas Banker, Stuart's accountant?'

They were suddenly interrupted by Edee's phone ringing on the bedside cabinet.

'Shall I get it?' asked CJ, still contemplating the likely murder suspect, and trying to retrieve Edee's underwear from a very playful Oscar.

'No. I'll get it. You just concentrate on getting my thong back,' said a laughing Edee, as she swept into the bedroom with a towel elegantly draped around her body, and another wrapped around her long ebony hair.

'Hi Charlotte. To what do I owe the pleasure?'

'Hi Edee. I'm at Stuart's cruiser in Padstow, and he *was* due to meet me here,' said a concerned Charlotte, before she was interrupted.

Edee could hear someone in the background, and the smile immediately left her face as Charlotte continued talking to the stranger.

'Oh! What are you doing here? And so soon?'

'Edee I'll ca.....'

'Charlotte. Charlotte! Are you there?'

Edee looked at the phone, but the call had ended.

'What is it?' asked a confused CJ, who was now playfully rolling on the floor with Oscar.

'It's Charlotte. She's in Cornwall, apparently expecting to meet Stuart at his cruiser, but someone has just arrived, and the call ended abruptly.'

'Call her back,' suggested CJ.

Edee pressed the *reply* button.

'It's gone straight to voicemail,' said a worried-looking Edee.

'She doesn't know about Stuart by the sound of things,' said CJ, suddenly wondering who could have arrived.

'What shall we do?' asked a now concerned Edee.

It Wasn't Me!

'I think we need to get to Padstow. PDQ.'

Chapter 77 – A Long Drive!

Having quickly got dressed, CJ and Edee, along with Oscar, were walking along the minstrel gallery when Mrs Wembley met them in her dressing gown, with her hair in curlers.

'What's the commotion, Master James, Madame Edee? Where are you going? You do know it's after midnight?'

'It's okay Mrs Wembley. We need to go to Cornwall, and unfortunately we need to go now,' replied a placating CJ.

'Oh. Are you going to *Pen Wethers*?'

'We may call in while we are down there.'

'Do you want me to come? It's been a while since we stayed down there. I do like your holiday home.'

'It's okay, I think we'll manage,' said CJ, who was keen to get away as soon as possible under the circumstances.

'Shall I make you some sandwiches for the trip, and perhaps a flask of coffee?' continued the fussing Mrs Wembley.

'We'll be fine.'

'What about poor Oscar?'

'It's okay, Mrs Wembley,' said Edee, recognising that a feminine touch may be required. 'I think James and I can manage. I suggest you get back to bed and look forward to a lie in.'

'Lie in?'

'Yes, James and I will be away tomorrow, so you can take it easy.'

It Wasn't Me!

'Oh, Madame Edee, I couldn't do that. Not change a habit of a lifetime.'

CJ smiled, recognising that perhaps Edee still had a little to learn about the running of Overhear Manor.

'Heaven forbid,' said a smiling CJ. 'But you can get back to bed. If we need anything, we can get it on the way.'

'If you're sure, Master James?'

'I'm sure. Goodnight Mrs W. I'm sorry we disturbed you.'

'Goodnight Master James, Madame Edee. Goodbye Oscar,' said a rather crestfallen Mrs Wembley, who was suddenly disappointed at not going on a trip to Cornwall. 'Please let me know when you'll be back.'

'Goodnight Mrs Wembley,' said a smiling Edee, who linked arms with CJ, as they marched down the stairway, Oscar leading the way as always.

'Do we need anything else?' asked Edee, now considering what Mrs Wembley had said.

'Don't you start,' said a sarcastic CJ. 'We've an overnight bag, I'll pick up my Gilet, with Oscar's essentials' and we'll get a flask of water, his food from the kitchen, along with his bowls. Then we're off.'

'Okay. I'll call Cliff while you sort that out,' said Edee.

Cliff instantly answered his phone as it rang.

'What is it Edee? Is the Governor all right?' answered a worried Cliff.

'Yes. He's fine. He's just getting things ready. We're off to Cornwall.'

'Oh, are you?'

'Yes. That's the reason for the call. Could you get down to Padstow Harbour ASAP?'

'Yes. For you and CJ, anything.'

'That's great. As you'll be on your bike, how quickly do you think you can get there?'

'Not long, I would think. I'll call you when I get there.'

'Now don't you go getting any speeding tickets. I know you, and that bike of yours,' said an anxious Edee.

'Okay. I'll crack on then,' said a cheery Cliff.

'Don't you want to know what it's about?' added a slightly confused Edee.

'Not really. I'm sure the Governor will let me know when I get there, but it's no doubt something to do with the recent murders.'

CJ quickly looked across at the sleeping Edee. She looked beautiful as always, despite her head being at rather an awkward angle, caused by leaning against the car window.

He promptly returned his gaze to the motorway ahead. Despite the early hour, there was as always, more traffic on the road than he expected, but the Audi RS6 had made good progress with CJ at the wheel.

Oscar briefly woke from dozing in his basket on the back seat and put his chin on CJ's shoulder.

'Okay boy,' he whispered. 'Just one treat. Now lie down.'

It Wasn't Me!

CJ pulled a treat from his pocket and Oscar wolfed it down, but didn't move. 'One more and that's it.'

Oscar content, then resumed dozing, while CJ went back to aimlessly considering the case, as the miles and time passed.

The original expected satnav journey time of just over 6 hours for the 360 mile journey was receding at a rate of knots, as CJ exceeded the speed limits whenever it was possible, and on numerous occasions, was exceeding 100 mph. He, however, kept an eye out for the speed cameras en route, especially on the managed motorways of the M1, M42 and M5.

CJ's phone rang, and the car's display showed it was Cliff. Edee stretched her arms and slowly opened her eyes

'Hi Cliff, how goes it? You're on speaker.'

'Hello Governor, Edee. I'm okay. I've just parked up in Padstow, near the harbour.'

'Bloody Hell! Did you fly down, rather than just ride your bike?' said a surprised CJ.

'No. but the bike can reach over 200 mph, as you're well aware. Anyhow, your instructions, sir?'

'We're worried that the killer may be after Charlotte. We don't understand why, but we believe she's in Padstow, and was due to meet Stuart at his cruiser.'

'Okay, I'll take a look around, but it's all quiet here.'

'Great. Keep us posted. Worst case, we should be there in less than a couple of hours. Bye Cliff.'

'Bye.'

'Apparently no Charlotte. Is that a good sign or a bad sign?' asked a sleepy Edee.

'Let's decide that when Cliff has done a quick recce,' replied CJ, putting his foot down again as they left the M5 motorway south of Exeter, and joined the dual carriageway of the A30.

It Wasn't Me!

Chapter 78 – Another Long Drive

Smith pulled up outside Jones' home to find him already waiting on the pavement. He was studiously looking between his notebook and a list.

'Morning, sir. I've something interesting to tell you,' he said, as he got into the passenger seat.

'Good Morning, Jones. What is it?'

'I've been going through the list that Audrey Templeton gave me. You'll be surprised who's on it.'

'Let me guess. Matthew Kipling?'

'In one. He's not down as an employee, but he's on the list from a couple of years ago,' added Jones.

'Mmm. That's odd. Let's give Ms Templeton a call.'

'It's a bit early isn't it sir?' said a considerate Jones.

'Murder investigations don't recognise the hour of the day. You should know that.'

Audrey Templeton, surprisingly, picked up on the second ring.

'Good Morning, Ms Templeton. I'm sorry to call you so early. It's DI Smith.'

'Oh. Good Morning, DI Smith. That's alright. I've been struggling to sleep since.... Mr Brownlough was found dead.'

'That's rather understandable,' replied for once a rather caring Smith. 'It's just a quick question. I'm sure you can easily answer.'

'Go on.'

'We note that Matthew Kipling is on the list you gave DS Jones. But he surely doesn't work for Brownlough Developments?'

'No, you're quite right. His father asked if he could do his *Work Experience* in the office, and it was arranged. I think he enjoyed the time here. Stuart, I mean Mr Brownlough, liked the boy, and they got on well.'

'Oh, did they now?' replied Smith disdainfully.

'Yes. Matthew has visited the offices on quite a few occasions since then.'

'So he had access to the keypad entry system and knew the number?'

'Oh yes. It's the year Mr Brownlough was born. He kept it simple, so he could easily remember it.'

'Ms Templeton, you've been very helpful. Thank you for your time, and again, I'm sorry I've disturbed you so early.'

'That's alright. Are you any closer to solving how he died?'

'I think we might be,' said a thoughtful Smith. 'Goodbye.'

'Goodbye DI Smith.'

Jones looked across at Smith. 'Fuel for the Fire?'

'Yes Jones, it certainly is.'

Shortly, they pulled up outside the Kipling home, and the two officers again walked up the gravel driveway. There were no lights on, and no obvious signs of activity.

Jones rang the doorbell, and after quite a while, a sleepy-looking Lucy Kipling answered the door.

It Wasn't Me!

'Hello. What do you two want now? You do know what time it is?'

'Good Morning, Mrs Kipling. We do know the time, and we're sorry to trouble you so early, but we would like a word with Matthew,' replied a sarcastic Smith.

'What's it about?' asked a concerned Lucy.

'If we could, please speak to Matthew. It's regarding the death of Stuart Brownlough.'

'Well, I'm afraid you can't.'

'Mrs Kipling, I advise you not to obstruct us in carrying out our duties,' said a forceful Smith.

'You can't, because he's not here.'

'Oh,' said Smith, rather taken aback. 'Where is he then?'

'He's in Oxford, or he had better be. It's *Freshers' week.*'

'Ah. Of course. He's starting Uni,' said Jones.

'Could you please give us his Oxford address and his phone number? We do need to speak with him, to eliminate him from our enquiries.'

Lucy fetched a piece of paper with the details, and Jones quickly made a note of them.

'Mrs Kipling, could you please tell us where Matthew was on the night Stuart Brownlough died?' asked an enquiring Smith.

'He was out with his mates. Having a last drink before they all went their separate ways to university.'

'What time did he get home?' asked Jones, his notebook at the ready.

'It was 2.30 am. I distinctly remember, as he woke me up. He was rather the worse for wear, and like most drunks, rather loud, albeit apologetic, when he got home.'

'Thank you Mrs Kipling. You've been most helpful.'

'Is there a problem?' she worryingly asked.

'Perhaps,' replied Smith. 'I think we still need to urgently speak to your son.'

'Oh,' said an anxious Lucy, as she abruptly shut the door, sensing she needed to ring her son as a matter of urgency.

'Goodbye Mrs Kipling,' said a rather dumbstruck Smith, as they turned and walked back to the car.

'I take it we're off to Oxford?'

'We certainly are, Jones. We most certainly are.'

It Wasn't Me!

Chapter 79 – A Safe Harbour

The pitch black of the night sky was slowly turning a deep blue as dawn approached, with the horizon in the east over *Rock* starting to lighten.

CJ's phone pinged with a message notification.

He handed the phone to Edee, who read out the message. 'It's from Cliff.'

Can't talk
Charlotte's with a man in the Jolly Rodger
Will keep you updated when I can.

'That's odd,' said CJ. 'I wonder who she's with?'

'I hope it's not the killer.'

'Me too, but I think it might be. Check out the *Jolly Rodger* on Google. We're not far from Padstow now.'

The wide dual carriageway of the A30 had long been replaced with tight, narrow roads on the approach to Padstow. Fortunately, it was still early and there were few vehicles on the road. CJ was, however, still frustrated by those they encountered.

Edee had learnt to accept CJ's impatience with slow drivers. She had a similar trait, but today, even she was at times hanging on for dear life, as he took what could only be called *high-speed risks.*

'Nothing for *Jolly Rodger*. No pub or anything similar. '

'That's odd,' said CJ.

'What if it's the boat's name?' suggested Edee.

'Good thinking. It's the type of name Brownlough might adopt.'

CJ turned the Audi off the A389 and took the B3276 down towards the harbour, taking the sweeping curves rather too fast for the conditions.

'Edee, try Cliff.'

'No answer. His phone has gone straight to voicemail.'

'That's not a good sign.'

At the bottom of the hill, CJ turned the steering wheel sharply left to negotiate the hairpin bend and sped on towards the harbour, passing *Rick Stein's Chip Shop* on the right.

He pulled up to an abrupt halt outside the *Old Custom House*, and looked to abandon the car in a disabled parking bay, as there was no one about.

The picturesque harbour with its quaint and much photographed buildings and boats was quiet, with only a few people going about their early morning work. It was difficult to imagine that shortly it would become the bustling holiday resort, full of tourists.

'No sign of Cliff,' said Edee, as she eagerly sought out their friend.

'Edee, please hand me that blouse that Charlotte borrowed,' said CJ, as he got out of the car and opened the rear door.

Oscar jumped out and quickly relieved himself.

'Here, boy,' said CJ, as he offered the blouse up to Oscar's nose. 'Go find!'

Oscar set off, nose down, tail up, sniffing profusely, with CJ and Edee in hot pursuit, but Edee was struggling to keep up in her high heels.

It Wasn't Me!

'Wait for me,' she cried.

'Edee, keep up, and keep a look out for a boat called the *Jolly Rodger*.'

Oscar raced down the link span walkway that led from the harbour quay wall to the floating pontoons where the boats and yachts were moored.

'The *Jolly Rodger!*' shouted Edee, pointing at a modest 55 ft cruiser.

As they reached it, it was pretty evident there was no one on board.

'That's odd,' said a surprised Edee.

Oscar though, did not stop at the *Jolly Rodger*, but carried on his search, to what was a rather more substantial, and impressive 120 ft Luxury Motor Yacht, *The Arabian Prince,* which was making ready for departure.

Oscar leapt from the pontoon onto the large seating area at the rear of the yacht and ran into the saloon cabin.

'Oscar, wait,' yelled CJ, but for once, the obedient dog ignored his master.

CJ and Edee finally caught him up and looked searchingly into the yacht.

They were surprisingly confronted by a relaxed Sheikh Twoammie, dressed unusually in traditional sailing attire.

'Ah, James, my friend, Madame Songe, a pleasant surprise as always,' said Masud gracefully.

CJ and Edee looked at each other, puzzled, and rather worried by the turn of events.

'I thought you'd flown out of the country?'

'I have. Officially,' said a smiling Masud.

'Welcome aboard,' he continued. 'Please join Oscar in the saloon. We are about to get underway. We have to go. It's high tide.'

'Do we have a choice?' asked CJ.

'Everyone has choices, my friend, but in this instance, I suggest you don't,' said Masud, as he pulled a revolver from his belt.

'Oh,' said an anxious Edee.

'Have you seen Charlotte? We're concerned about her wellbeing. Perhaps even more so now,' said CJ.

'Ah. Charlotte. A very enterprising and resourceful woman,' said Masud. 'A woman after my own heart.'

'Precisely,' said Edee. 'But have you seen her? And more to the point, is she safe, and... alive?'

Oscar suddenly bolted back from inside the saloon. He was clearly in a very excitable mood. He ran towards CJ, and then immediately back into the cabin, encouraging his master to join him.

'I think Oscar wants to show you something,' said Masud, gesturing to CJ and Edee to follow him.

They both stepped cautiously aboard the yacht, and they both worryingly noticed a tarpaulin on the lower rear deck, which looked very body shaped in appearance.

They warily entered the saloon, fearful of what they might find, but were surprised by what they saw.

Alongside Oscar, on one of the large luxurious couches, was Charlotte.

'Charlotte. Are you okay?' asked a clearly relieved Edee.

'I'm okay.'

It Wasn't Me!

'That's good. Let's hope it stays that way,' added a worried CJ. 'Have you seen Cliff? We sent him to rescue you.'

'Cliff *was* here earlier, but he's no longer with us,' said Charlotte.

'Please take a seat. Would you care for some refreshments? Breakfast maybe?' asked Masud.

CJ and Edee rather reluctantly sat down opposite Charlotte, who had been joined by Masud, while Oscar had decided that lying with his master was possibly the best option.

'As we appear to be a captive audience, I might as well have a cappuccino,' said a reluctant CJ.

'And perhaps, a *pain au chocolat?*' added a hesitant Edee, also unsure as to what had, or was about to happen next.

'Aziz. If you please,' said Masud, gesturing to the steward, who was preparing a buffet breakfast.

Edee finally summoned up enough courage and suspiciously asked, 'Did you kill Stuart Brownlough?' fearing the likely response.

'No. That was a more unscrupulous young man,' replied Masud.

Chapter 80 – Oxford

Despite numerous attempts to contact Matthew by phone, none was successful. The calls immediately went to voicemail.

'Keep trying, Jones, but it looks like we'll have to go all the way to Oxford.'

'Had you anything else on today?'

'A detective police officer always has things to do, but for now, this is the most pressing for us.'

'Do you think Matthew killed Brownlough?'

'Based upon the information we have to date, he might well have,' answered Smith. 'He has the means, and a motive, but as for opportunity, this question remains. Where was he on the night of Brownlough's murder?'

'If we knew that for certain, our case might just be solved,' replied a thoughtful Jones.

It Wasn't Me!

CHAPTER 81 – WAS THIS WHAT HAPPENED?

CJ contemplated Masud's denial. 'If it wasn't you, then who was it?' asked CJ, looking at Masud, but having perhaps already come to a likely conclusion.

'I think we need to recap recent events to establish what has occurred,' replied an assured Masud.

The steward politely offered CJ and Edee their refreshments and placed a bowl of water on the floor for Oscar.

'Thank You,' they replied, while Oscar carried on dozing.

'Pray continue Masud. I'm intrigued,' said CJ.

'Yes, go on Masud. I would also like to know the full story,' said Charlotte, clearly aware of many things, but not all of what had occurred.

'I think between us, we have all the pieces of the jigsaw, some more than others. I take it you're aware of most things, up until the murder of Andrew Kipling?' continued Masud.

CJ and Edee nodded in agreement.

'Did you know I'd agreed to help fund the *Edendale Project* and had transferred £35 million to a joint account to buy the Golf Club?' asked Masud.

'Wow! No,' replied a surprised CJ. 'So there's a lot of money at stake?'

'A lot of *my* money. So when I thought back over events, things eventually started to become clearer. But like most of us at the time, I couldn't understand why Andrew was killed. But we were obviously more concerned about Charlotte, who was arrested for the crime,' said Masud. 'Especially as I couldn't understand what would be her motive.'

'No. Neither could we,' added Edee.

'When Charlotte was suddenly called away from the Winners' Enclosure, it seemed rather strange, but knowing Charlotte, not unusual. I did, however, notice that Stuart didn't join us there, which did seem slightly odd in the circumstances.'

'I admit that when I let slip we'd found our copy of the Deeds, Andrew did appear to be getting nervous,' added CJ. 'I assume that Stuart also got worried that Andrew might lose his nerve regarding his involvement in producing the fake Deeds. He then decided he couldn't afford for Andrew to say anything, so made the decision to kill him.'

'That's my assessment also,' said Charlotte. 'If the deal failed because Andrew got cold feet about the false document, then there was likely to be no money to keep Brownlough Developments afloat. Stuart was therefore desperate for Masud's money for the development to go ahead.'

'When Stuart messaged me, I went straight to the stables,' added Charlotte.

'Yes. The killer wanted someone to take the blame for the murder. Deflecting all suspicion from them,' added Masud. 'They deleted most of the calls and messages from the phone and then sent Charlotte the incriminating message.'

'They then left the phone on Andrew to implicate her,' said CJ. 'Hoping the police would think she committed the murder when she and the body were found together.'

It Wasn't Me!

'Correct,' said Masud.

'Luckily CJ's checking of the CCTV, and the results of the Post Mortem, proved Charlotte couldn't have done it,' added Edee.

'Yes. I'm most grateful to you both for believing me when I said I didn't do it. Not like some,' said an extremely thankful Charlotte.

'I then had my first piece of good fortune,' said Masud. 'It was when you asked RSM Ledger – Cliff - to get involved in keeping an eye on Stuart.'

'What do you mean?' asked CJ.

'I have to admit that I asked Cliff to do a bit of moonlighting for me,' replied a contrite Masud. 'Following our chat at the races, you did say he was his own man.'

'That's true,' admitted CJ. 'So he was also keeping you informed of Stuart's movements?'

'Yes, and as you know, his army skills have made him very resourceful, observant, plus an accomplished killer.'

'He is that,' said CJ.

'So I believed Stuart killed Andrew, especially when Charlotte advised me of his plan.'

'Stuart's plan?' asked a bemused Edee.

'As Cliff no doubt told you, Charlotte and Stuart met up at the Watermill Arms after she was released,' added Masud.

'Stuart told me that he'd had his phone stolen, and he thought I'd actually committed the murder,' said an indignant Charlotte. 'But he then told me that he was never going to go ahead with the *Edendale*

Project. It was a complete scam just to get Masud's money.'

'You see, Charlotte then told me this,' said Masud. 'And he wasn't going to get away with that.'

'I agreed to go away with Stuart. What had I to lose?' added Charlotte. 'I didn't know what was about to happen though, and I left for Padstow by train the next morning, planning to meet Stuart on his boat.'

Charlotte, at this point, looked down at her feet, clearly regretting her actions.

'Cliff subsequently followed Stuart back to the office,' said Masud.

'We're aware of that. Cliff messaged us at midnight,' said a thoughtful CJ. 'And I assume he also told you.'

'He did. I wanted my money back. That was for certain. And I was going to make sure I got it, at whatever cost,' said a now rather evil looking Masud.

'So you killed Stuart and then went after Charlotte? When she called us, unfortunately for you, we sent Cliff looking for her, but he found you, and you killed him to shut him up,' stated Edee, looking daggers at Masud.

'Madame Songe, you do have a furtive imagination. I guess that comes from working so long with James.'

CJ looked at Edee, smiled and shrugged his shoulders. 'I guess he may have a point.'

Edee playfully punched CJ on the upper arm. 'You don't have to agree with him.'

It Wasn't Me!

'No, I didn't kill Stuart. That was a man with ice in his veins.'

'You can't mean you got Cliff to murder Stuart?' said a startled Edee. 'And then you killed him.'

'No. Cliff has higher morals than that. I think he would only commit the ultimate crime under orders from one man, and you know who that is.'

Edee immediately glanced at CJ, who returned her look, and they held hands. But they both already knew and accepted the unbreakable bond between Cliff and CJ.

'No, Stuart's killer did come to Padstow with the intention of killing Charlotte,' said Masud, looking fondly towards Charlotte, who looked back with deep affection.

'So who did kill Stuart?' asked Edee.

Chapter 82 – Revelations?

CJ again contemplated Masud's denial. 'As it wasn't you, then I can only assume it was Nick Banker,' stated CJ, looking directly at Masud for some acknowledgement or confirmation.

'You're correct, my friend,' replied Masud. 'But when and how did you come to that conclusion?'

'Only just now. I can't be sure, but he seems the most obvious person, based upon the available facts. But to be honest, even now I'm not totally confident as to the full circumstances and his involvement.'

'No. I'm not surprised. It also took me a while to fully figure out what was going on, and only a short time ago did the picture fully develop.

'Previously, when RSM Leger trailed Stuart to the pub, he also saw Nick enter.'

'Yes, Stuart and I saw him at the pub. I now assume he overheard us discussing our plans,' said Charlotte, piecing together the things she now knew.

'That was when Nick possibly realised that he wasn't going to get any benefit from the deal, and he wasn't as close to Stuart as he'd thought, or hoped.'

'Cliff also observed Nick going to the Brownlough Developments' office, in the green Tesla which he left at the scene, to again seek to throw suspicion on someone else. This time Sarah Brownlough.'

'I take it that Nick had access to the office, and because he loved Stuart, being a homosexual, he tried to seduce him,' suggested CJ. 'But when it didn't

It Wasn't Me!

work, he was enraged, and killed him in one final sordid sex act.'

Edee looked at CJ sideways. 'You didn't say anything to me about Nick being a homosexual?'

'Call it intuition,' said a smiling CJ.

'I thought that was purely associated with *females*,' said a smiling Charlotte.

'That's correct,' said an assured Masud. 'Nick killed Stuart out of *anger.*'

'How are you so certain?' asked a slightly confused Edee.

'You see Madame Songe, once these things started to fall into place in my mind, it could only be Nick,' said Masud.

'When Charlotte had absentmindedly walked off to the stables on the day of the races, I remembered Nick returning looking furtive and anxious, looking continually over his shoulder which, at the time, I didn't consider relevant. But it was.'

'He had committed Andrew's murder,' said CJ.

'To shut him up,' said Charlotte.

'Yes. To stop Andrew talking about falsifying documents,' said Masud. 'But I couldn't be certain if he did this on his own behalf, or under instruction from Stuart. You see, I believe Nick would do anything for his *friend.*'

'So Andrew was killed out of *fear*. In case the truth about the Deeds came out,' added CJ. 'Nick also saw it as an opportunity to remove Charlotte from the equation. She had eased her way into Stuart's affections and distracted him from Nick. Something that must have eaten away at him.'

'Ah, so he set me up?' said a clearly dumfounded Charlotte.

'Then the morning after Stuart's death, and realising where Charlotte was, I made a new plan,' said Masud. 'I decided to follow her, as I thought that was where Nick would head to next.'

'But you left the country?' replied Edee.

'As I said earlier, officially, yes. But private jets are not subject to the same security scrutiny that is observed on scheduled airlines. My PA left with a tall man in Arabic robes. That was officially me.'

'So, to all intents and purposes, you're not here?' said CJ.

'You're correct.'

'But why do that?' asked Edee.

'So he couldn't be implicated in anything that occurs or has occurred,' said CJ, gently shaking his head, and smiling in realisation of what had now happened.

'So how did you get here?' asked Edee.

'Cliff gave me a lift on his bike. He's an assured motor cyclist. But I suggest you don't ride pillion with him, especially if you are of a nervous disposition,' laughed Masud.

'I take it your yacht has been here for a while?' asked CJ.

'I guess another piece of good fortune, that was for once in my favour. I'd planned to visit here while I was in the UK. I remembered long ago, when you told me how beautiful the area was, and that it was one of your favourite places to relax. I then arranged

It Wasn't Me!

to travel on to Monaco. It was pure chance that Stuart also had his cruiser moored here.'

'That was very fortunate,' added CJ.

'Yes. I also had to convince the Harbour Master to allow me to moor here. This yacht is far too big to be allowed here normally. But money has a great way of convincing people to consider alternative options,' said a smiling Masud.

'But where's Cliff, and why didn't he pick up my call?' asked a puzzled Edee.

The Yacht was now slowly sailing through the open harbour gates, and it turned slowly to port into the River Camel estuary. On the harbour wall, sitting on his bike, was Cliff, who nonchalantly raised a finger to his head, saluting in acknowledgment of the onlookers.

'Ah. Cliff. Such a true and honest man. But I had to be sure about any potential loose ends. So I persuaded him to drop his phone into the harbour. I didn't want him to make any silly or unnecessary calls,' said Masud sarcastically.

'We need to leave now, only at high tide are boats allowed in and out of the harbour,' said Masud. 'Aziz, please ask the Captain to slowly make way towards *Doom Bar*, but to go no further for now.

'I gambled on Nick doing exactly what Stuart had planned. To take the money for himself, and sail off into the sunset, or in this case, the sunrise,' continued Masud, now rather serious.

'Do you think he planned to do that?' asked a quizzical Edee.

'I know he did.'

'How's that?' asked a rather confused Edee.

'Because Nick came to kill Charlotte. Kill her out of *envy*.'

'So that's who Cliff saw in the *Jolly Rodger* with Charlotte?' said Edee.

'Yes, my dear, it was.'

'Luckily, Cliff and Masud came along. I think they saved my life,' said a clearly relieved Charlotte. 'I'm convinced Nick would have killed me.'

'You see Madame Songe, once Nick was confronted by Cliff and me, he had no alternative but to confess everything. He couldn't unburden his soul quick enough, once Cliff had a gun pointed at his head.

'He was, as Cliff succinctly put it, "*shaking like a shitting dog.*" He squealed, like the pig he was.'

'But surely Cliff didn't kill him?' said a troubled and alarmed Edee.

Masud broke the silence. 'No, and Nick was desperate to save his skin. So I first got him to transfer the money - that he and Stuart had taken from the escrow account - back to my bank.

'I then encouraged him to tell the full story of the crimes he had committed and how he carried them out. Which I have recorded here,' said a resolute Masud, as he showed them a USB memory stick.

'So where's Nick now?' asked Edee.

'Nick's dead. He's lying on the lower deck under that tarpaulin,' said a solemn CJ. 'Killed out of *a desire* for revenge.'

'What!' said Edee.

It Wasn't Me!

'Yes, my dear. No one crosses Sheikh Twoammie and gets away with it.'

'So why not just give the evidence to the police and let them deal with it?' asked Edee.

'Madame Songe, for such a worldly wise woman, you do at times, show a wonderful innocence.'

'Islamic justice is rather more, shall we say, summary,' added CJ, understanding that western culture, and standards, aren't always shared by others around the world.

'Summary Justice, I think is about right,' added Masud. 'While I recognise that UK law is possibly one of the fairest systems in the world, their justice system is not in accordance with Islamic law.

'I'm not totally confident that Nick would have been found guilty in a UK court of law. Some *smart alec* lawyer might have got him off because the confession was obtained under duress. I couldn't risk that.

'And even if he was found guilty, what would be the judgement? A life sentence? Where he might be out on parole in 15 years? That's not in keeping with the crimes he committed.

'Fraud, extortion, and two brutal premeditated murders, I believe, required appropriate Muslim retribution.'

'An eye for an eye, and a tooth for a tooth?' said a stern but ironic CJ.

'Exactly, my friend. Nick had a little accident earlier. His body will now decompose in the Atlantic ocean, hopefully, never to be found.'

'The perfect crime?' said a reflective Edee.

'No. The perfect justice,' said Masud. 'But let's not dwell further on morbid things.'

'Let's not,' said a now more cheery Charlotte.

CJ and Edee took a few moments to take in the full revelations, but possibly understood Masud's motives, and struggled to argue with them.

Eventually Edee spoke, breaking the awkward silence.

'So Charlotte, what are your plans now?' already suspecting what the answer would be.

'Well, I was planning to go to the French Riviera, and Masud has now kindly offered to give me a lift. So I'm going to take him up on his generous offer of a trip to Monaco, and I hope to show my appreciation on the way,' said Charlotte, as she kissed a now blushing Masud on the cheek.

'Travelling, Charlotte style,' said Edee, smiling as she squeezed CJ's hand.

'What about us?'

'Ah yes. What about you two?' said a thoughtful Masud. 'The police, I think, have already decided on what they felt occurred. So what's to be gained by further action? The case will be closed, and without a body, or anyone to report Nick missing, what will happen?

'Nothing, so I think you two can go. I think a little dinghy ride may be the order of the day.'

'Dinghy ride?' enquired Edee.

'We're coming up to *Doom Bar*. A fitting place to set you free, and the tide should take you back towards *Daymer Bay*,' said Masud, pointing starboard towards the beach.

It Wasn't Me!

'My old hunting ground,' said CJ. 'I know it well.'

Oscar raised his head, recognising that it was possibly time to move.

'Just one thing, my friends, before you go free. Just pop your phones over the side. I wouldn't want to give you the opportunity to feel some remorse and consider calling the police. Well, not until I'm in International Waters.'

Chapter 83 – Where Were You?

Smith and Jones were walking in the college quadrangle, having established from the porter where they could find Matthew Kipling.

The sun was shining brightly, and the grounds looked wonderful.

'Did you go to Uni Jones?' enquired Smith.

'Nothing as grand as this. Northumbria University. I enjoyed it, got 2:1 degree. What about you?'

'University of life for me, and a long career in policing, has held me in good stead.'

'Ah, who's this approaching? It looks like our young suspect.'

'Hello Matthew.'

'Oh. Hello,' said a rather stunned Matthew. 'You're a long way from home.'

'Have you got a moment? We just want to ask you a couple of questions.'

'Yes. Of course. I've nothing to hide. Have you solved the suspicious deaths?' he said more confidently, having regained some composure.

'Where were you on the night Stuart Brownlough died, and more importantly between midnight and 2 am?' asked Smith.

'Oh, that's easy. I thought it was going to be a difficult question. I was out getting pissed with my mates before we all left for Uni. We had some drinks around Yorksbey, then about midnight we got Uber taxis to Etongate. We went to the new nightclub in

It Wasn't Me!

town. We then left about 2 am in another taxi. I got home about half-past two.'

Smith and Jones looked at each other, recognising their investigation was coming to an end.

'I had a terrible hangover the next day, but I met a wonderful woman on the train. I don't know if you know her or not. Charlotte Tate.'

'Oh yes. We know Charlotte.'

'She showed me a great time and gave me a wonderful bit of advice.'

'And what would that be?' enquired Smith.

'*Life is for Living.* Live it to the full. Seize the day - *Carpe diem* – by taking opportunities when they occur.'

'That definitely sounds like Charlotte.'

Meanwhile, two hundred and twelve miles north, Peel had convened a press conference. Or more to the point, he was delivering a press statement.

"Thank you all for coming at short notice.

I felt it appropriate that I updated you all as soon as possible regarding the recent suspicious deaths in Yorksbey."

The TV cameras were rolling, the digital cameras were flashing, with Felicity Feelgood up front and centre with her microphone.

"Due to speedy and efficient police investigations, I'm pleased to confirm the circumstances around the tragic deaths.

Mr Andrew Kipling was brutally murdered by Mr Stuart Brownlough, to prevent a fraudulent activity from coming to light regarding the proposed

Edendale Project. Unfortunately, Stuart Brownlough has subsequently died of a suspected alcohol and drug overdose.

As you will appreciate, this is a sad and difficult time for the family and friends of both the deceased. I therefore ask that you give them time and space to come to terms with their grief, and I hope you will respect their privacy at this challenging time.

Thank You."

Felicity sprang into action.

'Superintendent Peel, is it true Stuart Brownlough was engaged in BDSM Sex activities when he died?'

'No comment,' said Peel as he quickly turned and hurried back into the police station, perhaps now regretting calling the press conference.

'Is it true that DI Smith was taken off the case?' she stubbornly continued.

Peel continued, mumbling to himself, 'Why don't you fuck off, and pester someone that deserves your journalistic prowess.'

'I take it that's another, No Comment.'

It Wasn't Me!

Chapter 84 – A Dawn Beach Walk

The dinghy with CJ, Edee, and Oscar was slowly floating towards the beach. They were contemplating quietly what had occurred, and now more importantly, how they were going to get out of the dinghy without getting too wet.

CJ spoke up. 'Being the gallant gentleman I am, I'll get my feet wet for the love of my life.'

'My *Knight in Shining Armour,* as always,' replied a thankful Edee.

As the dinghy hit the beach, Oscar jumped out, and ran straight for the dry sand, vigorously shaking the water from his coat.

Oscar looked back as CJ ungainly got out of the dinghy and passed his shoes and socks to Edee to hold, while he picked her up and carried her to him on the dry sand.

'There you go, my darling. No wet feet for you.'

'Thank you. Very good. But how am I going to walk in these heels on the sand?'

CJ laughed, before adding, 'I suggest bare foot like me.'

Edee threw his shoes at him, which missed, but Oscar ran off with one of them, looking to be chased and to have some fun. Meanwhile Edee ungracefully hopping, took off her own shoes.

She then linked arms with CJ, and they walked off towards the village of *Rock*, the early dawn sun rising over *Brea Hill,* making a wonderful vista.

'How are we going to get the car back?' asked Edee.

'We can get the passenger ferry from *Rock* to *Padstow*. We should be there in about thirty minutes at a steady walk.'

'We're not in a hurry, are we?' she enquired.

'No. Why do you ask?'

'I'm just appreciating *You, Me and Oscar*,' replied Edee. 'Life is for Living. Let's live life to the full.'

'How about we spend a few days at *Pen Wethers*?' asked CJ. 'I would like to show you why I love this part of the world.'

'I would really like that,' replied Edee, as she hugged him tight and kissed him.

Oscar – as normal - was already racing about the beach, relishing the freedom it offered.

It Wasn't Me!

Epilogue

Father and daughter were on a Zoom call. CJ, for once, decided it was possibly appropriate, rather than their normal quick phone call, or WhatsApp.

'So, it sounds like Charlotte has been up to her old tricks,' said Jemima.

'Yes, it sure does,' replied CJ. 'She does seem to attract controversy.'

'Or seeks the attention of *Bad Boys*?'

'Perhaps.'

'So, how did you feel about Sheikh Twoammie's summary justice?'

'To be honest Jem, I feel that in the circumstances, it was possibly reasonable, but don't say anything about this to anyone. As far as the police are concerned, both the cases are closed.'

'From what you've said, I'm struggling to find a reason to disagree with you. How does Edee feel about it?'

'I think she is rather sanguine. I guess it's her gallic upbringing.'

'So, Nick Banker secretly loved Stuart Brownlough, and his devotion wasn't reciprocated.'

'That's about the top and bottom of it. It's not for the first time that unrequited love resulted in tragedy. This time, though, resulting in two deaths,' replied CJ sardonically.

'I guess everyone at the Golf Club is happy, though? Including you.'

'Yes. I'm not sure what would have happened if Brownlough had been serious about the development. But all's well that ends well.'

'Earl Hargrove and The Major must be over the moon?'

'Oh, their joy was short-lived. They soon forgot about the issues. They were more interested in just playing golf,' laughed CJ.

'What about Harry Tovaine? Will his business survive?' enquired Jemima.

'I gather that Sienna has asked Sarah if she'll help bail him out, with some of the life assurance money she'll receive on Brownlough's life.'

'That's good. It would have been a shame if his business had gone bust.'

'I also think Masud was impressed by his work. I think he might actually look to do a legitimate development in the UK, and use Harry for the architectural design.'

'Oh, that's positive,' replied Jemima, before adding. 'How was your stay at *Pen Wethers?*'

'Edee loved it. She loves the area as much as we do.'

'I must get Marcus to take Emmy and me for a holiday. It's been years since I visited.'

'Talking of Architects and Marcus. How is he?' asked CJ, dreading the possible answer.

'He's good,' replied Jemima, recognising that her father was fishing.

At that moment, Edee came into the Study with Oscar, who immediately jumped on CJ's lap, as he recognised Jemima's voice.

It Wasn't Me!

Edee leant over CJ's shoulder. 'Hi Jem. How are things?'

'I'm good. How are you?'

'Mmm. As your dad has possibly explained, we've had an interesting time since we got back from Dubai.'

'Yes, I gather so.'

'Well, how was your dinner with Marcus? Did you have a heart to heart?'

Jemima had been contemplating how to convey what had been going on with Marcus. CJ recognised the hesitancy in his daughter. He knew her too well and recognised there was news afoot.

'Well, you both knew I was concerned about Marcus suddenly going away. But I took your advice, and I booked a table for dinner to *confront* him.'

'Oh, and how did that go?' asked Edee.

'I didn't get a chance to ask him.'

'What do you mean?' enquired a concerned CJ.

'The big softy got down on one knee and asked me to marry him properly,' said a smiling Jemima. 'You know we quickly got legally married when I was pregnant, so we could live with Emmy in Dubai? But we had no real engagement or fancy wedding.'

'Whoop, Whoop. Congratulations,' said a really pleased Edee.

'Congratulations, Jemima,' added a joyous CJ.

'I said there was nothing to worry about. Marcus worships the ground you walk on.'

'I know. The reason he'd been secretively going off, was because he was designing the engagement ring - I never had - with a renowned jeweller, plus he's been looking at wedding venues.'

Jemima suddenly held her finger up to the screen, and on her wedding finger was the most beautiful engagement ring.

'It's stunning,' said Edee. 'You must be over the moon.'

'I am. I couldn't be happier.'

'So, when's the big day?' asked CJ.

'We haven't fully decided,' said a clearly emotional Jemima. 'We're going to enjoy our *engagement*. We'll probably get *properly* married next year. But that can wait for now.'

'And how is Emmy taking it? That Mummy and Daddy are going to get married.'

'She already knows we are. Legally. Our love for her remains eternal, so no change there. But I think she's really looking forward to being a bridesmaid at the wedding.'

'I'm so happy, everything is fine, I did say not to worry. Congratulations to you both,' said CJ.

'As usual, Dad, you know best,' added Jemima. 'And I've learnt something else during this past few weeks. Life is for Living, and you must live life to the full.'

'Hear, hear,' said Edee and CJ, and Oscar gave a short bark in agreement.

Life is For Living

It Wasn't Me!

C J Meads

It Wasn't Me!

ACKNOWLEDGEMENTS

Well, this time around, it's been a bit different. The family, as always have encouraged me, as I've already written and published *'Murder comes to Edendale?'*

After publishing the first book, Julie and Aileen both read it and liked it. That was good enough for me. So here we have it. Book No. 2 in the CJ Gray Mystery series, *'It Wasn't Me!'*

Sharon has read it as usual, and she enjoyed it as much as the first novel. James will no doubt read the book, and I also welcome his comments. They will be honest as always.

This time around, I have been very fortunate that Gemma and Aileen have provided great support, by editing my story as I've been writing. So I'm hopeful all the silly errors and any spelling mistakes have been eliminated. *Fingers crossed.*

I would also like to thank Michelle Campbell, the General Manager at Wetherby Racecourse, and her colleagues, who provided me with a valuable insight into horse racing, and their course.

Sales of *Murder comes to Edendale?* are steady at best, but I didn't primarily write that novel, or this book, for anyone else other than for me. I really do enjoy writing, and my retirement has given me the time and opportunity to do it.

If someone, as always, likes the latest CJ Gray Mystery adventure, then that is a wonderful bonus.

I have again self-published with Kindle Direct Publishing (KDP) which has given me the opportunity to put my work out into the world, and to them I remain grateful.

I do again hope that you like the punchy short chapters, which suit my writing style, and the hours I like to put in each day on the computer.

I also hope you like the entwined story, an easy read whodunnit plot, with a bit of love and sex interest, with some humour to boot. I would like to think there remain no plot holes, not like some novels, and if you solved who the killer was, before the reveal, then my work as always is complete.

It would be good if you got to the end, and also liked it, but I fully understand if you didn't. Some of the explicit content, I do recognise, is not for everyone, but it was instrumental to the plot.

Having learnt so much from last time, I completed the writing in 10 weeks, slightly ahead of my schedule. And with the editing being done in tandem, also publish ahead of schedule.

You'll note Book 3 is already swirling around in my head, so look out for that, possibly next spring.

So, as before, I'm just left with thanking you dear reader, for deciding to buy a copy. For that I'm truly grateful, albeit earning a living from writing is not really my aim, but I do enjoy writing fiction, and while someone else also likes my style, then we will continue on our journey together.

It Wasn't Me!

THE NEXT CJ GRAY MYSTERY

New Year's Eve at Hargrove House

The annual New Year's Eve Party at Hargrove House takes on a *Cluedo, Murder Mystery* theme, and is thrown into complete disarray when one of the Special Guests is *actually* found murdered.

Due to the bad weather, everyone is locked in at the stunning ancestral home, with no one able to get in or out. *So who's the killer?*

CJ Gray, his enigmatic partner, Eden Songe, and his loyal dog Oscar, are drawn into another adventure of murder, blackmail, greed, corruption, lust, and romance.

There are plenty of twists and turns in this roller coaster short story with the usual red herrings to throw you off the scent.

The story again provides an opportunity for everyone to enjoy the escapism, in a novel with something to please most tastes. Then, just when you think you have it all worked out, the final twist - as all good whodunnits - will have you stunned and again leave you longing for the next adventure in Edendale, with CJ Gray and the gang.

CJ Gray, Edee, and Oscar are back
Another easy-read Whodunnit Mystery

C J Meads

It Wasn't Me!

Follow CJ Meads at :-

https://the-world-according-to-spiel.com/

Contact:

email:- cj.meads@btinternet.com

Printed in Great Britain
by Amazon